BY CARPET

A gripping British crime mystery full of twists

P.F. FORD

A Slater & Norman Mystery Book 1

Previously published as *Death of a Temptress*

JOFFE BOOKS

Revised edition 2024
Joffe Books, London
www.joffebooks.com

First published in Great Britain in 2014
as *Death of a Temptress*

This paperback edition was first published
in Great Britain in 2024

Cover art by Dee Dee Book Covers

ISBN: 978-1-83526-456-0

With thanks to my amazing wife, Mary — sometimes we need someone else to believe in us before we really believe in ourselves. None of this would have happened without her unfailing belief and support.

PROLOGUE

In the dark gloom of the early hours, with lights extinguished, the estate car reversed slowly off the main road into a narrow side street and then continued to creep on down to the riverside, where it finally stopped at the top of an old, disused slipway.

A man, dressed from head to toe in black, emerged from the car and made his way stealthily to the back. There was a loud, metallic pop as the hatch opened, followed by a hiss as it glided upwards. Shocked by the apparent loudness of the noise, he froze and held his breath.

After what seemed an eternity, he began to relax. It seemed no one had heard the noise, so he began the business of removing what appeared to be a roll of carpet from the back of the car. It was roughly six feet long and was bound with string around the middle and over each end.

Somehow it seemed to have grown heavier on the journey and it was much harder to get it out of the car than it had been to put it in. In no time, he was sweating profusely from his efforts.

He eventually gave up trying to carry the carpet and settled for dragging it from the car and down the slipway. In the darkness, he didn't notice the string was being loosened as it caught and snagged on the rough concrete.

Finally, he reached the river's edge and there was a faint splash as he dropped the end he was holding into the water. Then he stepped back to the other end, dropped to his knees, and launched the carpet into the river like a torpedo. In the dim, murky glow from the distant streetlights on the far bank, he could just about see it bobbing along on the surface as it floated out into the river and the current began to carry it away.

He watched with great satisfaction as it began to gather speed and was drawn out towards the middle without sinking. He had thought carefully about this — if it sank too soon it might be visible when the tide went out, so he had taken great care to make sure it floated long enough to reach the middle before it became waterlogged and sank.

He stood watching the slowly sinking package until it was lost from sight in the darkness, then made his way back to the car. After carefully easing the hatch shut, he climbed into the driver's seat and started the engine. As he crawled back along the lane, the lights of a passing car flashed past, and his confidence began to waver once more.

Not for the first time, he wondered how on earth he had been foolish enough to allow himself to be drawn into this situation. It was like the worst sort of nightmare, but, he also realised, it was too late for regrets. There could be no turning back now.

As the man turned onto the main road and switched his headlights on, the now waterlogged roll of carpet reached the middle of the river and disappeared below the surface, just as was intended.

The tide was in full flow now, and the fierce current had begun to work at the loosening string. Over the next half hour, the roll of carpet was dragged and bumped along the bottom, and in the process, the string was further loosened, and the carpet was almost unrolled.

It was quite possible that, in a day or two, the precious contents within could work loose and be carried away by the tidal current, and from there anything could happen . . .

CHAPTER ONE

Detective Sergeant Dave Slater itched and scratched at the unruly stubble on his chin. To say he felt aggrieved would be something of an understatement. He was currently on so-called 'gardening leave', which sounded as though it should be quite enjoyable, but, in reality, it was a euphemism for 'suspended from duty pending investigation'. He had been tending his garden for two weeks now and he was bored out of his mind.

It's not as if there was anything in particular to investigate. The simple truth was that an operation had been both poorly planned and badly executed, which, coupled with some very bad luck involving an unexpected dustcart and an idiot police driver, had resulted in their failure to apprehend the villain they had under surveillance.

The whole fiasco was a team effort, and Slater thought if anyone should have been singled out for blame it should have been DI Jimmy Jones of the Serious Crime Unit, who had been parachuted in from London to take control of the operation. But Jones was one of those fast-tracked rising stars, so he was never in any danger of carrying the can for his own incompetence.

In fact, it had been embarrassing to see how quickly everyone from the SCU had gazed in the direction of Jones' finger, pointing straight at Dave Slater. The unfortunate Slater had swiftly been nominated as the official sacrificial lamb.

They had very conveniently overlooked the fact that even if the operation had gone as smoothly as a Rolls Royce, they still wouldn't have got their man. He seemed to have been aware of everything they were doing and stayed one step ahead of them the whole time. It was quite clear to Dave Slater that the guy either had a crystal ball or, more likely, he had a man on the inside feeding him information the whole time.

In Slater's opinion, what they should have been investigating was the amazing coincidence of how a London-based criminal who had never been to Tinton before in his life had managed to keep ahead of an operation being led by a DI brought in from London for this one operation. His point being that Tinton had never suffered from the effects of a leak before.

But, of course, it was less politically sensitive to just lay the blame on the local officer thrust in at the deep end to help run an operation he wasn't trained for, and ignore the possibility that a favourite, rising star might not actually be all he was supposed to be.

So yes, he was aggrieved.

Just a tad.

His brooding was interrupted by the sound of his mobile phone warbling to acknowledge the arrival of an incoming call. He checked the number on the caller display. It was his boss, Detective Chief Inspector Bob Murray.

In his mind, he played through the scenario he had imagined hundreds of times over the last two weeks. It was the one he most dreaded — where he was called in and dismissed from the service.

He thought about ignoring the call. They couldn't sack him if he didn't answer it, could they? But he quickly realised just how stupid he was being. If that was what was going to happen it would be far better to get it over with, wouldn't it? Either way, there was only one way to find out. He picked up the phone.

'Hi, Boss.'

'Good morning, David. How are you?'

Bob Murray was a strange mix of modern thinking and old-fashioned discipline. He was modern enough to allow the informality of calling Slater by his Christian name in this situation, but not informal enough to use the abbreviated form 'Dave'. Everything about him was contradictory in this way, but Slater liked him.

'I've been better,' admitted Slater. 'All this waiting around is driving me crazy.'

'That's what I'm calling about. I need to talk to you. Can you get here this afternoon?'

Slater felt his blood running a bit colder.

'Is this something I want to hear?'

'You'll find out when you get here, won't you?' growled Murray. 'About four o'clock suit you?'

'Err, yes, sir. Of course.'

'Good man. I'll see you then.'

There was a soft click and the line was dead.

Well, thought Slater, *that didn't sound like I was going to get the sack. Perhaps someone's finally going to ask me for my side of the story . . . but I have no idea what to think. I know a man who might, though. It's time to make a call of my own . . .*

'But why does he want to see me?' Slater asked, down the phone. 'Come on, Stan, you're my union rep so why haven't you been told? I've been suspended from work and kept totally in the dark for two weeks and now, suddenly, my boss wants to see me and no one knows why. What the bloody hell's going on?'

'Look, calm down, will you?' said the voice at the other end of the line. 'They can't sack you without me being there. Anyway, this isn't a disciplinary matter. I don't know quite what's going on but none of the usual procedures are being followed.

'You're not even officially suspended. I get the impression there's some sort of barney going on between our lot and the Serious Crime Unit. They want you to get the blame but we're saying you can't be responsible when you're not trained to run an operation like that. The feeling this end is Jones is responsible, not you.'

This was news to Slater. Maybe he wasn't on his own after all.

'And don't start thinking Murray's on their side,' Stan continued. 'He went ballistic when he found out you'd got the blame. He's definitely fighting for you, so I can't see how he's going to suddenly turn on you now. If you want my honest opinion, I don't think they know what to do with you.'

'Why, thank you, Stan,' said Slater sarcastically. 'You sure know how to make me feel better.'

'Listen, Murray's on your side and he's got the big chief's ear, which means now even the big man himself thinks you're being used as a scapegoat. If you want my advice, you'll stop feeling sorry for yourself, get in here this afternoon, and show these people they're doing the right thing by backing you.'

Well, when it's put to you like that, you can't really argue, can you? And to be honest, self-pity hasn't done me any good so far, has it?

He thought it might be a good idea to show a little respect to Bob Murray when he met him later. A shower and a shave certainly wouldn't go amiss.

* * *

'So, how come I get to take this over?' asked Slater, when Murray explained the situation. 'No, don't tell me, let me guess. I suppose it's a ticking time bomb that no one else wants to handle, but it's okay if it blows up in my face because I'm expendable.'

'Look,' said Murray, patiently, 'I understand how you feel and I'd probably feel the same if I was in your shoes, but I think you're looking at it from the wrong angle.

'This case has been kicking around for six months. It's been dismissed as a simple runaway by our colleagues in the Met, and with no evidence to suggest otherwise, and no dead body, you can hardly blame them. But the missing girl's sister won't accept it. She's found some barrister with a bit of clout to back her up, and now between them they've got the local MP on the case too.

'The Met insist they don't have the manpower to spend any more time on the case, so the local MP suggested it should be handed to us. He's got friends in very, very high places so he got his way.'

'And how much help can I expect from the Met?' asked Slater, wearily.

'I might be wrong, but, between you and me, I would expect to get bugger all. They might be glad to get rid of it, but, as you can imagine, they won't be pleased to find we're re-investigating one of their cases.'

'So I'm in between a rock and a hard place then.'

Murray nodded.

'Do I get any help from this end?' asked Slater, optimistically.

'The Met aren't the only ones who are short of manpower—' began Murray.

'But then I'm supposed to be suspended so I'm a spare pair of hands for any dirty jobs that come in,' finished Slater, before adding an afterthought. 'Am I working officially, boss? Or am I really surplus to requirements?'

'I'd prefer it if you kept as low a profile as possible, but let's get something clear. As far as I'm concerned there's no way you should be suspended. DI Jones should have been the one to blame for the Slick Tony fiasco, not you. And you should be aware that my boss agrees with me. We're doing all we can to reverse the situation, and getting your suspension lifted so you can carry out this investigation is the first step. So get that bloody chip off your shoulder and get out there and do your job. Do I make myself clear?'

'Yes, boss, crystal clear,' said Slater, sulkily, thinking to himself that he didn't have much choice.

Murray stood up, indicating the meeting was over. He came round the desk, shook Slater's hand and handed him a folder.

'I understand why you feel reluctant, but do one thing for me. Take this home and read through it,' he said, gripping Slater's hand. 'Go and speak to the missing girl's sister. Then if you decide you're really not interested and you'd rather take a chance on what happens, I'll understand. But I think you have a chance to shine here, a real chance to prove you're as good a copper as I believe you are. I think you should get out there and use that chance.'

'Yes, boss.'

'If you need anything, you let me know. And keep me informed. You never know what you might find.'

He led Slater to the door.

'Come back and see me in a couple of days. In the meantime, I'd keep quiet about this.'

'Ok, boss,' said Slater. 'I'll take a look and let you know.'

As he walked from the office, Slater figured it had probably gone as well as he could reasonably expect. Better, in fact. At least now he knew that his own superiors were on his side, and for that he really was grateful. Idly he wondered what Murray had meant when he said 'you never know what you might find'. Was there something he wasn't being told, or was he just being paranoid?

CHAPTER TWO

It's a police officer's lot to spend much of his, or her, life dealing with people who have reason to lie and cheat. This can make it difficult to maintain a positive outlook and many develop a rather jaundiced and cynical view of the world. Dave Slater was no exception to this experience, and he was finding it difficult to be anything but cynical having just finished going through the folder Bob Murray had handed to him.

At first glance, everything seemed to be in order, but Dave Slater knew better. He had experience in conducting investigations like this himself, so he had a good idea of the sort of information that should have been here. Having read through from start to finish, his experience told him that either this report was the result of serious incompetence, or, worse still, it represented some sort of cover-up.

He slid from his stool, stretched and yawned. He looked at the papers strewn across the breakfast bar in his tiny kitchen. So, was this the real reason he had been handed this particular hot potato? Was he actually being asked to investigate the investigators? And why choose him? They already had a branch of the police service that had been created for exactly this purpose. Why choose a lowly DS like him?

Once again, the sulky cynic within him came to the surface to direct his thinking. He had been handed this because he was expendable, of course. Let's face it, he was already halfway out of the door. If he messed this up, and it could well be a case of 'damned if you do and damned if you don't', it would be a simple matter to give him that final shove before they slammed the door behind him.

Well, sod 'em, he thought. *Why should I make it easy? If they want to get rid of me they'll have to do it the hard way. They can stick their investigation and find some other mug.*

Having made his decision, he ambled across to his fridge, swung the door open, and looked inside. As usual, there was precious little food inside, but there was half a case of lager. He reached in and grabbed a can. With the care born of years of experience, he managed not to shake it up too much so that when the ring pulled away there was no fountain of spray to deal with.

Carrying his precious can with him, he made his way through to the lounge and sank into his armchair. Using the remote control, he scrolled his way through the TV channels until he found a football match to watch. It was a recording of the previous night's Champions League football. It was a pity all the English teams were already knocked out but even so, this was an unexpected bonus. Like many armchair fans, Slater could barely kick a ball straight, but, of course, that didn't deny him the right to appoint himself chief critic.

As he watched the game unfolding, his mood began to improve. By half-time he was feeling reasonably good, and by the time the second half started he was mellowing quite nicely as he put his feet up and settled back into his armchair with a second can of lager. If the game now continued in the same vein, it would be entertaining enough to make him forget his problems for another forty-five minutes. And if it went to extra time and penalties, it could add another hour on top.

Fifteen minutes into the second half, his mobile phone began to ring. He wasn't quite sure where exactly it was, and anyway he was watching football, so he decided whoever it was could leave a message. It was probably some arsehole calling to try to sell him something, and if it was anything important he'd call them back. After a couple more rings it stopped.

Five minutes later, it began to ring again. It wasn't quite so easy to ignore this time, but he was enjoying the game and he knew it wouldn't be important. Again it stopped ringing, only this time it started again almost straightaway. Damn. Perhaps it was important after all.

Grudgingly, he climbed to his feet and began to search for the cause of his irritation, which he eventually found in the pocket of the jacket he had flung onto his bed earlier. The ringing stopped and started twice more during his search, so he figured it probably was important; but when he finally picked up the phone, he didn't recognise the number displayed.

'Hello?'

'Is that DS Slater?'

It was a female voice, strong and confident, a bit on the posh side, he thought.

'Yes it is. Who's calling?'

'My name's Jenny Radstock.'

'Well, Ms Radstock, I'm afraid I'm on leave right now. Perhaps you'd like to call Tinton station. I'm sure someone there would be able to help you.'

'On leave? I was told you had been suspended.'

Now that threw him. Who on earth was this woman, and how did she know so much?

'You're very well informed. Perhaps a bit too well informed. Do you mind telling me who you are and what you want?'

Before she could reply, his doorbell rang. Two thoughts suddenly filled his head. The first was wondering who the hell was coming round at this time of night. The second was the realisation that this could be a chance to get rid of his caller.

'I'm sorry, Ms Radstock,' he explained as he reached the door, 'I've got to go. There's someone at my door.'

'Yes, I know,' she said as he swung the door open.

A tall, slim redhead stood at the door, phone clasped to her ear. She gave him a beaming smile and waggled the phone at him.

'Hi,' she said.

Weirdly the voice came from his phone too. Puzzled, he looked at her and then at his phone. Then it slowly dawned on him she was the person he was talking to.

She ended her call, slipped the phone into her pocket, and then slowly and deliberately looked him up and down.

'Well, you're much better looking than I was told, so that's a good start.'

Slater's mouth opened but no words came out. Who was this woman?

'I hope I'm not disturbing you.' She gave him another warm smile.

'Actually, yes you are,' he said, irritated. 'I was watching the football.'

'The replay of last night's game?'

'As it happens, yes.'

'Good game,' she said, approvingly. 'Barcelona won on penalties.'

'Don't tell me that.' Now he was more than irritated. 'I was enjoying watching it. Now you've spoiled it for me.'

'I need your attention if we're going to talk,' she explained. 'And I won't get it if you're trying to watch football at the same time. Now you don't need to watch it and I'll have your attention.'

She smiled at him again as he struggled to find the right words to convey his feelings without resorting to swear words.

'Are you going to let me in?' she asked. 'I don't bite.'

'Why should I let you in? You've already spoiled my night. What possible reason could I have for letting you in?'

'Ruth Thornhill.'

'What? How do you know about that?'

'If you let me in, I'll tell you.'

Slater quickly sized up the woman on his step. She was well dressed; smart but casual. And quite good-looking too, thought Slater, with pale skin and red hair which was gathered in a bun. Her intense green eyes made her look a little fierce, but she certainly didn't look dangerous. Also in her favour, she claimed to know something about Ruth Thornhill. And the football was ruined now she had told him the result.

'You'd better come in.' He stepped back to make way for her. As she passed, he got wind of her perfume. Chanel Number Five. He liked that. Maybe this wouldn't be so bad after all.

In his tiny house, the front door opened into the lounge. She took in the room and wrinkled her nose.

'I'm sorry,' he said, using the remote to turn off the TV. 'It's a bit of a mess.'

'It's fine.' She smiled again. 'I'm not here to judge how you live, and I can assure you I've seen much worse. You keep this place tidier than most single guys I know.'

'Here, sit down.' He grabbed a pile of newspapers from the small settee to make space for her.

'Can I get you a drink?' he asked, making his way to the kitchen.

'What have you got?' she called.

He looked in the cupboard and then in the fridge.

'Not much, I'm afraid. I wasn't expecting company.'

'Lager's fine.'

'Really?' He hadn't expected that.

'I take it you have glasses. It doesn't do my reputation much good to be seen swilling lager from a can.'

He came through with a glass of lager and handed it to her before sinking back into his armchair.

'Here's to Ruth,' she said, raising her glass.

He raised his can in salute.

'Ok, Ms Radstock, I only let you in because you mentioned Ruth, so how about you cut to the chase.'

'I know you were given the file this afternoon, and I take it you've read through it by now?'

She looked pointedly at him.

He nodded. 'So far so good,' he said. 'But how come you know so much about this? Where do you fit in?'

'When the Met decided they couldn't be bothered to look into this case properly Ruth's sister approached me to see if I could help.'

'And why would you be able to help?'

'Because I know people who know people.'

Slater looked unconvinced, and Ms Radstock clearly realised further explanation was required.

'I'm a barrister. I grew up in this area and I know your boss through my father. I also know the local MP, who just happens to know the Home Secretary. And now, so do I. We all feel the Met could have done much better. As Ruth lived here in Tinton, we have managed to have the whole investigation handed to the local police to re-investigate. It's amazing what you can do when you know the right people.'

'But why me?' asked Slater. 'I mean I'm supposed to be persona non grata; the useless copper who couldn't find his arse with a map.'

'Self-pity doesn't suit you, you know,' she reproached him. 'We all know you've been used as a scapegoat. This is your chance to prove your critics wrong.'

'Yes, so I've been told. At least you're all singing from the same hymnbook.'

'Oh dear.' She sighed. 'Cynical, too. Is it really so hard to believe that there are some people on your side?'

'But why would you be? I mean, you don't know me from Adam, so why would you suddenly be so concerned for my career?'

'Now that's a fair question,' she said, smiling again. 'And I'm happy to admit that I didn't know you from Adam. However, I have crossed swords with DI Jimmy Jones before. Now there's a man I wouldn't trust as far as I could throw him.'

Slater perked up. 'Now this is getting interesting. Tell me more,' he said, leaning forward.

'Well . . .' She was clearly warming to her subject now. 'Do you really think you're the first person to be one of DI Jones' scapegoats?'

'I'm not?'

'Good heavens, no. Our friend Jones seems to have far more clout than he should in his position. I find that rather worrying. I've been watching him, and I know of at least three other good officers who've had similar treatment to you. He messes up, and they become the victim. Sound familiar?'

Slater nodded as she continued.

'Up until now I've been unable to do anything about it, but then Ruth's sister approached me and I realised maybe now is my chance to get involved and exert some influence. This time I feel I might actually be able to help. In fact, I already have by getting you involved.'

She sat up straight, looking pleased with herself.

Slater was puzzled.

'But I don't understand how this case will help me to prove he was wrong about me.'

'You leave that to me,' she said. 'As I said before, I didn't get where I am today without getting to know some pretty powerful people, certainly powerful enough to stop DI Jones from ruining any more careers.'

Slater thought about this. He had to admit it would be good to bring that arsehole Jimmy Jones down a peg or two, and being suspended with nothing to do was driving him mad. At least if he took this case, he'd have something other than his own problems to focus upon.

'I have some questions,' he said.

'I thought you might.' She looked at her watch. 'But I'm afraid I have to run right now.'

She stood, ready to go.

'Look,' she said. 'I understand why you might not want to get involved in this. But it's not just about you, or me, or even DI Jones. Go and talk to Ruth's sister. I'm sure once you have, you'll agree with me that the poor woman could do with our help.

'Now I really do have to go,' she said, looking at her watch again before plunging her hands into her pockets.

Slater really wanted to ask more questions but she obviously wasn't going to answer them so he led the way to his door to let her out. Once outside, she turned back to him and handed him a business card.

'There is an added bonus,' she said, looking straight into his eyes. 'My number's there. I'd like to meet up with you on a regular basis so you can keep me informed of your progress. I'm a very straightforward kind of girl and I like to think I'm good company.'

She opened her jacket just enough to reveal an attractive, slim figure, clad in expensive clothing.

'What you see is what you get with me, and I can be very accommodating.'

As Slater's mouth dropped open once more, she gave him a knowing smile, winked, turned on her heel and marched off.

He watched her as she walked away. Did he really hear that right? Was she offering what he thought she was offering? He shook his head. No. He must have got that wrong, surely.

CHAPTER THREE

Despite Bob Murray's assertion that he should keep a low profile, Slater thought that if he was going to do this job, he was going to do it his own way. He figured it would be a good idea to contact the original investigating officer, explain how he had been lumbered with the case, and get the guy onside right from the start.

'DS Donovan speaking.'

'Good morning. My name's DS Dave Slater from Tinton. I'm hoping you can help me.'

'Tinton? Where's that? Sounds sort of yokel. West Country is it?'

Slater sighed inwardly. Here we go again, he thought. He'd had dealings with detectives from the Met once or twice before. On each of those occasions, he had been made to feel like an inferior being who didn't deserve help from the superior race. He wondered if maybe it was part of their training. Whatever it was, he was just going to have to deal with it. Maybe he could even use it to his advantage.

'Miles out, I'm afraid,' he explained patiently. 'Tinton's in Hampshire, less than sixty miles from the centre of London.'

'Sixty miles, or six hundred miles. It's all the same to me, mate. This is where the real work's done. We deal with real police work and real cases up here.'

Of course, thought Slater wearily, *there is no crime anywhere else, and anyway, the rest of us are just too stupid to know our arses from our elbows.*

'Well, that's handy then,' said Slater, fighting a heroic battle with his desire to tell DS Donovan exactly what he thought of him. 'It's one of your cases I wanted to ask you about.'

'What do you mean "one of our cases"?' said Donovan, defensively. Then, far more aggressively, he added, 'Since when has one of our cases been within your jurisdiction?'

'Since it was handed to me and I was told to investigate it.' Slater was beginning to enjoy himself now he knew he was getting under Donovan's skin.

'What bloody case?'

'Ruth Thornhill.'

'Who?' Slater could tell by the tone of Donovan's voice that he knew exactly who, yet he was stalling, playing for time. *Now that's interesting,* thought Slater. *Why would he do that?*

'Ruth Thornhill,' said Slater, playing along. 'She went missing about six months ago. Her sister reported her missing, but you decided she was a runaway and took no further action.'

'Did I? You're probably right. We get so many of them I can't be expected to remember them all.'

'I am right.' Slater was enjoying Donovan's discomfort. 'I've got a copy of your report in front of me now.'

It was rather like lighting the blue touch paper on a firework. For just a short moment it seemed nothing was going to happen, then Slater heard a hiss as Donovan drew in his breath. This was followed by what could best be described as an explosion of profanity down the line. Apparently DS Donovan didn't approve of Dave Slater getting hold of his report.

Slater held the phone away until Donovan finally began to slow down sufficiently to become coherent, eventually re-joining the conversation at a point he felt was appropriate.

'And just who the bloody 'ell do you think you are, to be checkin' up on me?' finished Donovan.

'Let's get one thing straight, shall we?' said Slater, smiling broadly to himself. 'It's not my idea to be checking up on anybody. But, just like you, I have superiors, and just like superiors everywhere, every now and then they like to hand someone a pile of shit just to see how they deal with it. Right now, your case is my pile of shit and I have to deal with it whether I like it or not.'

'But what makes you think you can do any better than me? We don't have time to fart around, so when we found there was no body and no sign of anything untoward, it was put on the back burner. Then when we saw the text messages sent to the boyfriend from the missing girl's phone, that was good enough for us. Case closed.'

'I quite agree.'

'You do?' said Donovan in surprise.

'I've read the file and I agree with your conclusion,' Slater said, trying to pacify him.

'Oh. That's alright then,' said Donovan, evidently beginning to calm down. 'So, why the call?'

'The reason I've been handed this particular pile of shit,' explained Slater, 'is because the missing girl's sister, Beverley Green, won't let it go. She's even got the local bloody MP involved now.'

'That cow,' agreed Donovan. 'If you've got to deal with her you have my sympathies, mate. She's a real pain in the arse. Drove me mad, she did.'

'She's been driving my bosses mad too,' said Slater. 'And now I've been given the job of trying to convince her there's nothing we can do.'

'Huh! Good luck with that. We told her exactly that back then, but she just wouldn't accept it.'

'Yes, I know you did,' Slater said. 'But she still doesn't believe it, and I've still got to do what I can and hope I can convince her. I've read your report and it certainly looks open and shut to me.'

There was silence from the other end of the line so Slater decided it was time to apply a little pressure.

'I just wanted to check in with you before I go to see her. I thought letting you know was the right thing to do. I'm sure you wouldn't have been happy if you found out I was creeping around behind your back.'

Donovan's apology sounded grudging, and it took a long time coming, but finally he began to back down.

'Look, I was probably a bit hasty.'

'Probably?' said Slater. 'Do you know how many different names you called me? Do you think I want this job?'

'Okay. Point taken,' conceded Donovan. 'It's just, you know, when someone starts checking up on you . . .'

'Whoa. Hold on a minute. I'm not Professional Standards looking to catch you out. But I am going to have to go through the motions. I'm sure you understand that?'

'Well, yeah. I suppose you'll have to do that,' agreed Donovan, sounding reluctant.

'Here's how I was thinking of playing it,' explained Slater. 'I'm going to see the sister later today. I'll listen to her story and let her think I'm going to re-investigate. Then I'll just go through the motions, basically confirming all your findings and reaching the same conclusion. It should be a doddle if I'm careful, and both you and my boss will end up happy. What do you say?'

'Are you going to be poking around up here?'

'Well, I may have to, just to keep up appearances and make it look like I'm being thorough, you know? It'll be a nice day out for me,' Slater said, laughing.

'You're not such a bad bloke for a yokel, Dave Slater,' said Donovan, sounding relaxed now. 'Let me know if you're coming up here. I'll buy you a pint. I know some good places, know what I mean?'

'Sounds good,' said Slater. 'Now, before I go to meet her, what can you tell me about the sister?'

As Slater had suspected, DS Donovan had no time for Beverley Green. As far as he was concerned, she was clearly a total waste of space who just wouldn't accept the facts. He basically advised Slater to disregard everything she had to say.

'Look, mate,' he finished, 'Ruth Thornhill is just a runaway. She's an adult and she's allowed to do what she wants, when she wants. As far as we're concerned she's run off with another feller. There's no law against it, even if she didn't tell her sister. Maybe her sister didn't know her quite as well as she thought she did. Whatever, we've got better things to do with our time.'

CHAPTER FOUR

The Glades was a private, gated, and rather exclusive, estate to the south side of Tinton. The whole site occupied twelve acres, but such was the size of these houses, and their gardens, there were only twelve properties in total. An intercom outside the gates controlled access to the estate. Fortunately for Dave Slater, Beverley Green was expecting him and she buzzed him through straightaway.

The properties were all quite new, but that was their only similarity. The whole site had been developed as a collection of individual houses, all set in different places within their individual plots. This estate was less than five years old, yet Slater found he was driving along a lane with mature trees either side. It was as if the whole thing had been there for many years.

It certainly wasn't his style; all this money made him feel rather uncomfortable, but he could appreciate just how much these properties must be worth. If there was any change out of two million quid, he'd be very surprised. It was definitely a case of 'how the other half live'.

As its name suggested, Old Shrubs Cottage was at the end of a driveway bordered by an array of shrubs, which hid the house from view until he rounded a corner and found himself approaching an enormous six-bedroom house.

Slater knew Beverley Green was thirty-seven years old, with three small children, and from his conversation with Donovan earlier, he was rather expecting to be greeted by some sort of harassed housewife figure. He certainly wasn't expecting to find the confident, good-looking woman who was waiting at the front door. She was dressed for tennis, her short skirt revealing a shapely pair of tanned legs finished off with expensive-looking tennis shoes.

'If you're just off to the tennis club, I can always come back later,' he said, as he introduced himself.

'Good heavens, no, Sergeant. We have our own court in the garden, behind the house. It's an indulgence of mine, but I enjoy it and it keeps me fit.'

Slater thought she was definitely right about that. In modern parlance, she was indeed 'fit'.

She looked Slater up and down. 'Do you play, Sergeant?'

'Who? Me? Err, no. I never seem to get much time for sport.'

'You should try it.' She smiled saucily. 'I could teach you. It would be fun to play a game with someone different now and then. Don't you think?'

Her face told him nothing, but Slater had been round the block enough times to know an invitation when he heard one. This was a completely unexpected turn of events, and for a few moments it threw him, but he couldn't afford to let himself get distracted now. In different circumstances, he might even have been prepared to play her little game, but today he wasn't interested.

'Maybe another time,' he said, his expression deadpan. 'Now. About your sister.'

Slater noticed a little pout of disapproval momentarily cross her face, but it was gone almost straightaway.

'Ah, yes,' she sighed. 'My missing sister. Come on inside and I'll tell you what I know.'

She led him through the front door into an elegant hallway. As he followed her, he took in the photographs in the hall. *This must be the three children,* he thought, *and that's got to be Dad.*

And of course there's Mum, and finally the happy family group photo. Then they were through into a fabulous kitchen; Slater thought he could probably have fitted his entire house in this one room.

'This is a beautiful house,' he heard himself say.

'Only the best.' Beverley Green indicated the superbly equipped kitchen. 'I suppose I'm what you could call a kept woman. My husband has a very good job up in the City and he likes me to play the dutiful housewife and raise the children. I'd be a fool not to, really, wouldn't I? Especially when I can live like this.'

'What does he do?'

'Some sort of investment management. I'm not really sure, and I don't really care if I'm honest. As long as the money keeps rolling in, I'm happy.'

She must have taken in Slater's expression.

'Oh, don't get me wrong. I'm not one of those embittered women who feels she's treated like a doormat. I regard myself as very lucky to have a husband who looks after me so well, and he's a wonderful father to our three children. He works hard Monday to Friday, often away midweek, but come Friday evening work stops and he's very much a "hands-on" dad until the next Monday morning. He's a good man, Sergeant.'

'You must get a bit lonely if he's away in the week.'

'Oh, I manage.' She gave him a wry smile. 'There's a very good babysitting service in Tinton. That means I can always go out with the girls on a Wednesday. That's good enough for me. And, of course, there's always my tennis.'

She licked her lips and gave him that innocent look again, but he ignored it.

'About your sister,' he reminded her, pulling out a stool and perching on it at the breakfast bar. 'I know you've done all this before, and I have read the reports from the earlier investigation, but I want you to imagine I'm completely new to this investigation and I know nothing. Can you do that?'

She nodded, and perched herself on a stool alongside him. Then she jumped down again.

'Before I forget,' she said, 'I found these for you.'

She opened a drawer and handed Slater two photographs.

The girl in the photos was rather frumpy looking, with dowdy clothes that made her resemble a refugee from the fifties. She had long, lacklustre, brown hair, and dull brown eyes. In a crowd, she would have stood out as the one with the least amount of fashion sense.

'Did she always dress like this?' asked Slater in surprise. With Ruth working for a magazine, he had expected to see someone rather closer to the cutting edge of fashion.

'She wasn't exactly a sexy dresser in the family tradition, I'm afraid.' Beverley sighed, climbing back onto her stool.

Slater looked thoughtfully at the photographs for a moment, but then decided to let it lie.

'Ok,' he said instead, setting down his notebook and pencil. 'I need you to tell me everything you know. Start by telling me about Ruth and her job.'

'Ruth was my little sister,' Beverley began. 'I was ten when she was born and I think she was a mistake. My parents never seemed to have any time for her so I always seemed to be the one who looked out for her . . .'

* * *

Beverley spoke for the best part of an hour. Slater prompted her with a few questions here and there, but by the time they had finished, it seemed he had an extensive amount of background information to work on.

Ruth Thornhill had virtually been raised by her sister, to the point of living with her on and off for years, even after Beverley had married. She led a pretty unremarkable life for her first twenty-five years, but then, apparently, she had discovered a desire to become a journalist. She had managed to secure a job with a magazine up in London, working as a receptionist/clerk. At that time, she had been travelling to London by train every day.

But Ruth was ambitious and hard-working, and about fifteen months ago, the magazine had promoted her to staff writer. Of course, at first she got little or no credit for her writing, but then she was given the chance to write small features which she did under the pen name of 'Ruby Rider'.

As she began to develop her career, she began to benefit from some of the perks of the job. One of these perks included the magazine paying for her to stay in a small hotel (Beverley wasn't sure, but she thought it was called the Mistral) during the week, meaning she only had to travel up on Monday morning and then home again on Friday afternoon.

She was having a relationship with a Tinton man called Tony Warwick. Beverley didn't seem to know much about him, and she certainly didn't seem to like him, but she also didn't appear to have any particular reason for her dislike.

Everything had seemed to be going well for Ruth, and then, suddenly, about six months ago she had disappeared. Apparently, she had sent text messages to her boyfriend in the days following her disappearance, which indicated she had run away with another man; but Beverley insisted it couldn't be true. She claimed Ruth was crazy about her boyfriend and would never have run away. She had a good job and had everything going for her. Why would she have thrown it all away?

He left with Beverley's final words ringing in his ears. 'And she would have told me first whatever she had decided to do. She had even told me when she got pregnant a few years ago. I had helped her arrange an abortion. So, you see, we had no secrets. She would have told me.'

* * *

Slater knew people rarely told each other everything, and he thought it more than possible that a girl spending the week in London on her own could meet someone else and decide to run away, but he had kept his own counsel, deciding he wasn't prepared to argue the point just yet.

As Slater was saying goodbye, a young man came cycling up the drive. He was dressed for tennis.

Slater looked at Beverley Green, who looked back at him straight-faced.

'My tennis coach and sometime mixed doubles partner Sebastian,' she said, her face giving nothing away. 'Come to play with me.'

'Yeah. Right. Of course he has,' said Slater.

As he climbed into his car he thought about the frumpy looking girl in the photographs Beverley had given him. A girl who dressed like that working as a receptionist for a magazine — it seemed rather unlikely, didn't it?

CHAPTER FIVE

Next on Slater's list was the boyfriend, Tony Warwick. He rented a tiny, rather tatty looking, terraced house near the centre of town. Whoever the landlord was, he clearly didn't seem to think he should spend any of the rent on improvements. The front door was old, not the 'antique, worth preserving' sort of old, but the 'should be condemned and replaced' sort of old. It didn't even fit the frame properly.

Dave Slater was a great believer in his ability to quickly size people up, and he wasn't often wrong. He quickly took in the tall, thin figure in the doorway and his first impression was that there was something distinctly odd about Tony Warwick. And, whatever Beverley Green might say to the contrary, Slater just couldn't imagine Ruth, or anyone else for that matter, being crazy about this man.

The first thing Slater noticed when he was invited through the rickety front door was the huge crucifix hanging from the wall. Two candles burned on a sideboard beneath it. Beverley hadn't mentioned anything about Ruth being religious and Slater was already struggling to see how she would have become involved with this rather strange man.

Tony Warwick's version of events was a good match for Beverley's, as far as Ruth's job and disappearance were concerned, but Slater was interested to learn a bit more about their relationship.

'So how did you come to meet?' he asked.

'At church. After Ruth committed her sin, she came to the church to repent. I met her there and took pity on her.'

'Her sin?' Slater was puzzled.

'She had intercourse with a man outside of marriage, and was with child. Then she had *that* operation,' explained Warwick.

'Ah, right,' said Slater, not sure if Ruth had committed one, two or three sins in Warwick's eyes. 'And you took pity on her?'

'I offered to stand by her and help her achieve repentance.'

Slater didn't like the sound of this.

'And how exactly was she going to do that?'

'Through prayer, of course,' said Warwick, as though he were addressing an idiot. 'She used to come here and we would pray together.'

'And that was the full extent of your relationship?'

Warwick looked shocked by Slater's question.

'What are you suggesting, Sergeant?'

'I mean, were you in a sexual relationship with Ruth?'

'Sex outside of marriage is a mortal sin, Sergeant. I was trying to help Ruth repent,' replied Warwick, clearly trying to be patient. 'She had already committed that sin once, it would have been a terrible thing if I had committed the same sin with her, don't you think? If that had happened, then I, too, would have been a sinner.'

His holier-than-thou attitude was beginning to get under Slater's skin, but before he could speak, Warwick continued talking.

'Sadly Ruth couldn't control her lustful urges. She ran off with another man.'

He opened a drawer and produced a mobile phone.

'Here,' he said, handing it to Slater. 'You can see what she had to say for herself.'

Slater took the phone and began to thumb his way through the text messages. There were four in total, spread over seven days, starting two days after she had last been seen. As he read through them, Slater became more and more convinced there was something very odd about them.

According to Warwick, he and Ruth had a very non-sexual relationship. In fact, the way he told it they hardly had a relationship at all — they just prayed together. Yet the tone of the text messages suggested Ruth had been apologising for breaking off a warm, loving, and obviously sexual, relationship. Here was something else that didn't make sense.

'These texts would suggest that your relationship with Ruth consisted of rather more than just praying together, don't you think?'

'Who can say what goes on in the mind of such a sinner, Sergeant? It's true we had talked of the possibility of us perhaps getting married one day, but first she had to prove her repentance and I thought that was still a long way off. In fact, it looks as though she's never going to achieve it now. I tried but I failed. Such is life, I'm afraid.'

Slater looked hard at Warwick, almost as if he was trying to see right inside the man's head, but of course, he couldn't. He wondered why Warwick would keep the messages when he seemed to have so readily dismissed Ruth as a waste of his time, and yet there seemed to be no anger at her wasting his time and cheating on him.

'Don't you feel angry that she let you down?'

'What good would anger do, Sergeant? Some of us are strong and some of us are weak. Anger is the property of the weak.'

Slater felt he couldn't take much more of this sanctimonious bullshit. He had to get out of there before he did something very unprofessional, so he made his excuses and left. As he drove away, his mind was spinning into overdrive. What on earth was going on here? And why did the previous investigation turn a blind eye to all these inconsistencies?

Was it simply the case that with the texts as evidence, no body, and nothing to suggest foul play, they just chose the easiest way out? It crossed his mind that it would be quite easy for him to do exactly the same. After all, it would be a lot less hassle.

But Dave Slater was tenacious, rather like a dog that has discovered a new smell. And he felt this particular smell was becoming more interesting by the minute. He wasn't going to stop sniffing around just yet.

* * *

'So what do you think? Are you going to take it on?' asked Jenny Radstock.

Slater shifted the phone to a more comfortable position.

'You're very persistent, Ms Radstock,' he replied.

'It's a good way to make sure I get what I want,' she said. 'And in my experience, it usually works.'

'And what is it you want?'

'I want to make sure you take this case.'

'And if I say no?'

'I'll be very disappointed,' she said. 'This case needs someone who can be relied upon to do a thorough job; someone who's tenacious enough to see it through to the end. I know you've spoken to Beverley Green. You seem to have a fan there; she was very impressed. I think she would be *very grateful* if you could find out what really happened to Ruth.'

The implied innuendo made it quite clear how Jenny thought Beverley might show her gratitude, but Slater was unimpressed. In fact, he was rather insulted by the suggestion he could be persuaded by such an offer.

'Really,' he said, dryly. 'I'll be sure to bear that in mind when I make my decision.'

'But surely you've seen enough by now,' she protested. 'Don't tell me you're not intrigued.'

'I suppose I could easily go mad if I sit here staring at four walls much longer.'

'So you will take it then?' she asked, sounding triumphant.

'It's not as if I've got anything else to do right now, is it?' he said, sighing.

'You won't regret this, Sergeant. And, like I said before, I'd like to meet up so you can keep me up to date with your progress.'

'Would these meetings be official, or simply to satisfy your curiosity?' he asked.

'Oh, I have lots of curiosity, Sergeant. Don't you?'

He declined to comment.

'Well, you've got my number,' she said. 'Give me a ring when you're ready. I have a weekend house near Tinton — we could meet there. I have to go now. Bye.'

Slater looked at the now dead phone in his hand, and made a mental note to ignore her invitation. He was quite sure his boss would be less than impressed if he even suspected Slater was sharing information with a member of the public, and the last thing he needed now was more hassle.

CHAPTER SIX

His appointment with Camilla Heywood, owner and editor of the *Magazine*, was fixed for three thirty p.m., so Slater had a leisurely morning to effect some sort of recovery from yet another sleepless night before catching an early afternoon train up to London.

He was surprised to find the offices of the *Magazine* were quite small. He had been expecting some sprawling open-plan building, but what he found was a small, compact group of offices in a shared building. He thought it was hardly Fleet Street, then realised how stupid it was to think like that, remembering that most of Fleet Street's finest were no longer anywhere near it.

Slater had done his research, and knew that Camilla Heywood was a great example of what hard work and forward thinking could achieve. Being young and inexperienced when she had started the *Magazine*, she had not been entrenched with preconceived ideas about glossy paper and circulation figures. She had quickly realised the opportunity offered by the increasing use of the internet and had started her venture online. This had given her a head start over many rival publications, whose much older editors had scoffed at the very idea that a magazine could work online. They were also rather put out that she had the audacity to call it the *Magazine*. They regarded her as crazy. People just wouldn't read a magazine online no matter what it was called, they agreed behind her back.

Now, as the others saw their circulation figures falling and struggled to catch up and match her online performance, Camilla had the luxury of being regarded by the industry as the 'go to' person for advice about online magazines. To her credit, though, she never seemed to gloat, and freely shared her thoughts with anyone who cared to listen. The upstart had come good, and was now well respected in her own right.

* * *

Slater had liked her straightaway. She had the sort of cut-glass accent that might have led him to describe her as a posh bird, and her clothes suggested no shortage of money in her life. There was no doubt she was both successful and busy, but she had welcomed him into her office, put everything else on hold, and given him her complete attention. Another thing he liked was the fact that she was happy to lead him across to a pair of comfy chairs either side of a coffee table and didn't use her desk as a barrier between them. The coffee and biscuits (chocolate Hobnobs were a favourite of his) were like icing on the cake.

She told him she was willing to help him in any way she could, so he had started as if with a blank canvas and asked her to describe how Ruth had managed to secure her position at the magazine. This was to be the first of a number of surprises.

'Ah, yes.' She laughed. 'It's not often I get caught out, but Ruth certainly pulled the wool over my eyes. Normally I wouldn't give house room to any sort of fraud, but the thing was I genuinely liked her, and so did everyone else, especially visitors to the office.'

Slater was puzzled, and he was obviously doing a poor job of hiding it.

'You look confused, Sergeant.'

'Totally,' he conceded. 'According to her sister, Ruth had sent samples of her writing and you had taken her on as a clerk/receptionist with a view to developing her talent as a writer.'

'Oh she sent samples,' agreed Camilla. 'And they were very good, but they weren't written by Ruth, and it became obvious within the first week that Ruth couldn't write for toffee.'

'She couldn't?' Now Slater really was confused, but he chose to keep quiet for the moment.

'Sadly,' said Camilla, shaking her head, 'Ruth was dyslexic. But it wouldn't have made any difference because she just couldn't string a few sentences together on paper.'

'So how come you kept her?'

'That was a no-brainer decision.' Camilla flashed a smile. 'It sounds terribly sexist, I know, but with her looks and dress sense she was a different sort of asset to this place. She had a gift for making people feel welcome and she could talk to absolutely everyone no matter what their background. Having her as the first point of contact here was just perfect. I was seriously disappointed, as were many of our male visitors, when she asked if she could go part-time.'

'Part-time?' Slater slumped in his seat. He thought Camilla must surely be describing another girl altogether. This couldn't be the same girl, could it?

'Is there a problem?' asked Camilla. 'Only I get the feeling I'm not telling you what you wanted to hear.'

He didn't want to give too much away, so he said nothing as he reached into his pocket and produced one of the photos of Ruth given to him by her sister.

'We are talking about the same girl, aren't we?' he asked, passing the photograph to Camilla.

She smiled as he handed over the photo, but the smile disappeared as she glanced down at it. She looked closer, squinting to get a better look.

'Goodness,' she said, sounding surprised. 'I suppose it could be her.' She walked over to her desk, returning with spectacles in place. They gave her a more serious air as she studied the photo again. After about thirty seconds, she looked up at him.

'Yes, it is her,' she agreed. 'But where on earth did she get these awful clothes, and that old-fashioned hairstyle? I've never seen her looking anything like that! She's always looked like a million dollars as far as I can recall. And super sexy. That's why all the men liked her so much.'

'Whoa, whoa, whoa!' said Slater. 'Are you telling me she was some sort of sex bomb?'

'Let's put it this way, Sergeant. If I could be half as sexy and sassy as Ruth was, I would be a very, very happy girl.'

From where Slater was sitting, he reckoned Camilla was already a very attractive lady. And yet she thought Ruth Thornhill was the epitome of sexiness. *Oh boy, what had he stumbled upon here?*

'I don't want you to think I don't believe you, Miss Heywood, but I'm having a great deal of difficulty making sense of this. You see, the picture you're painting of Ruth is almost exactly the opposite of the picture painted by her sister.'

'Now I'm intrigued,' said Camilla. 'What's her sister been saying?'

'I'm not sure I should be telling you,' began Slater.

'Come now, Sergeant. You've almost accused me of being a liar. At least tell me why.'

She walked across to her desk and picked up the phone.

'Amber?' she said, 'More coffee please, and can you find me a couple of the photos from the Christmas party? The ones with you and Ruth together would be good. Thank you.'

She replaced the phone and walked back to her seat.

'Now, Sergeant,' she said, smiling, 'your turn to talk, don't you think?'

'I'm sorry,' he replied defensively. 'I didn't mean to imply you're not telling the truth. Let me explain and you'll see why I'm somewhat confused. According to Ruth's sister,' he continued, 'Ruth got the job here on the strength of her writing. She started as a receptionist/clerk and began to work her way up. She had been appointed as a staff writer not long before she disappeared, and she got the odd credit under the name of Ruby Rider.'

At that moment, there was a knock on the door.

'Come in,' called Camilla.

A young girl with striking red hair came in, looking nervous and carrying a tray of coffee. She looked about sixteen, but Slater guessed she was probably nineteen or maybe twenty. She walked across and placed the tray on the coffee table, then handed an envelope to Camilla.

'This is Amber,' said Camilla. 'Amber, this is Sergeant Slater. He's looking into Ruth's disappearance.'

Amber obviously wasn't used to dealing with police officers. She regarded Slater with wide eyes, as though he were so different from the rest of them he was perhaps a Martian.

'I thought she'd run away,' she said, 'with some bloke.'

'That may well be the case,' agreed Slater, 'I'm just trying to prove it.'

'Thank you, Amber,' said Camilla. 'That will be all for now.'

Then, as Amber turned to walk away, she added, 'One more thing, please. When you get back to your desk, could you ask Ruby if she would pop her head around the door?'

She waited for the girl to leave before resuming their conversation.

'It's a funny thing,' she said, 'but Ruth never mentioned anything about a boyfriend. You'd think she might have mentioned it if she was keen enough to run away with him.' She pondered the thought for moment. 'Then again,' she mused, 'now I think about it, she never really told anyone anything about herself.'

'I thought you said she was good talker,' pointed out Slater.

'Oh, she could talk alright,' said Camilla. 'She could talk for England. But she never actually told you anything about herself. She had that gift for getting others to talk about themselves, so she never needed to tell anyone anything about herself.'

She suddenly seemed to realise she was still holding the envelope Amber had given her. She pulled the three photos out and took a quick look before handing them over to Slater.

'Admittedly these were taken at our Christmas party, so everyone was dressed up, but this is the Ruth we knew here. Now what would you say? Frumpy? Or sexy?'

He took the photos and studied them carefully. Each one showed two girls. One was obviously Amber, with her long, flowing, red hair and pretty face. On her own she would have made a pretty picture, but the girl beside her, being ten years older and about a hundred years more sophisticated, was the one who caught the eye.

The dress she wore accentuated a fabulous figure and she had the classic face of an English rose, framed with fashionably styled, glossy hair. Slater thought Ruth Thornhill looked absolutely stunning. He looked again at the photo he had been given by her sister. If you looked closely you could see they might be the same girl, but just as obviously they weren't the same person.

'Wow!' was all he could say.

'Wow, indeed,' agreed Camilla. 'Who do you think all the men had eyes for? There were a lot of jealous wives that night, that's for sure.'

There was another knock on the door. This time it opened just enough for a woman to appear. She was obviously well into her late forties, with the well-worn look of a harassed mother.

'You wanted to see me?' she asked.

'Ah, Ruby. Thank you for coming by. The sergeant here wanted to see the real Ruby Rider for himself.'

Slater had more or less seen that one coming as soon as Camilla had asked Amber to send Ruby along, but even so, he still managed to feel embarrassed.

'Err, yes. Right,' he said, uncomfortably. 'Hello, Ruby. Thank you for coming down. I just wanted to eliminate you from my inquiry.'

'Does that mean you won't be arresting me?' asked Ruby, with a smile.

'I'm afraid so.' He smiled back.

'Damn.' She grinned. 'I never get to have any fun.' She winked amiably at him, then closed the door and was gone.

Camilla turned to Slater.

'I'm sorry if I've made your inquiry go all pear-shaped,' she said with a half-smile. 'But is there anything I can do that might actually help?'

'Pear-shaped is more interesting,' he said, jokingly. 'Can I have a copy of this photograph? That would help.'

'I can do better than that. I've got some with her dressed for work rather than for a party. That would be better, wouldn't it?'

'Yes. Yes, it would,' he agreed, 'Thank you. You've been very helpful.'

'I'll get onto that right away,' she said heading for her desk. 'I'm sure I've got them in my desk. Is there anything else?'

'There is one thing, although as she wasn't a staff writer it probably won't mean anything to you. Do you know of a hotel in London called the Mistral? Apparently you paid for her to stay in this hotel now she was a staff writer.'

Her face told him her answer before she spoke.

'I'm sorry. I've never heard of the Mistral Hotel, and I certainly don't pay for my staff writers to stay in hotels. We're an online business. That's why this place is so small. It serves mainly as a place for me to meet clients to discuss advertising. Most of my writers work from home and just come in once a week. On any other day you would have missed Ruby.'

'Oh well. I had to ask,' said Slater, unsurprised to have drawn another blank.

She rummaged in her desk, finally producing two photographs of Ruth immaculately made-up and finely dressed.

'She could have been a great model.' Camilla sighed, handing the photos over. 'She had everything.'

Slater looked at the two photos. He had to agree with Camilla. Ruth certainly appeared to have everything.

He had just one last question.

'Is there anyone here she might have confided in?'

Camilla thought for a moment before answering. 'The only one who might know anything would be Amber. They used to share reception and Ruth taught Amber how everything worked. Maybe they shared gossip.'

'Is it okay if I talk to her?'

'Of course, but you might find it easier after work. She's very busy and conscientious. You're welcome to try, but if you try to talk to her here she might tend to be distracted. And, you should know that she's not very worldly. Being a police officer, you'll probably intimidate her.'

'I'll ask her on the way out. Thanks for these.' He waved the photos in the air before putting them carefully in his pocket.

She led him to the door and shook his hand warmly as he left.

'If there's anything else I can do, or if you have any more questions, just let me know.'

* * *

Just as Camilla had predicted, Amber seemed to be totally overwhelmed by, and engrossed in, her work. Slater figured that maybe it would be better to meet her in a different environment, and she agreed to meet him outside, after work at five o'clock.

He had half an hour to kill, so he sauntered across to investigate a small park which nestled behind the buildings opposite. He took a quick look around. This really was a nice little park. It would be a good place to have a quiet chat with Amber. There was even a coffee shop just two doors down from the *Magazine*. He could meet Amber, buy them coffees, and then bring her across to the park. Perfect.

He ambled slowly back to the offices and sat on a bench nearby to wait, slowly becoming lost in his thoughts about the case. There was no doubt it was getting more complicated by the minute, and his instincts were telling him he was beginning to open up a whole can of worms — and who knew where that was going to lead?

* * *

No matter what Ruth's sister might believe, it seemed there was no doubt Ruth had been leading a double life. She was the dowdy, forgiveness-seeking prayer-monger at the weekend, but the sassy, sexy, complete opposite during the week. So what, he wondered, had she really been up to?

The possibilities this double identity offered made him feel uneasy. In his experience, people who led such lives rarely did so from good intentions. Whatever was really behind Ruth's behaviour and disappearance, he had the uncomfortable feeling it was going to be a whole lot more complicated than a simple runaway.

He was roused from his thoughts by a tap on the shoulder.

'Amber! I'm sorry. I meant to come and stand by the door.'

'That's ok,' she said, sounding shy. 'You weren't exactly hard to find.'

He jumped to his feet.

'Come on, I'll buy you a coffee. We can talk in the park over the road, if that's ok?'

'Yeah,' she said, falling into step alongside him. 'Great.'

She insisted on waiting outside while Slater queued for two coffees. She was wearing a light waterproof coat which hung open to reveal a short blue skirt and a sensible white blouse. Watching her through the window, he could see her fidgeting and fiddling with her skirt under the coat. It was a good six inches above her knees to start, but as he watched, it seemed to lengthen until it stopped just above her knees.

Observing her, he thought she was a bit on the skinny side, and she obviously lacked a bit of confidence which made her stand small rather than tall. He thought about the photos he had seen of her with Ruth, and how happy and confident she had looked then. He guessed Ruth had given her that confidence. Camilla had said Ruth had that ability to make people feel good.

* * *

'Amber. It's a pretty name,' he said, as they walked slowly over to the little park.

'My mum chose it. As soon as she saw what colour me hair was,' she explained.

'It was a good choice. Do you get on with your mum?'

'Oh, yeah. She's great. It's me dad who's hard work.'

'He doesn't like the short skirt, then?'

She looked embarrassed.

'I watched it growing longer while I was waiting for the coffees,' Slater explained.

'He says it makes me look like a tart,' Amber said. 'He seems to think fashion's a crime. He'd wrap me up in cotton wool if he had his way. He never lets me go out with boys or anything.'

Slater thought that would explain her lack of confidence.

He led her to a bench and invited her to sit with him.

'Are you sure you don't mind talking to me?'

'I don't mind,' she began. 'But I'm not sure I really understand why you're asking questions. I mean, I told 'em what I knew before. They said she ran away. She did, didn't she? That's what the other policemen said back then.'

'I understand,' Slater said. 'And I know you spoke to them before, but sometimes you remember things after the event, you know? We just want to make sure we got it right and didn't miss anything back then. You're not in any trouble or anything like that. Okay?'

She nodded her head and smiled. He smiled back. Slater got the impression that Amber wasn't used to being listened to, and was enjoying being the focus of someone's undivided attention.

'Did you like Ruth?' he began.

'Oh, yeah. She was like the big sister I never had, you know? She was funny and kind. I'd never met anyone like her before. At first, she just showed me how to do my job. She taught me what to say to people, how to answer the phone in the right way . . .'

She had a smile on her face just from the memory. Slater thought Ruth had meant a lot to this slip of a girl.

'And then she started to help me with my clothes, and my make-up. She was really good to me, you know? She was a fun person. Just being with her made me feel so good.'

She looked into his face for the first time, and he could see the tears in her eyes.

'And then she just left. She didn't even tell me she was going. Just didn't turn up no more.'

The tears were flowing now. Slater fumbled in his pocket for a tissue and handed it to her. She wiped her eyes and sniffed hard.

'Sorry,' she said, quietly.

'Don't apologise,' Slater said, gently. 'You really miss her, don't you?'

'Yeah.' She nodded. 'I really do. There's not much fun in my life right now.'

'I think you were probably a little bit in love with her,' he explained, adding hastily when he saw the look on her face, 'like you'd love a big sister. So it's quite natural to be upset when you think about how much you miss her.'

'Yeah. I suppose so. But I can't understand why she didn't say goodbye. I mean, it's not as if I could have told anyone where she'd gone or anything.'

This was a blow. He'd been hoping Amber would be able to fill in the blanks regarding her life up here in town.

'You can keep a secret, then?'

'I didn't have to.' She looked at him. 'She never actually told me anything. I've spent hours thinking about it since she left. It wasn't until she'd gone that I realised she had never told me anything about herself. I knew she went home every weekend, but I can't remember her ever telling me where home was. Isn't that strange?'

'Did she ever talk about her sister?'

'Not really, no. She did say she was a bit bossy and interfering, but that was something of a one-off, you know? She never really talked about her family or her home.'

Slater was getting the feeling this interview was going to be a fruitless exercise. It seemed as though Amber, the nearest thing to a friend Ruth had seemed to have, knew even less about her than he did. Maybe he needed to change his approach.

He spent another fifteen minutes trying to get Amber to remember any little detail that might help, but he quickly realised he was wasting his time. And it wasn't that Amber was keeping things from him; he was convinced she genuinely didn't know anything. The only slight glimmer of hope was that Amber thought Ruth may once have mentioned staying with a cousin in a flat in Clapham. But even that wasn't backed up with any degree of certainty.

'I'm sorry,' she said at last. 'I'm really not helping much, am I? I'm just a waste of your time.'

'It's ok,' he reassured her, 'you can't tell me what you don't know. I'm grateful you could spare me the time. And anyway, you've told me a bit more about what sort of person she was. And that helps, honestly.'

He gave her a smile of encouragement and she smiled shyly back. He thought she was quite pretty when she smiled and he could imagine how someone like Ruth would have been so good for this girl's confidence.

'Anyway,' he said, looking at his watch, 'I'd better let you get off home.'

'Oh, that's alright. There's no rush,' she said, a bit too hastily. 'Me mum's a nurse. She's working late. And I'm in no hurry to face me dad. He'll want to know where I've been, who I've been with.'

She didn't say any more about her dad, but Slater could imagine what she meant.

'We can talk some more if you like,' she said, sounding hopeful. 'It's nice talking to you. You don't try to make me feel small, you know? And you listen to what I say, just like Ruth did.'

This conversation was taking a turn Slater hadn't bargained on. She was a nice enough kid, but the last thing Slater needed now was a girl half his age developing a crush on him. It wasn't the first time he had inadvertently attracted the attentions of the opposite sex, and to be honest, he quite enjoyed the game when it involved the right sort of woman, but Amber didn't meet his criteria at all.

'I'm afraid I have to catch a train,' he explained. 'And you need to get yourself home, even if your dad is the only person waiting for you.'

'But at least tonight I can tell him I've been helping the police,' she said gloomily. 'He can't find fault with that, can he?'

'I certainly hope not,' agreed Slater. 'But if he does, give him this.' He handed her one of his cards. 'Tell him he can call me any time if he wants to know why I'm talking to you.'

She looked at the card as if it were something really precious. Then she looked up at him and back to the card.

'Can I keep it?'

'Of course.'

'Really? Wow!' she said breathlessly, clutching the card to her heart. 'You're the first man who's ever given me his phone number.'

Now Slater was becoming just a tad alarmed. This was supposed to be an interview, but Amber was beginning to treat it like a first date.

'It's just a business card, Amber. In case you think of anything else that might help me. It's quite possible you'll think of something in the next day or two. It often happens like that, and if it does, I'd like you to give me a ring. Do you understand?'

'Oh yeah,' she said, unconvincingly. 'I get it. If I think of anything else, I'll ring. And I will, I promise.'

He walked with her, down to the tube station where, at last, they said their farewells; Slater trying to be as professionally formal as possible, but with the overwhelming feeling that Amber was expecting something more, like perhaps a hug or even a kiss goodbye.

* * *

As the train gathered speed on the way back to Tinton, Slater asked himself what more he had learned today. Not much, if he was being honest. But it wasn't all bad news. At least now, on the plus side, he knew Ruth was definitely leading some sort of double life, and during the week it was based up in London. But that was where the pluses ended. So far, he didn't have a clue *where* exactly the London part of her double life was based.

It seemed the Mistral Hotel almost certainly didn't exist.

There was a possible cousin, but this seemed unlikely too. Surely her sister would have known that and told him about it. And there might be a flat in Clapham, but even that was only a vague possibility.

The only thing he could really be sure about was that finding where she lived was going to be like looking for a needle in a haystack. A bloody huge haystack.

But the thing that was nagging away at him more than anything was this: it hadn't taken any great detective work to find out what he now knew; the information had been there at the *Magazine* the whole time. All anyone had to do was ask. So why was there no mention of most of it in the original investigation?

CHAPTER SEVEN

The previous inquiry had supposedly done all the possible searches to find something to prove Ruth Thornhill had lived in London, and it claimed it had drawn a blank. Nevertheless, Dave Slater went painstakingly through the procedures again.

First, he tried to find some reference to her as an individual. But this drew the very same blank as it had for those before him. There appeared to be no record of her anywhere. He thought that was bizarre in itself and should have warranted a mention in the original report, but he wasn't really surprised that it hadn't.

Next, he tried looking for the Mistral Hotel. Camilla Heywood said she had never heard of it. He had had no reason to disbelieve her, but now Dave Slater knew for sure that she was telling the truth. There was no hotel by the name of the Mistral in London. Unless, of course, it did exist but was so exclusive no one knew where it was.

Yeah, he thought in frustration. Right.

He had spent the entire morning searching everywhere he could think of, but the place just didn't exist. He felt the needle he was seeking had just got a lot smaller — and the haystack a damned sight bigger. If only he knew what he was looking for. Was it a hotel, or a flat, or what?

A phone call to Beverley Green earlier in the day had revealed no knowledge of a cousin or any other sort of relative living in London, but he had taken this news with a large pinch of salt. After his visit to the *Magazine* yesterday, Slater wasn't sure what to think of the story Beverley had originally told him.

He knew he was going to have to tell her what he'd found out eventually, but that was a problem that could wait until he was sure what the facts really were. Right now, he was beginning to think the only thing he was sure of was that he wasn't sure of anything.

He had been hoping a two-hour lunchtime walk around town would clear his head and enable him to think more clearly, but it had failed to work. Now it was mid-afternoon and he had been sitting gazing at a large map of Clapham for the past half hour.

He had focused in on the Clapham area because Amber had said Ruth might have mentioned a cousin in Clapham. Admittedly, Beverley had already told him there was no cousin anywhere in London, but with nothing else to go on, he was clinging rather desperately to the hope that something might jump out at him.

And then, finally, just as he was about to give up, he spotted something. In amongst the jumble of streets, almost too small to spot, he saw the word Mistral. It wasn't the Mistral Hotel. It wasn't even Mistral Street. It was called Mistral Court and it was small enough to easily miss. It appeared to be a small side street, or perhaps a courtyard, that couldn't have contained more than a handful of houses.

He went to the kitchen and made himself a cup of tea, then returned once more to the map. He studied it again. Now he'd found Mistral Court he couldn't keep his eyes away from it. A part of him was saying this was likely to be another waste of time. But another part was reminding him that his hunches had paid off before, and they'd never let him down. So why should this one be any different?

And anyway, what else did he have to go on?

CHAPTER EIGHT

It was ten thirty a.m. on a warm, sunny, May morning when Dave Slater emerged from Clapham Common tube station. He didn't really need to consult the notes he'd made on a scrappy piece of paper but he did it anyway. Then, having got his bearings, he headed up a bustling Clapham High Street. Being part of the main A3 into London from Surrey, it was thick with the noise of traffic on his right side, and the occasional blare of music from shops on his left.

As he walked he swung his gaze from side to side, checking every building name and number for anything that might relate to the Mistral, but nothing caught his attention. He counted the turnings on the left. He passed one, two, three. Now he could see the turning he was looking for up ahead. As he rounded the corner, he stopped to make sure. *Yes. Clapham Manor Street. This was it. Fourth on the left, off Clapham High Street. Mistral Court should be down here on the left.* Sure enough, after about a hundred yards he found it.

He had expected to find a small street, or perhaps some sort of open courtyard, and maybe back in the past that was what it had been. But now he was confronted by high walls, a gated entrance, and a keypad. There was nothing else, not even a list of flat numbers or residents. Presumably, if you didn't know the code to get in you just weren't welcome.

He could see beyond the gates, and sure enough, there was a courtyard surrounded by small terraced houses that were probably once pretty shabby. But whatever this place might have been in the past, it was obvious it was now a rather exclusive complex of luxury homes. He didn't really have a clue about property values up here, but he knew enough to know he was looking at megabucks. Even if she had been renting and not buying, this place would have been beyond the means of a part-time receptionist, that's for sure.

Cursing quietly to himself, Slater wondered what he should do next. Maybe this particular hunch was going to be the one that let him down. He supposed it was bound to happen sooner or later. But it would be a great pity if he'd had to come all the way up here to find out.

He decided that now he was here he might as well have a wander up and down the road. You never know, he might find something. But although he walked the full length of Clapham Manor Street and back again, he couldn't find a single thing that might help.

He was disappointed but, he conceded, it had always been a long shot. He stuffed his hands disconsolately into his jacket pockets as he walked slowly back towards Clapham High Street. In his left pocket, he felt the sharp corners of the two photos of Ruth.

There was just one, small, positive thing he could think of: at least he wouldn't have to catch a rush hour train back to Tinton, so he might even get a seat this time.

* * *

At the junction where Manor Street met the High Street, there was a corner shop selling newspapers, cigarettes, etc. He decided he might as well buy a newspaper to read on the train. As he waited to be served, he wondered how many people from Manor Street must pass through this shop every day. Probably loads, he thought. Even those from Mistral Court might well call in here if they were on foot . . .

'Can I help you?' asked a voice.

Slater looked up. It was his turn to be served.

'Err, yeah. Sorry. I was miles away.' He smiled. '*Daily Mail*, please.'

The young Asian behind the counter was obviously not in the mood to be pleasant. He scowled at Slater as though he was a fool. He handed over the newspaper and took his money without a word.

'I wonder if you can help me,' Slater began.

'Sorry, mate. Too busy.'

Slater looked around. He was the only customer in the shop.

'But there's no one else here,' he said.

'I'm not the talkative sort,' was the curt reply. The shop assistant made a point of opening a magazine and ignoring Slater. It was a top-shelf magazine.

'You like your girls, then?' asked Slater, nodding at the magazine.

The youth looked suspiciously at him.

'It's none of your business what I like.'

'If you like girls,' Slater continued, 'I've got a couple of photos you might like to see.'

Now the boy was interested.

'Yeah? What, dirty like? Titties and that?'

'Well, not exactly,' said Slater, producing the photograph of dowdy Ruth and placing it on the counter.

The boy looked aghast.

'What the bloody hell's that? I thought you was going to show me somethin' nice!'

'You don't recognise her?'

'What? You think I'd be interested in somethin' like that? Why don't you piss off and stop wastin' my time?'

'The next one's better,' promised Slater as he produced the photo of sexy Ruth. 'This one's really nice.'

The boy looked at the new photo and his eyes widened. That told Slater the boy knew her. He felt the adrenaline rush that told him he was finally onto something.

'You know her, don't you?'

The boy looked uncomfortable and guilty. That was interesting.

'Is she a customer?'

'No.' He shook his head. 'She used to come in here but I haven't seen her for months.'

'Like her, did you?' insisted Slater.

The youth looked down at the photo again and licked his lips.

'Err, well. Yeah. She was real nice. But I never, sort of, knew her. You know what I mean?'

'Ah, right,' said Slater, conspiratorially. 'But you fancied her, didn't you?'

The shop assistant's face told Slater he was guilty as charged.

'It's okay,' Slater reassured him. 'It's not against the law to fancy someone. Do you know where she lives?'

'You seem to want to know a lot about her,' challenged the youth. 'What are you? Some sort of stalker or somethin'?'

Slater produced his warrant card.

'No, son. I'm some sort of copper. This girl is missing and I'm trying to find out what's happened to her.'

The boy had gone several shades more pale than his normal colour. He obviously felt guilty about something. Slater kept quiet and waited. Sure enough, the boy felt he had to fill the silence.

'Well, I ain't done nothin'. I just followed her one day, that's all. I never touched her or nothin' like that.'

'When did you follow her?'

'Must have been a year ago or more. I jus' wanted to see where she lived.'

'And where did she live?' Slater asked.

'Them posh places up the road.'

'Mistral Court?'

'That's right, yeah. Them posh places.'

'You know which one?'

'No way, mate. They wouldn't let the likes of me in a place like that, would they?'

Slater looked hard at the boy, but he was pretty sure he was telling the truth.

'Well now, that wasn't so hard, was it?' he said, finally. 'Being helpful is good, don't you agree?'

The boy shrugged his shoulders resentfully. Slater got the impression he had been about to make a smart remark, but had then thought better of it. 'By the way,' said Slater, as he gathered his two photos back from the counter. 'You should never judge a book by its cover.'

'Eh?' The boy looked confused.

Slater showed him the two photos again.

'The girl you said you wouldn't be interested in. It's the same girl.'

'What?' said the boy, in disbelief. He looked hard at the photos again. 'No way. You're takin' the piss.'

'I'm not. Seriously. It's the same girl. Just the clothes and the make-up are different.'

The boy studied the photos again.

'Jeez.' He whistled. 'You're right. But why would she want to look that bad when she scrubs up so well?'

'Now that,' said Slater as he gathered the two photos and slid them back into his pocket, 'is your starter for ten.'

'What? You've lost me now, mate.'

'It's a TV show. *University Challenge*. It's what the quiz-master says,' explained Slater, but the boy's eyes seemed to have glazed over at the mention of the word 'university', and now his nose was back in his dirty magazine.

'Don't watch poncey crap like that,' he mumbled.

'No? Now there's a surprise. Oh well, never mind,' said Slater, as he turned and left the shop.

He started to head back up the road to Mistral Court. At least *now* he felt he might be getting somewhere. It was a start.

* * *

He peered through the gates at the empty courtyard, wondering how he was going to get inside. Normally in this sort of situation, there would be a row of buttons to push and he would just work his way through them until someone answered. Then the magic words 'police officer' tended to get him inside quite easily.

That wasn't going to work here for two reasons. First, there were no buttons, and second, he didn't want to use the magic words if he could avoid it. The original investigation had failed to mention this flat and that could only mean one of two things: either it was down to incompetence or it was a cover-up. Whichever it was, he wasn't going to be very popular when it was discovered he'd found it, so the longer no one knew he was here, the better.

He scratched his head as he tried to come up with a plan. Perhaps he should just press all the keys? No. That would be stupid. There might be some sort of alarm system that alerted the local police. That would make a mockery of his desire to keep a low profile.

After five minutes, the best he could come up with was to wait until someone actually used the keypad. It wasn't a great plan, but he didn't have anything better. He settled back against the wall and opened his newspaper. He started with the football results.

He was bemoaning the fact that Spurs had lost yet again when he became aware of a familiar noise. Someone was sweeping. He looked around, expecting to see someone sweeping the street, but there was no one there. Yet he could still hear the noise. He peered through the gate. There, at the back of the courtyard, a little old man was sweeping. He was obviously happy in his work, singing quietly to himself and shuffling some fancy footwork in time to his singing.

Slater guessed the little man must be in his seventies, his white hair perfectly matched by an equally white moustache. He wore round wire-rimmed glasses, and a flat cap which seemed the perfect accompaniment to his faded blue overalls. He looked like a throwback from the fifties, but he also had the unmistakable air of a man who took pride in his work, no matter how humble that work might be.

'Excuse me,' Slater called through the gates.

The little old man continued to sweep and sing, apparently oblivious to the voice calling him. Then he turned slightly to his left and Slater saw the unmistakable white lead trailing from his ears down to an iPod clipped to his belt. He might look like something from the fifties, but he was no stranger to modern-day pleasures.

'Excuse me,' called Slater again, only a bit louder this time, and with some arm-waving thrown in. 'Over here.'

The sweeper looked up at Slater, smiled and waved back, then pirouetted neatly in time to the music before turning back to his sweeping.

Slater waited patiently as the sweeper waltzed slowly back along his line, and then as the man reached the end of the line and did his next pirouette, he called again, this time shoving his arms through the gate and waving even more frantically.

The sweeper waved back to him but continued his little dance for a few more seconds. Then, with a flourish, he made a little skip in the air and stamped his feet together. Slater watched fascinated as the man then bowed gracefully to his broom before leaning it against the wall.

'I'll be right back,' he promised the broom. 'The next one's a foxtrot.'

As he walked over to Slater, he reached down to pause his iPod.

'Yes, mate,' he said. 'What can I do for you?'

'Morning,' replied Slater. 'How do I get in?'

'If you don't know how to get in, then you ain't supposed to get in.'

'But I need to get in to see someone,' insisted Slater.

'Well, perhaps you do, son, but if they haven't told you how to get in, maybe they don't want to see you.'

Slater produced the photo of sexy Ruth.

'I'm trying to find this woman,' he said, showing the photograph. 'I think she lives here.'

The old man studied the photo, and then looked suspiciously at Slater.

'You're not one of those weird people, are you?'

'What weird people?'

'One of them whatchacallums. Errm, ah, yes. A stalker.'

This was the second time Slater had been accused of being a stalker in less than an hour. He wondered if maybe he needed to change the way he dressed or something.

'Do I look like a bloody stalker?' he asked, irritated.

'Dunno,' came the reply. 'I never seen one before. But I suppose you must look like one if you are one.'

'But I'm not one. I'm an undercover police officer.'

The little old man stepped back and looked Slater up and down. He sucked on his teeth as he considered this newcomer who claimed first to be a stalker, and now to be a police officer.

'Well,' he said after some consideration, 'if you are an undercover police officer, you ain't a very good one, are you?'

'What?' Slater was puzzled.

'You won't stay undercover for long if you go around telling everyone you're undercover, now, will you? I mean, I was quite happy to believe you were a stalker.'

'But I'm not a bloody stalker,' said Slater, his patience wearing thin. He took a couple of deep breaths and made a decision.

'Look,' he said, producing his warrant card, 'I'm a police officer. The girl in this photograph has gone missing. I believe she lives, or may have once lived, here, but I need to confirm this. That's why I want to come in.'

So much for keeping my identity quiet.

The old man studied the warrant card, then looked again at the photograph of Ruth Thornhill.

'Nice looking girl,' the old man said. 'But she don't live here. I've been working here for the last four months and I ain't never set eyes on her. And I would have remembered a face like that!'

'She went missing about six months ago,' explained Slater. 'There must be someone who would know if she lived here.'

'They'll know in the office,' the old man told him. 'They got records an' that.'

'And where's the office?' asked Slater.

'I'll take you there.'

He walked to the side of the gate and pressed the keys on the inside. The gates glided smoothly open and Slater walked in. The gates closed behind him.

'This way.'

Slater followed the old man across the courtyard to the corner of the buildings where a door was marked *Office.*

'If you'd said you was a copper I'd have let you in straightaway,' explained the old man, 'but when you said you was a stalker. Well. I mean. We don't want none of them in 'ere, now, do we?'

Slater ground his teeth in frustration.

'Do I really look like a stalker?' he asked.

They were outside the office door now. The old man knocked on the door and then turned to look at him.

'I dunno, son.' He smiled. 'Like I said, I never seen one before.'

He winked at Slater and doffed his cap.

'Now, if you'll excuse me,' he said, as he started walking away, 'my partner's impatient to be swept off her feet. If you get my drift.'

Slater couldn't help smiling as he watched the old man return to his broom, where he bowed and offered his hand. Then taking up the broom he carefully clicked play and took his position.

'Foxtrot. It's our favourite,' he called to Slater as he spun away to his left and began sweeping and singing in time to the music.

Slater thought this man was either very happy with his lot, or just plain mad. He finally decided he must be happy, because whatever else the old man might be, he was certainly no fool.

'Can I help you?'

He turned to find a pleasant looking woman in the doorway of the office.

She held out her hand.

'I'm Janice,' she said, introducing herself. 'I run the office here.'

Slater took the hand and shook it.

'DS Dave Slater,' he said, showing her his warrant card. He thought the old man would almost certainly tell her was a police officer, and besides, she might be more helpful if he told her the truth.

'Ooh! We don't often get the police coming here. Come on in.'

She backed into the office and he followed her in. It wasn't exactly the biggest office he'd ever seen. She saw his expression.

'Yes,' she said. 'It's a bit pokey, isn't it? You'd think the office would be as lavish as the flats here, but I suppose they had to save some money somewhere.'

'The old guy's a bit of a character,' he said.

'You mean Sid? Yes, he's a lovely old fellow.' She smiled, sadly. 'He's my dad. He dances with his broom every day. He and my mum used to be champion ballroom dancers. They used to dance all the time. But she died last year just before Christmas. He took it very badly; they were very close. I got him the job here keeping the place tidy so I could keep an eye on him. You have to look after your family, don't you?'

'I'm sorry. I didn't mean to be disrespectful.' Slater suddenly felt a bit small.

'No. It's alright. He'd much rather you called him an old guy. He is an old guy. He doesn't want to be treated special or anything. He just wants to be treated like anyone else.'

With the tiniest of shivers, she seemed to shake her sadness away and then she was ready for business again.

'Now then, Sergeant. What can I do for you?'

'I'm looking for a missing girl.' He showed her the photograph. 'Ruth Thornhill. I believe she used to live here, or she might even still be living here.'

Janice looked at the photo.

'Used to live here,' she said. 'She doesn't live here anymore. And she hasn't done for about six months. She left before the lease expired, which is a bit odd considering how much these places cost to rent.'

'How much?'

'Five thousand a month,' she told him.

'Wow! They must be pretty special.'

'At the end of the day they're just pokey little terraced houses that have been done up inside. I think the rent's extortionate, but people are prepared to pay it. I suppose they must have more money than sense.'

Having said her piece, Janice looked embarrassed.

'Listen to me. Not very professional am I?'

'You're probably right, though,' Slater agreed. 'And anyway, I'm not going to run to your boss and tell him what you said. So what's happened to her flat now?'

'It's vacant, waiting for a new tenant.'

Slater could hardly believe his luck.

'Could I take look inside?'

'I'd have to get permission,' she said.

'How long would that take?'

'They're not quick at that sort of thing. It could be days.'

'But I only want to have a look, to try and learn a bit more about her. Seeing where she lived might give me a bit more insight.'

'Have you ever thought about renting a place like this?' she asked.

'You have to be joking,' he said, disappointed by her refusal to let him see inside the flat. 'On my salary?'

'It's just that when people are interested I'm allowed to show them around,' she continued.

He was trying to think what to do next, so he wasn't really listening to what she was saying. She pushed a form across her desk towards him.

'If you were to just fill this form in, stating your interest, I would have a good enough reason to show you around.'

'What?' He had just caught the last bit.

'The form.' She waved it at him. 'Fill it in and I can show you around as a potential tenant.'

* * *

'And this is the exact flat Ruth lived in until six months ago?' he asked, as Janice opened the front door.

'Who?' she asked.

'Ruth. The missing girl.'

'That's not the name we knew her by,' said Janice. 'She called herself Ruby. Ruby Rider. She said she was a writer and it was her pen name.'

The plot thickens.

'Did she pay the rent in that name?'

'It was her publisher that paid the rent. Or, at least, she said it was her publisher. To be honest, as long as the money comes in on time it doesn't really matter who pays, you know?'

'Can I see who the payee was?'

'I think you'd need a warrant for that, to be honest,' she replied. 'I can get away with this because I can plead ignorance. I can tell them you're just a bloke who enquired about the flat and I showed him round. How am I to know you weren't who you said you were? But I can't plead ignorance to showing confidential stuff to someone who just walked in, can I?'

She had a point, and Slater knew it, so he didn't think he should push his luck.

'I didn't realise it would be furnished,' he said.

'They're not usually, but she left everything behind. The boss kept it in lieu of notice. He figured it made up for his losses.' She pulled a face. She obviously wasn't a big fan of her boss or his ethics.

'So, she left everything?'

'Yep,' said Janice. 'Every little thing, right down to her make-up and lipstick.'

'Didn't anyone think that was a bit strange?' he asked. 'Don't women take their make-up everywhere? Especially their lipstick?'

'When I asked my boss, I was just told that she'd left, and if she chose to leave her stuff it was none of my business.' She pulled another face. 'Whatever that means.'

The building may have looked like an old terraced house from the outside, but inside it had been gutted to create an open-plan living space with a kitchen built on at the back. The old staircase had been replaced with a modern spiral staircase.

'Okay if I look upstairs?' he asked, nodding towards the staircase.

'Carry on,' she said. 'As a potential tenant you can go anywhere you like.'

He walked slowly up the spiral, emerging onto a small landing. A luxurious bathroom and dressing room were at the back, and a huge bedroom to the front. The bed appeared to be big enough to have filled the entire upper floor back in his little house in Tinton. Janice informed him it was a super king size. He had to admit, he had never seen a bed that big before.

He pulled open a drawer in the bedroom, hoping he might find something of interest, but it was empty.

'What happened to all her personal stuff, and clothes?' he asked.

'I think they're in one of the lock-ups out the back,' she told him. 'I can check if you like.'

'Any chance I could see them?'

'I'll ask my boss,' she said. 'Maybe if I explain there's a missing girl he might be a little more inclined to help you out. If you've finished up here, I'll make a phone call and see what I can do.'

He didn't think it would do any harm, and he desperately needed to see these personal things, so Slater agreed to her plan.

Back in the office, he waited while Janice made the phone call.

He heard her start with 'Hello, Mr Chan. It's Janice here . . .'

He expected his request to be turned down, so he tuned her out and thought about other ways he might wangle his way into the lock-ups.

Twenty minutes later, he was making his way back out of the gates to Mistral Court. To his surprise, Janice had managed to convince her boss that it would be a good idea to let him have a look at Ruby/Ruth's personal stuff, and even more surprising he had agreed, but only if he could also be there. So Slater had had to agree to go away and come back again in the morning.

It was a pain, but if that was what he had to do, then that's what he would do.

CHAPTER NINE

As the gates closed smoothly behind him, Slater caught a movement from a window opposite. There was someone at the window, watching him. And they had a camera.

'I wonder if you can help me,' he muttered to himself, making a beeline straight across the road to the house opposite.

He rang the doorbell and banged on the door. Nothing happened so he hammered on the door again. He pressed his ear to the door and listened hard. Eventually he could hear someone on the other side.

'Just a minute,' called the voice. It sounded like an older woman. Then he could hear a quieter muttering. 'Gawd, dear oh dear. Can't a person be left in peace? Hammering on the door like that. You'll wake the blinkin' dead, you will.'

Eventually the door opened a crack until the chain inside took the strain. Part of a face and a baleful eye peered around the door at him.

'What you want?' demanded a grey-haired old woman.

'I want to know why you were pointing a camera at me,' said Slater.

'Eh? You must be seein' things. I ain't got no camera.'

'Then you won't mind if I come in and take a look, will you?' insisted Slater.

'You can't do that!' she snapped. 'Go away or I'll call the police!'

'I am the police.'

'You don't look like a policeman to me. Where's your uniform? I know what you're up to. You're trying to get in so you can steal my stuff. Well, you can piss off! Go on! You ought to be ashamed of yourself.'

Patiently, Slater rummaged in his pocket and produced his warrant card. At least this time he wasn't being accused of being a stalker.

'We don't all wear uniforms, luv,' he explained. 'I'm in plain clothes.'

She looked up at him doubtfully. A scrawny hand reached around the door and grabbed the warrant card.

'I'll have to find me glasses to look at this,' she said, pushing the door closed.

She was gone for so long Slater was beginning to think she'd fallen asleep or something. Then he had the horrible thought that maybe she had phoned the local police station. That would have been a disaster, and he began to regret giving her the card.

Eventually the door did open again, but now her attitude was quite different as she ushered him inside.

'So how come a police officer from Hampshire is knocking on my door?' she asked, handing back his warrant card. 'Shouldn't it be a London boy?'

'Ah, yes. I know it seems a little odd,' he explained, 'But, you see, the inquiry I'm working on is a Hampshire case.'

'It's alright,' she assured him. 'I'm not against police officers. It's just that some of the wankers we get around here couldn't find the nipples on a pair of tits!'

Slater hadn't been expecting a comment like that and his face showed his shock.

'Oh don't be shocked, luv,' she said. 'It's true. There's all sorts goin' on right under their noses and they do nuffink about it. They're either useless or on the take. I'm not sure which it is. I kept telling them about the prostitute who was workin' over in them fancy places across the road, but they never done anythin' about it.'

'Which house was the prostitute using?' he asked her.

'That one over there, right in the middle.'

She parted her curtains and pointed to the house opposite. Even through the fancy gates, Slater could see which house she meant. It was Ruby Rider's.

'I haven't seen her for a while, mind,' she continued. 'When I saw you looking at it, I thought maybe she was starting up again and you were a new client.'

'You're sure she's a prostitute?'

'There's only one reason that many different men come calling at regular times,' she assured him.

He reached in his pocket and produced the two photos. He showed her the dowdy one first.

'Is this her?'

'Oh no,' she said, shaking her head. 'She was far more attractive than that.'

He showed her the second photo.

'That's her,' she said straightaway. 'But she didn't often have brown hair like that. She used to change it quite often. Black, blonde, red, you name it. Why does a lovely looking girl like that want to sell herself? I think it's such a shame.'

'Is that why you have the camera? To spy on her?'

'It sounds terrible when you say it like that. I didn't want to get her into trouble. Just to make her stop and see sense. I thought if I could get some photos then the police would have to stop her. The joke was on me anyhow.' She laughed ruefully. 'I haven't seen hide nor hair of her since I got me camera.'

'You still take photos?'

'Bloody camera's useless,' she said, pointing to a digital camera lying on the sideboard. 'It ain't got no film in it. I bought a roll, but I can't work out how to load the blinkin' thing.'

Slater resisted the temptation to laugh out loud.

'Can I have a look?' he asked.

'You can take the bloody thing if you want.'

He took a quick look, hoping she might have some shots on the memory card, but although there were plenty of pictures of the inside of her curtains and the carpets, and one or two blurry images that could have been the buildings across the road, there was nothing that could have been recognised as a face. *Oh well,* he thought, *that really would have been too much to hope for.*

He thanked her for taking the time to talk to him and made his excuses to leave. As she showed him out of the door, she spoke again.

'I'm sorry I mistook you for a punter,' she said. 'It was a silly mistake to make. I mean, she was real classy, and look at you.' She looked him up and down. 'There's no way you could have afforded her.'

She closed the door behind him without further comment. As he started to re-trace his steps back to the tube station and on to home, he thought about what she had just said. Was that an insult or a back-handed compliment? He really couldn't be sure.

* * *

He was early enough to beat the rush hour and catch the four fifteen train back to Tinton. Apart from one man immersed in a book at the far end, Slater had the entire carriage to himself. He also had plenty of time to consider what he had discovered so far.

He already knew Ruth was leading a double life as meek, mild and humble Ruth Thornhill back in Tinton, and sexy, sassy Ruby Rider up in London. The evidence now seemed to suggest Ruby Rider (Ruth's alias and not the writer from the *Magazine*) was making her living as a high-class prostitute.

This only served to make Ruth/Ruby, and the entire situation, much more intriguing in Slater's eyes, and he could only begin to imagine what her sister was going to say when he told her. He thought that was going to be one very interesting conversation.

What he found even more intriguing and interesting was her flat. How could it be possible that he, a so-called 'yokel' incapable of doing real police work, as suggested by DS Donovan, working entirely on his own, had managed to find the flat without too much trouble, yet the supposedly superior police force based in London hadn't? He knew he was a reasonably good detective, but he also knew he was one of many and didn't see himself as particularly special.

So, in his opinion, anyone could have found that flat, which left him with a rather uncomfortable question he'd really prefer not to be asking. Were the original investigating officers really so incompetent they couldn't find it? Or had they just not bothered? Or was there another option? Had they found it and then chosen to ignore it? Or, even worse, had they found it and then been directed to ignore it? He really didn't know what to think, but he knew a man who might be able to shed a little light on the subject if he was approached in the right way.

One of Dave Slater's pet hates was mobile phones in restaurants and on trains, especially when the user was one of those morons who thought it was okay to share their side of the conversation with everyone within shouting distance. But this was an empty carriage, bar one guy at the far end, and he had no intention of shouting.

* * *

'Yeah, Donovan,' said a tired, bored-sounding voice in his earpiece.

'Hi. It's DS Dave Slater here.'

'Who?'

'Dave Slater from Tinton CID, investigating the disappearance of Ruth Thornhill.'

There was a short pause, during which Slater could have sworn he could hear Donovan's brain working, and then finally the expected response, designed to offend, but carefully ignored.

'Oh yeah. I remember. The copper from, where was it? Toytown?'

'Tinton,' corrected Slater, patiently.

'That's it, yeah. Still think you yokels can do a better job?'

'If you mean am I still doing the job I've been given, investigating the disappearance of Ruth Thornhill, then yes, I am.'

'Hey. Loosen up, Davey boy. Don't go all stiff and official on me.'

'Try being just a tad less offensive and maybe I'll be a little more amenable,' said Slater. 'Try to recall our last conversation when I explained to you that I didn't choose this job, I was lumbered with it. And that I don't like it any more than you do, but I still have to do it.'

There was another pause. Slater hoped it meant Donovan was considering what he had just said. To his great surprise, it seemed he was.

'Look, I'm sorry mate, alright? We've having a shit time up here right now and you're an easy target to have a go at. But you're right. It's not your fault.'

'That's okay,' said Slater, far more graciously than he felt. 'Apology accepted.'

'So what can I do for you, Davey? Are you planning on coming up anytime soon? I'll buy you a pint as a peace offering.'

Slater hadn't bargained on an opportunity like this. He hated being called 'Davey', and the last thing he wanted to do was share a drink with Donovan, but it might be the best way to get the guy to talk. And you don't look a gift horse in the mouth, now, do you?

'As it happens,' he replied, 'I was planning on coming up tomorrow, just to talk to the people at the *Magazine* and make it look like I'm doing my job, you know? I'm planning on being finished early afternoon. Maybe we could meet up then. I'd like to compare notes. Make sure we're singing from the same hymn sheet, if you see what I mean.'

Donovan took the bait straightaway.

'Good boy, Davey. Make sure your story matches mine. You know it makes sense,' he said, sounding earnest.

'Can we meet up, then?'

'I tell you what, there's a pub called the Three Crowns,' Donovan said. 'It's on Marshall Street, just a few minutes' walk from the *Magazine*. I'll meet you there at about two thirty-ish.'

'I'll be there,' agreed Slater. 'Now I'm sure you must be busy so I'll let you go. See you tomorrow.'

He ended the call before Donovan had a chance to say any more. There was something about the man and his attitude that annoyed Slater. He really wasn't looking forward to meeting him, but he figured he would learn a lot more over a couple of pints than he ever would over the phone, so he was sure it would be worth it in the end.

He couldn't be sure over the phone, but it seemed Donovan was unaware that he'd already been to the *Magazine*, or that he had found the flat. This was good news, if it was true, and meant he would be able to catch Donovan unawares with some of his questions. It could be a very interesting meeting.

CHAPTER TEN

'This is Mr Ling,' said Janice, the next morning, indicating the smartly suited young man standing in the office. 'He will take you round to the lock-ups. Mr Chan is waiting there.'

Slater held out his hand, but the young man bowed politely before shaking it. This made Slater feel awkward, as he didn't know if he should also bow — and he got the impression that was what Mr Ling had intended.

'Will you come this way, Sergeant?' he said, opening the door.

Slater followed him down a passageway which led round to the back of the buildings. There were half a dozen small lock-up garages.

'This is our storage area,' Mr Ling explained.

'So what's your position here?' asked Slater.

'Mr Chan does not speak English so I interpret for him.'

Slater smiled to himself. *Okay, I can play games too.*

One of the lock-ups was open and Ling led Slater through the open door. An older Chinese man dressed in a smart suit waited to greet them.

The two Chinese men exchanged a few words in what Slater assumed was some sort of Chinese dialect. The only word he understood was his own name. The older man bowed to him and this time Slater bowed back.

'Mr Chan has asked me to tell you he will answer any questions you have, but you need to address them to me so I can interpret.'

'Very well.' Slater nodded. 'Perhaps you could ask him when he forgot how to speak English?'

Ling tried to look suitably confused, but failed. Mr Chan was obviously made of sterner stuff, but even so his eyes flickered, just enough to signify he had understood the question.

'I don't understand what you mean,' blustered Ling. 'I already told you, Mr Chan does not speak English.'

'But he managed to speak English with Janice yesterday afternoon.' Slater smiled. 'So, has he lost the ability to speak English since then?'

The younger Chinese man looked at Mr Chan, who was still keeping his straight face.

'Look guys,' sighed Slater patiently, looking straight at Mr Chan. 'I don't know what dodgy dealings you're trying to hide, and frankly I don't care. All I'm interested in is a missing girl. At the moment, I want to keep things nice and friendly, and respectful.

'Now I know you guys are all about respect, right? And I don't have a problem with that. Unless, of course, you want to continue to show me disrespect by playing games designed to make a fool of me. If you want to play that sort of game, I can think of a good one that involves me contacting my boss, the taxman, VAT inspectors, health and safety, and just about anyone else you can think of who can make your life difficult. So we can either stop messing around and start being respectful, or I can start a shitstorm. It's your call.'

He really didn't know if he could cause these guys any trouble, but he wanted to make a point.

Mr Ling was looking daggers at Slater, but the older Mr Chan kept his straight face for about fifteen seconds, then he broke into a broad grin.

'Ah, Sergeant,' he said, bowing again, 'I must apologise for misjudging you. Please accept my apology. No offence intended.'

Then he turned to his younger colleague and barked an instruction in Chinese. The younger man had obviously been humiliated and his gaze seemed to turn even more evil, but even so, he bowed politely to Slater, and then to Mr Chan before turning on his heel and walking from the lock-up.

'I hope you will forgive me,' said Chan. 'You are right, that was disrespectful, but one cannot be too careful these days.'

Slater looked sceptical, and wondered exactly what Chan meant by that, but he inclined his head sufficiently to acknowledge the apology.

'I have no desire to interfere with your business, Mr Chan. As I said before, I am simply trying to find a missing person who once lived in one of your flats. I believe you have some of her belongings and I would like to take a look at what you have. Maybe there will be something that will give me a clue about what happened to her.'

'Of course,' replied Chan. 'Everything she left is here in this storage unit. Please help yourself.'

Slater looked around. There were four wardrobes and three chests of drawers. He felt sure there must be something in here that would help him.

'Is this everything?' he asked.

'Absolutely.'

'Does anyone else know it's here?'

'I only kept them because I have no address to send them on to. I thought the girl might come back to collect them, or send for them, but she never did.'

'No other police officers have been here?'

'No one else has been here to enquire, Sergeant. You are the first.'

'Thank you, Mr Chan,' said Slater looking around, trying to decide where to start. 'I'm sure this won't take too long.'

'Do you need me here?' asked Mr Chan. 'I will be on site until you finish but I have work to do.'

'No, no. Please carry on. I'll find you when I've finished if I have any more questions.'

Chan gave another little bow and then left Slater to it.

Wardrobe number one contained a few plain and simple skirts and jackets, and a few pairs of rather dull and boring shoes. This was definitely the property of Ruth Thornhill. The next two wardrobes were packed with very expensive clothes and shoes. Designer labels seemed to adorn just about every item. This certainly wasn't the wardrobe of a hard-up part-time receptionist.

Wardrobe number four was the most interesting from Slater's point of view, revealing some additional, very interesting, outfits that certainly wouldn't be found in the average young woman's wardrobe. Unless, of course, she had a particular sort of client to amuse. This was most definitely the Ruby Rider working wardrobe.

The chests of drawers followed the same pattern, ranging from the sensible underwear he thought should be associated with Ruth, through to the much sexier and much more expensive items that he would have expected to find in the Ruby Rider area.

Two whole drawers were filled with expensive make-up (why would she leave that behind?) but once again, the most interesting items were to be found amongst the Ruby Rider range, with a selection of weird objects and devices in one drawer which could only be described as sex toys.

He stepped back and looked around the room again. Sure, the clothes proved the point that there were two identities. They also proved she was a high-class hooker, but after that it didn't make sense. There wasn't a single shred of evidence to even suggest these things really belonged to Ruth/Ruby. Where were all her personal effects? There wasn't a single scrap of paper to prove she even existed. There was no diary, nothing.

If Mr Chan was right and no one else had been in here, someone had obviously gone to a great deal of trouble going through Ruth/Ruby's flat before her disappearance had even been noticed. Someone appeared to have removed every single item that might have actually told him something.

Up until now, Slater had kept an open mind about what had happened to Ruth, but now he was beginning to get a bad feeling about this whole thing. Now he felt she hadn't chosen to run away, but someone else had chosen to make her disappear. And that was a different ball game altogether.

He spent another twenty minutes with Mr Chan, but it didn't matter how he phrased his questions, Chan remained adamant he knew nothing about the missing personal stuff. He also claimed not to know who had been paying the rent. Slater was tempted to believe him about the first part, but he was equally certain he was being lied to about the rent. He would leave it for now. He could always get a search warrant if necessary.

Promising Chan he would be back, Slater finally made his way through the gates of Mistral Court and back onto the street outside. There was a large Bentley parked opposite. He could see the young Chinese man, Ling, glowering at him from the back seat, and he gave him a cheery wave as he set off. He felt the younger man's eyes burning into his back as he walked off down the road.

Oh well. It's true what they say. You can't please all of the people all of the time.

He pulled a piece of paper from his pocket. Scrawled upon it, in his rather spidery handwriting, were the directions to Marshall Street and the Three Crowns. It was time DS Donovan answered a few questions.

* * *

Even though it was gone three p.m. by the time he made it to the Three Crowns, the pub was still crowded with lunchtime drinkers. Slater hadn't bargained on the pub being crowded and for a moment he thought it was going to be difficult to find his man. He'd seen a photograph of Donovan so he knew the appearance of the man he was looking for, and he began to scan the drinkers' faces. He spotted Donovan straightaway. It wasn't his face that gave him away so much as his height. DS Declan Donovan would never be lost in a crowd. At six feet six inches tall, he stood out like a sore thumb.

At six feet one inch, Dave Slater was tall enough to look most men in the eye, and big enough to be confident in the knowledge he could look after himself if necessary. DS Declan Donovan, on the other hand, was a veritable giant and Slater imagined he was no stranger to the idea of using his size to intimidate. Donovan towered over Slater and gave him a crushing handshake, but Slater didn't flinch much to the other officer's disappointment.

Having been subjected to Donovan's feeble attempts to rile him over the phone, this attempted intimidation was no more than Slater had expected. He knew he was supposed to play the part of the feeble-minded country bobby to Donovan's superior breed of London copper, but if that's what Donovan really thought was going to happen, he was in for a surprise.

There were so many holes in Donovan's investigation, it was already leaking like a sieve, and Slater's respect for both his opposite detective sergeant, and the Met, was pouring down the drain at the same rate. This attempted intimidation simply cemented his determination to show Donovan that this was now his inquiry, and he intended to make sure it was as thorough as hc could makc it.

'Now then, Davey boy!' Donovan said. 'Let me get you a pint. What'll you have?'

'Just an orange juice and lemonade for me,' answered Slater. Then seeing the look on the other man's face he added, 'I don't drink.'

It was a lie, of course, but he wanted to make sure he kept a clear head.

'Can't handle it, eh?' sneered Donovan.

Slater smiled, nodded, and let the insult fly harmlessly over his head.

Donovan handed him his drink and grabbed his own pint.

'Cheers!' He raised his glass and Slater raised his in return.

'Over here.' Donovan pointed to an empty table in a corner and led the way over.

The conversation started off in a friendly enough fashion, and Slater learned that although Donovan's father was Irish (hence the name) his mother was very much London born and bred (hence the non-Irish accent).

In turn, Slater patiently tried to explain that there was a world outside London, and that Tinton wasn't on another planet, and in fact was actually just sixty miles from where they were sat at that very moment — but it was obvious Donovan either didn't believe him, or just wasn't interested. Slater wasn't surprised.

Pleasantries over with, Slater thought they might as well get down to business.

'I guess we ought to start talking about the elephant in the room,' he suggested.

Donovan looked around the room with a puzzled expression.

'I can't see no elephant.'

For a moment, Slater had the sinking feeling he really was dealing with a complete idiot, but then he caught the little smile that was creeping across Donovan's face.

'Ah! Right.' He grinned, sharing the joke.

'Now, come on, Davey. An elephant in the room is something people don't wanna talk about or don't agree about. So, to my way of thinking, just as long as we reach the same conclusion, there ain't gonna be an elephant. Ain't that right?'

He slowly, and carefully, placed his pint down on the table. Then he looked hard at Slater.

'We are reaching the same conclusion, ain't we?' he asked, his tone menacing.

Slater took a slow, deliberate sip of his drink, just to keep Donovan waiting.

'Well now,' he began, placing his own drink on the table. 'To my way of thinking, there might be a bit of a problem with that.'

'Problem? What problem?'

'It's like this.' Slater smiled. 'I seem to have uncovered one or two discrepancies. I mean, I'm just a country bumpkin, right? So I've not been using fancy interrogation techniques like you clever blokes up here in town use, and yet I seem to have found out lots of stuff that you guys didn't find.'

'What stuff? What are you bloody on about?' snarled Donovan, his face reddening and looking as if he would like to punch Slater in the face.

'How about Mistral Court?' asked Slater, quietly.

Just for a second, Donovan's face paled slightly and a look of panic flashed across it. He quickly regained control, but it had been enough.

'Mistral Court? What's Mistral Court?' he said, clearly attempting a bluff.

'You knew about it, didn't you?' asked Slater, knowing he was right. 'You knew about it and yet you didn't mention it in your report.'

He sat back, folded his arms, and watched Donovan squirm.

'To my way of thinking that's a cause for concern. So now,' Slater continued, 'I have to ask myself what possible reason you could have for doing that.'

'I told you before,' explained Donovan. 'Once we found the text messages there didn't seem to be any point in looking any further. The flat made no difference.'

'So you admit you knew about it then?' Slater said, pressing home his advantage.

'I admit nothing,' growled Donovan. 'You think you're so bloody clever, don't you? But I'm telling you this girl's just a runaway. That's all there is to it. All you're doing is poking your nose in where it's not wanted. You're going to make a lot of enemies, and for what? Just so you can find out where she went? You might have time to waste on unnecessary investigations where you come from, but up here we don't, see? Now the best thing you can do is agree with me and close your case.'

'Or what?' asked Slater. 'Are you threatening me?'

'Just do us both a favour, eh?' said Donovan, standing and towering over Slater. 'You really don't want to cross these people at the Unit. Go back to Toytown or wherever it is you come from, write your report same as mine, and don't come back.'

He turned on his heel, pushed his way through the crowd and out into the street, and was gone.

CHAPTER ELEVEN

Well, well, well, thought Slater as he watched the huge figure ploughing through the other drinkers. *Did I rattle his cage, or did I rattle his cage?*

He smiled ruefully as he climbed to his feet and slowly made his own way out. One thing was sure now, he thought, as he reached the street, whatever this was, it definitely was not a simple runaway.

He looked up and down the road. He could make out the top of Donovan's head quite clearly as he strode away into the distance. He was just so easy to spot. Slater turned in the opposite direction and started to make his way towards the nearest tube station.

As he walked, he had the distinct impression someone was following him, but when he turned to look he couldn't see anyone looking remotely suspicious. Maybe he was just getting paranoid. Perhaps Donovan had managed to intimidate him without him even realising. One thing was for sure — there was no way Donovan could be following him without Slater noticing.

He walked on a bit further, but the feeling he was being followed stayed with him. He looked around again. This time he thought he saw a familiar looking Chinese man dive into a shop, but when he walked back and looked there was no one there. He looked around and realised there were quite a few Chinese people around. In Tinton this would have been a surprise, but this was London. *What do you expect?*

He suddenly realised he needed to take the next turning on the left. It was just ahead on the other side of the street, so he needed to cross the road now. Unfortunately, he needed to cross right where there was a crowd of people waiting at a bus stop.

As if determined to prove the English don't always form the perfect queue, the mass of waiting people seemed to want to make it as difficult as possible for him to know where they started and where they ended. Of course, the polite thing to do would be to go around the queue, but as it was impossible to tell exactly where it began and ended, Slater decided it wouldn't do any harm to go through the middle.

He 'excuse me'd', and elbowed, his way through the crowd to reach the kerb, just as the bus was nearing the stop. He teetered on the edge of the kerb, knowing he couldn't have timed it any worse if he'd wanted to. Now he would have to stand his ground as all these people swarmed on board the bus. As the bus began to slow, the crowd surged forward, everyone fighting to claim their place the moment it stopped.

For a moment, he had a jocular vision of being carried helplessly onto the bus by this seething wave of humanity, but then something happened that shocked him back to reality. There was a hand in the small of his back pushing him in front of the bus. Instinctively, he leaned back against the hand and for a moment it seemed he was winning and he began to lean back, away from the bus, but then there was a massive two-handed shove and he was hurtling off the kerb.

Fortunately, he had managed to delay his attacker just long enough. As he hurtled forward, he crashed against the side of the bus close to the wheel arch and then, luckily, he bounced back towards the crowd. In that moment he knew he had been spared — he could just as easily have gone under the front wheel.

There seemed to be a brief hush and the heaving crowd momentarily stepped back to give him enough room to land, which he did with a dull thud, and then almost instantly they were swarming all around him again, busy as ants, far more concerned with claiming their place on board the bus than worrying about some guy lying in a crumpled heap on the ground.

The breath had been knocked from him, and his wrist was throbbing, but he was relieved to find he didn't seem to have suffered any major damage. It could have been so much worse.

'Are you alright, mate?' A man had emerged from the crowd at the bus stop and was kneeling down to attend to him.

'Yes. I think so. Just a bit winded,' Slater replied.

'No point trying to get on the bus until it's stopped and the doors open, you know,' said the man. 'Unless, of course, you wanted to end up under the wheels.'

'What?' said Slater. 'I wasn't trying to get on the bus, and I wasn't trying to jump under the wheels. Someone pushed me!'

'Is that right?' asked the man sceptically, helping Slater to his feet. 'Look,' he began in a concerned tone as he brushed Slater down, 'there are people you can talk to if you're feeling depressed. Whatever your problem is, it can't be so bad you need to jump under a bus and end your life.'

He took Slater by the arm and began fussing around him.

'I'm not trying to end my bloody life,' snapped Slater. 'I'll admit I'm pretty pissed off right now, but that's because someone has just tried to push me under a double decker bus.'

The man didn't seem to hear him. Instead he turned Slater around, gripped his other arm and started to brush his back down, much as he might have done with a five-year-old who had just fallen over.

'Will you let go of me?' said Slater, shaking the man off, his patience wearing dangerously thin. 'I don't need to be treated like a little boy.'

'Well, pardon me for being the only person who cares about you lying in the street,' said Slater's saviour, stepping back and looking at him with distaste. 'A little bit of gratitude would go a very long way, you know,'

Slater felt just a little embarrassed.

'I'm sorry,' he began. 'You're right. I owe you an apology, and I owe you a big thank you for helping me up. But, in my defence, I have just been pushed under a bus. It hasn't exactly put me in the best of moods. I'm sure you can understand that.'

'Are you sure you were deliberately pushed? I certainly didn't see anyone push you. These things happen when there's a crowd fighting to get on the bus. I'm sure if anyone did push you it would have been an accident. You'd be surprised how often it happens.'

There had been a big crowd waiting, and bus stop crowds did tend to surge forward when a bus arrived, so Slater could understand why the guy hadn't seen anyone push him. He looked at what was left of the crowd, the last four or five now funnelling onto the bus around them. It could have been any one of them. He felt the urge to get on the bus and see if any face seemed familiar, but a stronger urge told him he didn't need to go looking for trouble right now. Instinct told him he needed to get away from here. He needed to think.

'Thank you,' he said, regaining his composure now he was back on his feet and seemingly in one piece. 'No serious damage done. I'll be fine now.' He suspected he may have broken his wrist, but he could worry about that later.

The bus, now tightly packed with passengers, began to wheeze away from the stop, its driver quite unaware of the near-fatal incident that had just occurred. All that was left of the crowd were Dave Slater and the man who had stopped to help him.

'Are you sure you're ok? I can call an ambulance.'

'No, thanks. I don't want to appear ungrateful, but I just need to walk it off. Thank you for stopping to help me, but I'm fine now, honestly.'

'That's okay,' said the man. He pointed to Slater's left wrist. 'Just make sure you get that arm checked out.'

'Sure, I will. And thanks again.'

They went their separate ways, Slater walking a little gingerly at first, but then with more confidence. The throbbing in his wrist told him the man was right, he needed to get it checked out. He placed that hand in his pocket to try to immobilise it a bit. Absently, he wondered about the man. He hadn't asked the guy his name. He wasn't even sure he could describe him, although he did seem to have an air of authority about him, almost like he was a police officer or someone similar.

Then he began to think about what had just happened. Had someone really tried to push him under a bus, or was he mistaken? Perhaps it was an accident? But deep inside he knew there was no mistake. If it had just been the original one hand, he might have considered the possibility it was an accident, but there was no mistaking the two-handed shove that had finally sent him flying into the bus.

But why would someone want to push him under a bus? There was only one reason he could think of.

He had been given this case just to keep him out of the way. The Met had only allowed it because they thought it was a waste of time, just like they thought he was a waste of time — but they were wrong. He was onto something and he was making progress, but this wasn't supposed to happen. He wasn't supposed to be making progress, he was supposed to be a waste of space who would simply agree to do whatever he was told, and because he wouldn't do that someone wanted to stop him. Someone was trying to scare him off.

He smiled to himself as he reached this conclusion. *Well whoever you are, you've just made a big mistake, because now I know for sure I'm making progress.*

He was going to solve this case, and he was going to find out who tried to push him under a bus. Waste of space? He'd show them just how wrong they were. But there was something he needed to do first thing tomorrow: he needed to speak to Bob Murray.

As he walked, he clenched his left fist and a sharp stab of pain reminded him that he might well have a broken wrist. *Ouch, that's something else I need to do. As soon as I get back to Tinton I need to get to the hospital.*

CHAPTER TWELVE

'You look awful, if you don't mind me saying,' were Bob Murray's first words next morning. Pointing at the now-plastered wrist, he added, 'And what have you done to your wrist?'

'I look so great,' said Slater, 'because I spent most of yesterday evening in A & E getting this fixed, and then I sat up into the early hours writing this report for you. I think you'll find it proves quite conclusively that the case you gave me is far more than just a simple runaway. You'll see what I mean as soon as you've read it.'

He placed the report on Murray's desk.

'What makes you so sure?' asked Murray, ignoring the report and looking at Slater.

'I got this,' he said, holding the wrist out rather proudly, 'when someone tried to push me under a bus. Fortunately, I was able to push back just long enough to avoid going under the wheels, but not long enough to stop me being slammed against the side of the bus.'

'What?' said Murray, sounding aghast. 'Are you sure it wasn't an accident?'

'Does a good, hard shove from two hands placed in the small of your back sound like an accident, guv?'

'Hold on, Dave. I'm not questioning your judgement. This is a serious matter. If someone's trying to kill one of my officers I'm not going to just sit back and do nothing, but we have to be sure. That's all I'm doing, making sure. Are there any witnesses?'

'No, sir. There was a guy who helped me get back on my feet afterwards, but he said he didn't see anyone push me. But then we were in a heaving bus queue.'

'A bus queue sounds like the perfect cover,' murmured Murray, stroking his chin. 'Is it in the report?'

'Of course. You know me, guv. Just the facts.'

'Right,' said Murray decisively, 'I haven't got time to read your report right now, but if someone's out to stop you, you must have found something out. Give me a quick run-through.'

Slater gave Murray the short version of his progress to date, starting with his first impression of the original report and working his way on from there.

'I've even found out where the missing girl was living,' continued Slater. 'The other guys claim they didn't feel the need to look that far because they knew she was a runaway, but I'm one hundred percent sure they found it and then didn't do anything about it. I reckon they were told to forget about it by someone up above them. The whole thing smells bad to me, sir.'

'Hmm,' growled Murray. 'Maybe we should hand it over to Professional Standards. Let the police who police the police do their job . . . if you see what I mean.'

'I'd rather you didn't, sir,' Slater objected. 'I'd quite like to sort this one out myself. You know why.' This, of course, was a reference to Slater's chance to get back at DI Jimmy Jones.

'The problem with a vendetta,' warned Murray, 'is it can cloud your judgement and blur your focus.'

'I understand that, guv. But I think this has got a whole lot bigger than just me trying to get one over Jimmy Jones. This is a cover-up. I think I've stumbled across something serious, something that needs investigating properly. I've got this far, and I'd like to see it through. Besides, how do we know who we can trust up there? It could have been pressure from someone in PS that's kept the lid on it up until now.'

Murray paced up and down his office as he contemplated the situation, finally coming to a halt at the window where he clasped his hands behind his back and stared out at the world. Slater knew Murray was thinking he *should* hand the case over . . . but he also knew his boss, like him, would be wondering who they could trust.

'Can I remind you, sir,' said Slater, cautiously, 'you did tell me this would be my opportunity to put the record straight and prove everyone wrong. How can I do that if you take that chance away from me just as I'm starting to make some real progress?'

'Fair comment, David.' Murray nodded his head, keeping his back to Slater.

Slater watched Murray's back anxiously. Every detective working in this station knew that Murray always looked out of the window when he was making a decision. They even joked that it just depended on the weather. If Murray looked upon sunshine, he would make a positive decision and if it was raining, it would be bad news. That was the joke, but in reality, they all knew Murray took his responsibility very seriously and to a man, they valued his judgement. He was rarely wrong, and on those odd occasions when he was, he would always be prepared to admit he'd made a mistake. It was one of the ways respect was won, and they all had great respect for Bob Murray. Finally, he stepped away from the window and turned back to Slater.

'Right. This is what we're going to do. First, you're not going to hand this in,' he said, handing the report back to Slater, and hushing his protests. 'If I read it I'll have to pass the information on, but I can't read it if you don't give it to me. I'm sure you understand.'

Slater nodded as he took the report back from Murray. Oh yes, he understood.

'You're going to need some help,' added Murray. 'Reason number one — to watch your back. Reason number two — to make it much harder for anyone to claim you're making it all up. And reason number three — because I said so.'

'Do I get to choose?' asked Slater, optimistically.

'Who do you want?'

'Steve Biddeford,' said Slater without hesitation. They'd worked together before.

'Wasn't he one of the guys with you on that operation that went tits-up?' asked Murray.

'Yeah,' agreed Slater, 'But it wasn't his fault. He was one of the few things about that operation that didn't go bad.'

'He's young though, and inexperienced,' said Murray. 'I don't think he's ready to get involved in something like this. It could get seriously nasty and I'm not sure he's equipped to deal with that sort of thing just yet. I think you'd be better off with someone more experienced.'

He responded to the grimace on Slater's face.

'I know you like him, Dave, but I have a duty to help develop his career and look after him. It's all part of my job and you know it. Throw a young guy like him into a situation like the one you were in the other day, and he might not have the instincts to keep out of trouble. We could destroy a promising career before he's really got started.'

Slater knew Murray was right, but he couldn't hide his disappointment.

'I'll tell you what,' said Murray. 'He can help out down this end, but only if he's free. If he's busy you leave him alone. Okay?'

'Ok, boss,' agreed Slater. It was a compromise, and he knew there was a good chance he might not see Biddeford at all if he was kept busy elsewhere, but it was better than nothing. But that left one question.

'So who's the lucky person with the experience then?' he asked. There were a lot of detectives here that Slater would prefer not to work with, but he knew he'd have to make do with whoever Murray offered.

'DS Norman's free right now.' He smiled at Slater. 'You can work with him. He originally came from London so he might have some useful local knowledge.'

'DS Norman?' repeated Slater, thinking things couldn't get any worse.

'Is there a problem?' Murray said, sounding challenging.

'Err, no. I guess not,' mumbled Slater. 'I suppose help's help, at the end of the day.'

'Listen,' said Murray. 'Forget what you've heard about Norman from the other men. He's not the fool they make him out to be. Give him a chance.'

Slater thought he had little choice, but he kept it to himself.

'Yes, boss. Of course,' he said through gritted teeth. 'Where can I find him?'

Murray looked at his watch.

'He's probably in the canteen, right now. He's not attached to any other investigations at the moment so you can grab him now, get him up to speed, and you're good to go. You can start by giving him your report to read. At least then you won't have wasted your time writing it.'

With that, Murray returned to his desk and began going through the morning post. That was it. Meeting over.

Slater made his way to the door.

'Oh, David,' Murray called.

'Yes, boss.'

'Don't forget to keep me up to date.'

'Yes, boss.'

'And give Norman a chance. Alright?'

'Yes, boss.'

* * *

Slater made his way quietly to the canteen. At this time of the morning, just after nine thirty, it was too late for breakfast and too early for tea breaks, so there was hardly anyone around, just one lone, solitary figure at a corner table. He had his back to the room and was hunched over a newspaper spread out on the table before him. A used cup and saucer had been pushed to one side of the table.

As there was no one else in the canteen, Slater guessed this must be the already legendary Detective Sergeant 'Knocker' Norman. Slater hadn't met him before, having been suspended when Norman had arrived, so he only knew him by rumour. What he'd heard wasn't exactly inspiring, and it would be difficult to ignore, but he was going to try and do as Bob Murray had suggested and give the guy a chance.

It appeared Norman had recently arrived in Hampshire, from the Met, via three years in the cold wastes of Northumberland. Rumour had it that he'd been put out to grass in Hampshire while he waited to reach retirement age. Rumour also suggested he had been given the nickname 'Knocker' because the only thing he was good for was going door-to-door asking the same questions over and over.

There was an unfortunate thing about rumour. It always provided plenty of information, but most of that information tended to be incorrect, and vastly exaggerated. A lot of it also tended to consist of speculation. The rest was often just downright lies.

Slater knew not one member of staff at Tinton (apart from Bob Murray) had actually taken the trouble to speak to Norman and get the real story direct from the horse's mouth, so to speak.

The entire legend had been created from a few rumours planted, like seeds, over the grapevine from Northumberland, and then nourished by the fertile imaginations within Tinton itself. To be fair Slater hadn't been around much until now, but he had been quite happy to dine on the feast provided by rumour without once questioning its accuracy.

He grabbed a cup of the pale grey liquid that passed for tea in this place and slowly made his way over to the corner where Norman was sitting. As he approached, he could see that his new partner wasn't exactly going to be the fittest he'd ever had. He seemed to sag into his seat in such a way that he appeared to be spilling over the edges. His clothes had the crumpled air of a man living alone who had never mastered the art of ironing. On closer inspection, Slater thought it was possible he didn't even know what an iron was.

He coughed as he made his way over to Norman's table, keen to make sure his arrival wasn't totally unexpected.

'Err, is there room for one more?' he asked.

Norman looked round in surprise. His face was mostly hidden by an unruly mop of thick curly hair, which had obviously decided to adopt a style all of its own on this particular morning, and a heavy, thick pair of glasses perched on the end of his nose. He looked at Slater over the top of the glasses for a moment, turned to look at his table, and then back at Slater.

'Looks like there's plenty of room to me,' he said, waving at the table. 'Come on down, take a seat.'

Slater sat down next to him and placed his cup on the table. The front of Norman's suit was as crumpled as the back, and perfectly matched the equally crumpled appearance of his face. Slater had been told he was fifty-three, but he could easily have passed for ten years older.

Slater felt there was an air of sadness about Knocker Norman. It was as if he'd had the stuffing knocked from him and all the substance had been sucked out. And it wasn't just his scruffy appearance. Everything about his demeanour seemed to signal an air of defeat.

He couldn't understand why he felt this way, and he certainly couldn't have explained why, but he felt an immediate affinity with Norman.

'You must be Dave Slater,' said Norman extending his hand.

'You're expecting me?' said Slater shaking the proffered hand. *So Murray had arranged this before they'd even met this morning . . . But, why me?*

'I've been expecting you for a couple of days,' said Norman. 'I was beginning to wonder if maybe this was some sort of cruel initiation joke. Make the new guy drink crappy tea until he throws up, or something like that. I have to say, there's only so much shit tea one man can drink.'

'There is?' asked Slater. *So this has been arranged for days and Murray didn't tell me.* Norman was talking again.

'I reached my personal shitty tea limit at the end of the first cup. I tried another one this morning, thinking it couldn't possibly be that bad two days running, but I'm afraid it was even worse.'

He looked into Slater's cup.

'Of course,' he continued, 'It could be that we're both being punished by being force-fed shite tea.'

Slater just looked at him. Norman sighed heavily and studied Slater for a moment. He got the impression the scruffy police officer was appraising him — and not entirely happy with the results.

'Bob Murray tells me you're the only guy here who might accept me for who I am and not listen to all the rumours circulating about me,' Norman said.

'He did?' Slater started to feel a tad guilty now. After all, he had been taking in the gossip along with everyone else. Even if he did take it with a pinch of salt, he knew he would have been quite happy to accept it as gospel just like the others.

'But he didn't tell me you only speak two words at a time.' Norman smiled. It was a warm smile that changed his whole demeanour for those few moments it lasted.

Slater was briefly non-plussed, but finally he caught up. He smiled back.

'Oh, I can do more than two words,' he laughed. 'Sometimes I even do whole sentences.'

'I can't tell you how relieved I am to hear that,' sighed Norman. 'I was beginning to think Bob Murray was telling me porkies.'

'What else did he tell you?'

'He told me that you and I have something in common.'

Slater looked sceptical. He found it hard to believe that he could really have anything in common with Knocker Norman.

Norman read Slater's face, looked down at his spreading bulk and then back up to Slater.

'Yeah, I know. It's hard to believe I'm a sprint champion too, right?'

Slater couldn't help but laugh. He couldn't put his finger on what it was, but despite his air of defeat, there was definitely something about Norman that he liked.

'Okay. You don't believe me?' asked Norman. 'I hear you've just been made a scapegoat for the Serious Crime Unit. Welcome to the club, my friend.'

'You too?' asked Slater.

'There you go with the two-word thing again,' said Norman. 'You're gonna have to stop doing that. It'll drive me crazy!'

'Okay, okay. Point taken.' Slater smiled. 'I promise I'll try to use whole sentences in future.' Then, he became a bit more serious as he continued. 'So tell me more,' he urged Norman. 'What happened to you?'

'We can talk about that later,' said Norman. 'First, you tell me about this case you're on that needs my help? You've heard the rumours, right? Knocker Norman's only good for knocking on doors and doing house to house. Ergo, you must be pretty desperate if you need my help.'

'I didn't say that,' said Slater.

'No,' agreed Norman. 'But having heard the rumours you must be thinking it. If you're not, you must be mad. I would be.'

'Look,' said Slater, 'I'll admit I've heard one or two rumours. But I've not been in the station much lately so I've not heard it all. And I do like to try to make up my own mind about people, whatever the rest might think.'

'Do you succeed?' asked Norman.

'Mostly. I'm known for having my own opinion. When you make your own decisions about people, or anything else, you only ever have yourself to blame if you're wrong.'

'That's good to hear,' said Norman nodding and looking thoughtful. 'Anyway, you were going to tell me about this case you're on.'

Slater looked around at the dull drab canteen. It made him feel like hibernating, and he was used to it. God knows what Norman must be feeling if he'd been sat here for two days waiting for him. If it had been the other way around, Slater would have been going crazy by now. He made a decision.

'Come on,' he said. 'Let's get out of this dump. I'll show you where you can get a decent cup of tea around here, and while we're drinking it I'll tell you what we've got.'

They stood together.

'Your car or mine?' asked Norman.

'You drive, I'll show you the way,' said Slater, showing his plastered wrist. 'It's not far.'

'What happened to you?' asked Norman, clearly noticing the wrist for the first time.

'Close encounter of the big red bus kind,' was all Slater said.

CHAPTER THIRTEEN

It wasn't a long walk from the canteen to the car park, but by the time they got there, Norman was puffing and blowing like a damaged steam engine. Slater regarded him with genuine concern.

'I know,' wheezed Norman, obviously noting the expression on Slater's face. 'I'm not the fittest. I do try though. Believe it or not, I count calories and I eat mostly salads. And I eat my five a day. It's all healthy stuff, you know. It just doesn't seem to make any difference.'

'You can say that again,' agreed Slater doubtfully, under his breath.

'I might be overweight, and a bit unfit,' warned Norman, 'but I'm not deaf.'

'Sorry,' admitted Slater guiltily. 'But you've got to admit you're in a bit of a state. What do you do if you have to chase someone?'

'Oh, I don't do chasing,' said Norman, leaning back against his car to catch his breath. 'In fact I don't do any sort of running. At my age there's no point. They're all years younger than me and twice as fast as I ever was. You have to use your assets, and speed isn't one of mine. I use my head instead.'

'What? You mean you nut people?' Slater asked, laughing. 'You still need to get close to do that.'

'No. Of course I don't nut them,' said Norman reproachfully. 'I might get hurt myself doing that. No, what I mean is, I use my brain to outwit them.'

'And that works?' asked a sceptical Slater.

'Look,' explained Norman, fumbling for his keys, 'I might have been pushed into a siding, but I wasn't fired, was I? And the reason I didn't get fired is because I'm a bloody good copper. I just happened to be in the wrong place at the wrong time.'

He held up his car key triumphantly and looked across the car roof at Slater waiting patiently at the passenger door.

'From what I've heard,' continued Norman, 'that sounds exactly like what happened to you. You're a bloody good copper who happened to be in the wrong place, at the wrong time, and got dumped on from a great height. Am I right?'

Slater was flattered that he should be considered a good copper, but at the same time he was aggrieved at being reminded of the injustice of his situation. And now it seemed he had a partner with exactly the same problem.

He heard Norman plip the door locks and opened his door. A small sea of empty sweet wrappers filled the footwell on his side.

'Hang on a minute. I'll clear that up,' said Norman, seeing the look on Slater's face. He reached across and grabbed for the wrappers, but two hands were never going to be enough. With a sigh, Slater began to help him. Eventually they managed to clear enough of the sweet wrappers to find the carpet underneath and Slater climbed in.

As he took his seat, Slater looked around. The car had the appearance of a mobile rubbish tip.

'If I put this down in here,' he indicated the report he was still carrying, 'will you be able to find it again?'

'Look, I know it's a bit untidy—' began Norman.

'A bit?' said Slater. 'It's like a dustcart!'

'I'll have you know that it's actually very clean underneath all that rubbish,' said Norman indignantly.

'Yeah. Right.' Slater smiled. 'Of course it is.'

He turned and swept some of the rubbish from the back seat onto the floor and placed the report in the cleared space.

'My report on the case so far,' he said. 'I'll talk you through it in a minute, but read that later in case I miss out any details.'

'Anyway,' said Norman as he started the car. 'As I was saying, we've both been crapped on from a great height. But it gets worse because we were both in the same situation, helping to run a surveillance operation we weren't trained for, helping out a DI from the SCU. Now, I don't know about you, but I think there's something very wrong when the SCU can balls up whatever they like with their own incompetence but can then get away with it by blaming the nearest DS from the local nick.'

He turned to look at Slater. 'What do you think, Dave? You don't mind if I call you Dave, do you?'

'Yes, I think you're right, and no I don't mind if you call me Dave,' answered Slater. 'And knowing you feel like that makes me think you're going to like the case I'm on. Now, out of here and turn right,' he instructed Norman. 'So what's your name then?'

'Norman,' said Norman, keeping his eyes on the road.

'No, what's your Christian name?' said Slater.

'Norman,' insisted Norman. 'That's my name, Norman Norman.'

Slater eyed him suspiciously. Norman glanced quickly his way and then back to the road.

'It's a family name,' he said.

'Seriously?' asked Slater.

'Seriously,' admitted Norman. 'My mum and dad were pretty unimaginative.'

'What was your dad's name?' asked Slater.

'Norman, obviously,' answered Norman, and there was that infectious smile again, just for the briefest of moments.

There was an awkward silence, broken only by Slater's directions, but it didn't last long. It was Slater who broke it.

‘So tell me, what happened to you?’ he asked.

‘I was asked to assist the DI from the Serious Crime Unit on a surveillance operation. Mark Clinton was his name. When it went pear-shaped, I was made the scapegoat and he went on to be promoted. He’s the bloody DCI there now and I got shunted up north where I could “rebuild my career”. Where I couldn’t do any harm was more like it.’

Slater looked across at him sympathetically. He realised how lucky he was that he was still at Tinton with Bob Murray on his side.

‘Take a good look,’ said Norman, his voice sad. ‘If you had been based in London with a boss like mine, this could have been you too. The SCU have far too much influence, especially in London, and I had the misfortune to have a boss who’s in their pocket. I had no chance. You’re lucky because you’re just outside their real sphere of influence, and, even better, you’ve got a boss who’s on your side.’

‘So they really messed up your career, then?’ said Slater.

‘Worse than that.’ Norman sighed as he pulled into the car park Slater had suggested and eased into a space. ‘I was just seeing out my time, ready to retire. Me and my missus were going to do all those things we never had time to do because of my job . . .’

He seemed to choke on his words, and for a minute or so he just sat staring through the windscreen. Then, with a huge sigh, he started again.

‘You know what it’s like. You always end up working your days off. You get dragged out when the family come round.’

Slater nodded. Oh yes, he knew all right. That was exactly why he’d never managed to keep a steady girlfriend.

Norman sighed again ‘The thing is she put up with all that. She didn’t mind because she had all her family close by so she was never really lonely. She always said we’d make up for it later. Then the bastards sent me to bloody Newcastle. What choice did I have? It was that or lose my pension, and without the pension we wouldn’t have been able to do all those things . . .’

He began to choke up again, and Slater finally saw where this was going. *Oh shit! No wonder this is such a sad man.*

'But she wouldn't come,' Norman continued. 'Wouldn't come all the way up there where she'd be away from her family. So now I've lost her. And she was the one thing that made my life worthwhile. And all because some arsehole called Mark Clinton didn't have the balls to admit he'd screwed up. He didn't ruin my career; he ruined my life. Bastard!'

Slater didn't know what to say next. He really hadn't been expecting a story like that. He actually felt rather guilty that he thought he had been hard done by. Talk about other people's problems putting your own into perspective.

'I've not come across Clinton,' he said. 'The problem I had was called DI Jimmy Jones.'

'Who just happens to be,' said Norman, turning to look at him, 'Mark Clinton's golden boy. He's obviously taught Jones how to use others to protect his own arse when the fire gets a bit hot, don't you think? In fact, I'd go as far as to suggest it was Clinton's idea to hang you out to dry.'

It was Norman who was first to break free of the rather depressing atmosphere that had enveloped the car.

'Right,' he said, opening his car door, 'that's enough bitterness for now. Where do we get this decent cup of tea?'

'Follow me,' said Slater, climbing from the car.

'And you need to fill me in on this case,' Norman reminded him.

'As soon as we've got a real cup of tea,' replied Slater. 'Come on, you'll like this place.'

* * *

Sophia's Tea Shop was situated in a little side alley off Tinton High Street. It was owned by Sophia Ingliss, a cool, sophisticated, fifty-something lady Slater had a lot of respect for. Ironically, it had been her ex-husband they had been trying to catch in the operation which had led to his current situation.

In fact, if DI Jimmy Jones from the SCU had got his way, Sophia would have been arrested on some sort of conspiracy charge; but Slater had managed to spirit her away from the action before that happened. It had been a risky thing to do, but by that stage, he'd gone past caring about consequences and had been more concerned with making sure he kept her out of trouble.

They had been acquaintances before that particular fiasco, as Slater was friends with Sophia's boyfriend Alfie Bowman, but his actions that night had moved them on to become firm friends.

During the events of that chaotic night, Slater had been sent a bizarre text from a mobile phone number he hadn't recognised. It turned out to have been sent by Sophia's niece Jelena, a stunning young woman Dave Slater thought he would definitely like to get to know a whole lot better than he currently did.

It would be fair to say he found Jelena rather attractive. In fact, it would be fair to say he found her very, very attractive. He had saved the text message with the intention of sending a reply asking her out, but although he wasn't usually backwards in coming forwards when it came to the fairer sex, for some reason he had yet to send that reply. He'd thought about it plenty of times over the past couple of weeks but somehow he just couldn't do it. He didn't understand why, there was just something different about her. He couldn't explain it, and it worried him a little.

Yet here he was walking into the tea shop that she now ran. There was a good chance she would be here and he would have to talk to her, yet he had no qualms about that. How did that work, and what did it mean? Did it mean anything?

He was roused from these thoughts by the voice of Norman Norman.

'Earth to Slater, earth to Slater. We appear to have lost contact. Come in, Slater, come in, Slater.'

Slater looked around. They were outside the shop.

'Sorry,' he said to Norman. 'I was miles away.'

'You're telling me,' agreed Norman. 'I thought I'd lost you there for a minute.'

'Long story,' Slater said, sighing. 'I'll tell you about it another time.'

Norman began to push the door open.

'Come on. Let's see if this tea's as good as you say it is.'

* * *

The tea shop was situated in what might be described as a backwater, and used to be quiet and mostly empty when it was run solely by Sophia. But then long-lost niece Jelena had arrived and decided to stay. She had been more than willing to get involved in working in the shop and with her delightful mix of good looks, charm and sense of fun, allied to her keen business brain, things had soon begun to pick up.

It was now a thriving business. Sophia had been happy to take a back seat and allow Jelena to run the shop. Now they even employed two waitresses, such was the popularity of the place.

Norman led the way to an empty table in the corner where they sat and studied the menu. After a couple of minutes, one of the waitresses came over to take their orders. Slater was disappointed it wasn't Jelena, but then realised it was probably a good thing. She would be a distraction and he needed to focus his attention on the job at hand and Norman.

'Right, Norm,' he said. 'This case.'

'Fire away,' said Norman. 'I'm all ears.'

'According to the report from the original investigation, carried out by your old friends in London, Ruth Thornhill just up and disappeared one day. Over the next few days, she sent some texts to her boyfriend telling him she was sorry but she'd found someone else and run away with him to start a new life. As she was an adult with a mind of her own, and there was no suspicion of foul play, they were happy to conclude that she had run away of her own free will. Case closed.'

'Seems fair enough,' said Norman.

'Yeah,' agreed Slater. 'If you assume the investigation was thorough. But Ruth has a sister called Beverley. And Beverley is convinced there's more to it than that. She's also convinced the original investigation was half-hearted and gave up too easily when they saw those text messages.

'So Beverley starts to complain and she won't give up and she won't go away. Eventually she catches the ear of a lady barrister with some friends in very high places.'

'Like, how high?'

'Like Home Secretary high, and local MP high,' Slater informed him.

'Ah! People with a bit of clout, then.' Norman smiled. 'Don't tell me, she's called in some favours.'

'Exactly. So Tinton were then asked to re-examine the case. I was doing nothing, so I got lumbered. Apparently the Met have okayed it, but I suspect they weren't given any choice.'

They both sat back quietly while the waitress delivered their order and then continued.

'I can assure you they won't be happy about it,' said Norman. 'But then if you've spoken to anyone up there you've probably found that out already. Feel a bit unwelcome, do you?'

'More than a bit unwelcome,' agreed Slater. 'I seem to be finding out things that they didn't find, or maybe didn't want to find.'

'Oh, go on,' urged Norman. 'I'm beginning to like the sound of this.'

'The girl was leading a double life. She was a dowdy, mousy nobody when she was in Tinton, but she was a high-class hooker up in London.'

'And her sister didn't know?'

'It seems nobody knew. There's certainly no mention of it in the original report. And she had a flat up there too, a very expensive one. No mention of that in the report either. And when I challenged the DS who wrote the report about it, I got the distinct feeling he knew about it but had hushed it up.'

Slater could tell he had Norman's undivided attention now.

'Isn't this a job for Professional Standards?'

'The thing is, it might be someone from there who's behind the cover-up.'

'So basically,' summarised Norman, 'we're working on the theory that something may have happened to this girl and that there's some sort of police cover-up going on.'

'That's it more or less, yeah,' agreed Slater.

'Bloody hell.' Norman whistled. 'No wonder you're so unpopular and unwelcome. I bet they'd love to get shot of you.'

'Oh, they've tried.' Slater smiled, raising his damaged arm. 'Some arsehole tried to push me under a bloody bus.'

'Wow! That is unwelcome. You must be treading on some seriously big toes if they're prepared to go that far. But are you sure it's bent coppers behind it?'

'I'm not really sure of anything right now, if I'm honest,' said Slater. 'There seem to be suspects on every corner, but I've no idea what it is I'm supposed to suspect them of doing. It's certainly a weird one, but the fact evidence has been deliberately kept out of a report gives the whole thing a whiff of corruption, so my money's on the bent copper scenario, don't you think?'

'Oh yes, for sure,' agreed Norman.

'So what do you reckon?' asked Slater. 'Are you up for this?'

'After three years being treated like shit, you offer me a possible opportunity to get my own back on the Met, and you're asking if I'm up for it? What do you think?' asked Norman. 'Of course I'm up for it. I might even rekindle some of my old enthusiasm for the job.'

He picked up his knife and fork. 'Can we eat now? You've given me an appetite.'

'Yes.' Slater laughed. 'Of course you can eat now.'

Slater looked at Norman's plate.

'What have you got there anyway?'

'Salad. It's healthy. All part of my five a day diet.'

There was a selection of salads on his plate. There was coleslaw, Florida salad, potato salad and a couple of others Slater wasn't sure about. Each was blended with a rich mayonnaise sauce.

'Don't you think all that mayo rather takes away the benefit of the five a day?' asked Slater.

'Do you think so?'

'Norm, that stuff's heaving with calories! You must know that. If you think that's healthy eating it's no wonder you're not losing any weight. And you've got chips. Everyone knows they're fattening.'

'But they're potatoes. Vegetables, right? One of my five a day.'

'Right.' Slater chuckled, shaking his head. 'I think I see the flaw in your so-called healthy eating regime.'

Norman looked crestfallen, but nevertheless, he managed to plough his way through the plateful of salads. Eventually he sat back, pushed his empty plate away and burped happily. He congratulated Slater on his choice of venue.

'I'll definitely come here again,' he said. 'And that's a cracking cup of tea.'

He smacked his lips happily.

'So what do you want to do next then, boss?' he asked.

'If we're going to work as partners,' replied Slater, 'I need to know how you think. So, what I want to do next is hear what you think we should do next.'

Norman looked surprised at this. Slater wondered if he had been expecting just to be used as a runner.

'Look, I know it's my inquiry,' continued Slater, 'and if the shit should hit the fan for any reason, I'm happy to take the blame, but I don't see you as a junior partner in this team. You've got a lot more experience than I have, and you know London far better than I ever will. The way I like to work is to share ideas and agree on the best way forward.'

'That's going to take a bit of getting used to,' said Norman, cautiously. 'For the last three years I've been treated like I just don't matter. I'd forgotten what it's like to have my opinion respected.'

'I'm not saying I'm necessarily going to agree with you,' explained Slater. 'But I would like your input. Two heads are better than one, right? Especially when one of those heads is filled with experience and knowledge.'

Slater knew that a little respect could go a long way when someone's been through the wringer, and Norman's demeanour appeared to change right before his eyes. It was nothing dramatic, just a tad less defeat and a little more pride, but it was a good start.

'Coo. You're actually serious, aren't you?' said Norman with a smile. 'Right then, here's what I think we should do next . . .'

* * *

As Norman and Slater huddled over the table discussing the way forward for their inquiry, the waitress came to clear their table. She wasn't the same waitress who had taken their orders. This one was much more petite, and very attractive. Her long dark hair had been piled up on her head and two chopsticks appeared to have speared it into place, leaving just a wisp of hair, here and there, spilling loose.

'You enjoy meal, yes?' she asked in heavily accented English, as she began gathering their plates.

Slater knew that voice. He looked around.

'Oh. Jelena. Hi,' he said.

'I thought was you.' She smiled, her beautiful dark eyes threatening to swallow him up. 'Have not seen for long time. You are okay?' Then she noticed his wrist. 'Oh my goodness, what happen to your arm?'

'Oh, it's nothing bad. Just a little accident at work,' he replied, embarrassed. 'Apart from that I've been working hard but I'm fine. How about you?'

'Keep very busy here,' she replied. 'But that is good thing, yes? Better busy than no work, huh? And who is this?' She smiled at Norman.

'This is DS Norman. We call him Norm. He's going to be working with me for a while.'

'Ah. Please to meet you DS Norman.' She smiled again. 'I think I prefer Norm. Is nice name, yes?'

She had finished gathering up the plates now and she turned back to Slater, balancing the plates on her arm.

'Did you lose phone number? I thought perhaps you call.' She looked disappointed and Slater felt guilty. Why hadn't he called her?

'It all got a bit complicated at work after that night,' he explained. 'I got into a bit of trouble.'

'Because of Aunt Sophia?' she asked, sounding concerned.

'Oh no, I was in trouble before that.'

'Because of Alfie and me?'

'No. It wasn't your fault, honestly. It's a long story.'

'You could buy me drink and tell me story,' she suggested.

'Yeah?' said Slater with surprise. 'I like that idea. I'll call you and make a date.'

'I like idea too.' Jelena beamed. 'Is good, yes?'

She turned and walked away, both men's eyes watching her go.

'Now there's a nice young lady.' Norman sighed. 'And aren't you the lucky guy, getting asked out by her.'

'Yes,' agreed Slater. 'She's a very lovely young lady, and yes I am a very lucky guy.'

He was also thinking what an idiot he was to have put off getting in touch with her when she was waiting for him to call all the time.

CHAPTER FOURTEEN

'This is absolute rubbish!' Beverley Green fumed. 'How dare you come here dragging my sister's reputation through the dirt. She was a good God-fearing girl. She didn't even know what sex was. How could she possibly be working as a high-class hooker? She worked for a magazine. I thought I told you all this. Are you suggesting I'm some sort of liar? Or perhaps you think you know my sister better than I do?

'I was told you were an excellent police officer, one of the best, and yet here you are telling me some sort of fairy story. No. I'm sorry. I just don't believe it.'

She seemed to have run out of steam at that point, but Slater waited politely. Norman, however, had obviously heard enough.

'Have you finished, now?' he asked.

Beverley looked horrified that an underling like Norman should have the audacity to speak to her in that tone, but rather than put him down, the way she looked at him seemed to fire him up even more.

'You see,' he continued, 'the problem with people like you is you think you're always right. So, when we come along and tell you something you don't want to hear, you don't like it. And when that happens, you seem to think you have the right to berate us, insult us, and generally put us down.

'You asked DS Slater here to do a job. I happen to know he's gone to a lot of trouble to get to the truth. He's even endangered his life in the process. What he's come up with are facts. Now, I'm sorry if you don't like those facts, but that's life, isn't it? Understand this: it's not our fault your sister's a hooker, and it's not our fault you didn't know.

'We just find facts out. That's what we do. We don't get to pick and choose all the nice ones you want to hear and discard the rest. We have to work with all of them, even if we don't like them. As long as they're genuine facts, that's good enough. Now like I said, you may not like them, but that's tough. Whether you like them or not doesn't change them, and it doesn't give you the right to abuse us for finding them out.'

Norman seemed both surprised by his own outburst, and pleased with himself, at the same time. Slater enviously wished he'd said it, but also wondered how much trouble they might get into as a result.

Meanwhile, Beverley Green seemed totally lost for words. Slater thought that having someone finally stand up to her and put her in her place had come as a severe shock.

'Have I made myself, clear?' asked Norman.

'Crystal,' snapped Beverley. 'But if you think I'm going to apologise—'

'Of course not,' interrupted Norman. 'I'm sure you wouldn't know where to start.'

'I think you should leave,' she hissed.

'I think I want to,' retorted Norman.

'Er, right, yes,' said Slater. 'We'll see ourselves out, shall we?'

* * *

'That was some speech.' Slater congratulated Norman as they drove away.

'I'm sorry,' said Norman, sheepishly. 'I don't know where that came from. I think she must have hit one of my buttons when she went off on one.'

'Don't apologise,' Slater said, smiling. 'It was spot on. Exactly right. And she knows it.'

'D'you think she'll make a complaint? Only I don't want to drop you in it,' said Norman, sounding cautious.

'I bet it's a long time since anyone spoke to her like that,' mused Slater. 'I'm actually envious. I wish I'd said it. But no, I don't think she will complain. She'd have to explain why you said what you did, and she wouldn't want everyone to know how small-minded she really is, now would she?'

* * *

They spent the next couple of hours trying to figure out the best strategy to take their inquiry forward. They decided their first problem was to find out who had tried to push Slater under the bus. Going on what they knew so far, they figured the finger of suspicion pointed towards either DS Donovan or the mysterious Mr Chan.

They knew for sure Donovan couldn't have pushed Slater himself, but equally they knew he had colleagues. It seemed likely that if there really was a cover-up, it would involve more than one man and could include many, so there could be plenty of willing accomplices. Quite how they were going to proceed with that they had no idea at this stage, so they decided to first focus on Mr Chan.

They decided Slater would make the journey up to town, and Norman would start digging and see what he could learn using the resources available at Tinton. This made perfect sense. No one at Tinton knew or cared what Norman was doing, so in the increasingly unlikely event there was a mole at large, it was unlikely he, or she, would identify Norman as a threat.

And so, next morning at ten thirty, Slater found himself exiting Clapham Common tube station and following the now familiar route to Mistral Court and an appointment with Mr Chan.

* * *

An hour later, he was making his way back out of Mistral Court. His early optimism had been replaced by pure frustration. Whatever Mr Chan might be, he was certainly no fool. Slater's frustration was quite simply a result of Mr Chan's ability to remain polite and pleasant for the entire interview and yet tell him nothing. He had successfully answered every one of Slater's questions without giving him one single piece of information that was going to be any help.

Slater considered he was pretty good at what he did, but right now he felt as if he'd just sat through some sort of master class delivered by a disinformation guru. He even felt a grudging sense of admiration for Chan's performance.

Right from the start, he had been adamant his assistant, Mr Ling, could not leave his side, and after toying with Slater for a further half hour, he had finally shot him to pieces by pointing out that there are over 100,000 Chinese people in London, so it was hardly surprising Slater had seen them wherever he went.

'So, Detective Sergeant Slater,' he had said, with a knowing smile, 'unless you are suggesting they all work for me, I really can't understand why you are here.'

Slater had no answer to that, and he had the uncomfortable feeling Mr Chan had plenty more ammunition to fire in his direction if he so desired. Eventually he had decided a strategic withdrawal was the best option. He couldn't have claimed to be getting out while he was still ahead, because in his heart he knew he'd never even been in the race — hence his frustration.

It had been a wasted journey and he wondered if maybe he should have brought Norman along — his London experience might just have made all the difference. But, if he was being honest, he rather doubted it would have changed the outcome. Chan was as wily as they came, no doubt about that. If they were going to get anywhere with him, they would need something on him; something that would give them plenty of leverage. Of course, Chan could be completely innocent, but Slater figured that was extremely unlikely.

He had switched his mobile phone off while he was talking to Chan, but now he was back in the real world, he fished it from his pocket and switched it on. It was time to call Norman. Slater hoped he was having a more productive morning back in Tinton. But before he could make the call, his phone beeped to indicate he had voicemail.

'Hi. It's Amber. I need to speak to you. Please call me when you get this message.'

He found her number and pressed call.

'Hello?' she said.

'Hi Amber. It's DS Slater. You asked me to call.'

'Oh, hi. You said I should call if I thought of anything.'

'And have you?'

'Errm. Well. I wondered if we could meet up,' she said, falteringly.

Their last meeting flashed through his mind, and he remembered thinking she had a crush on him. He wondered if this was going to be a waste of time. Suppose she actually thought he would want to see her?

'It's just that I found something.' Her voice interrupted his thoughts. 'I'd forgotten all about it and then I found it at home last night.'

'What have you got, Amber? I hope you're not wasting my time.' Slater regretted it the moment the words had formed in his head, but it was too late to stop now.

'Why would I be wasting your time?' she asked indignantly. 'I thought you wanted my help.'

'I'm sorry, Amber,' he mumbled, wishing he could crawl under the nearest stone. 'It's just that I've had a bad morning. I've come all the way up here to see someone and they have been wasting my time. But that's not your fault and I shouldn't take it out on you. I'm sorry.'

'I've had a pretty crappy morning myself so far.' Amber sighed. 'I was hoping you might be pleased to hear from me, seeing as how I've got something that might help you.'

'Now I feel terrible,' he replied. 'Look, how about I come and meet you for lunch and you can tell me what you found.'

'Really?' she said. 'You want to take me for lunch? Wow! No one ever takes me for lunch.' She sounded genuinely surprised and pleased.

'Amber, this is business,' he warned.

'I know.' She sighed. 'You wouldn't want to be seen dead with me otherwise.'

'No,' he said firmly, 'that's not what I meant, and you know it.'

'Sorry. Sorry,' she said quickly, obviously fearful Slater's lunch invitation was going to be withdrawn.

'Okay,' he said. 'That's okay. Now, what time do you have lunch?'

'One,' she said.

'Right. I'll meet you outside the *Magazine* at one,' he said, and she agreed.

'I have to go now,' he lied, 'I have another call waiting.'

'See you later, then,' she said, sweetly.

As he cut the call, he congratulated himself on making a complete pig's ear of that situation, but the truth was he had no idea how to handle Amber. He was used to flirting and chatting up women his own age, but Amber was young enough to be his daughter. On the other hand, they needed all the help they could get, so if she really did know something, he couldn't afford to miss this opportunity.

As he called up Norman's number, he tried to gather his thoughts. *Pull yourself together. You're a professional. She's just a kid. You can handle this.*

* * *

'Ha!' Norman laughed when Slater had finished moaning about his morning so far. 'So Mr Chan was every bit as inscrutable as we thought he might be.'

'Hmm,' mumbled Slater, gloomily. 'Every bit, and then some. A whole lot more in fact. I probably would have learned more if I'd stayed home in bed.'

'Then it's just as well I've not been wasting my time down here,' said Norman, brightly.

'You've found something?' asked Slater, perking up at the sound of Norman's optimism.

'It could be,' agreed Norman. 'I've got a lot more to do yet, and it could prove to be completely innocent, but it appears our Mr Chan is a bit of a benefactor.'

'What's that got to do with—'

'Especially when it comes to our wonderful boys in blue,' interrupted Norman.

'Aha,' said Slater. 'Tell me more.'

'Mr Chan owns a chain of restaurants, and to show his appreciation for the work our wonderful boys do, he offers very generous discounts to anyone showing a warrant card.'

'Well, I suppose it's a start,' said Slater, his enthusiasm fading. This was no big deal. It happened in lots of places.

'SCU officers get the biggest discount,' said Norman. 'They don't pay at all.'

'I don't want to piss on your bonfire,' said Slater, grimly, 'but that's not exactly the sort of serious corruption we're looking for, is it?'

'Well, if you don't want hear the rest of it, that's fine,' said Norman, the disappointment clear in his voice. 'I'll keep it to myself and you can read it in my report.'

'Don't be an arse,' said Slater. 'But it's not a big deal, is it? We'll need a lot more than that if we're going to go after anyone.'

'He also owns several clubs. Oriental themed places with beautiful Oriental girls doing all the pampering. Massage, sir? Anything else I can get you, sir? Should I take my clothes off, sir? You know the sort of thing.'

'Now you might be getting warmer,' Slater said, encouragingly. 'Keep digging around there.'

'I already have been.' Norman sounded as though he was enjoying himself now. 'I have a feeling the membership list could prove to be quite interesting.'

'Yeah,' Slater said, gloomily, 'but we're not going to be able to get hold of that without alerting everyone to what we're doing. With all the data protection bollocks they hide behind now, we'd need a search warrant.'

'Well, you could do it that way,' agreed Norman, slyly. 'Or you could do it another way.'

'This sounds dodgy.' Slater sighed.

'Best if you know nothing about it then, eh?' said Norman.

'No, that's ok,' said Slater. 'You can tell me.'

'Ever heard of "need to know"?'

'Of course I have.'

'Well, right now, you have no "need to know", so I'm not going to tell you,' said Norman decisively.

'No!' cried Slater. 'You tell me now.'

'Sorry, I can't hear you. It's such a bad line, you're breaking up,' Norman said. 'You'd better get off to your hot lunchtime totty while I carry on slaving away here. I'll try not to get too jealous.'

Slater realised Norman had ended the call.

Hot lunchtime totty? Cheeky bugger. I bet he's going to keep on reminding me about that. He'd had to tell Norman he was meeting Amber, but now he wished he'd left it at that and not mentioned that she had a crush on him.

* * *

Last time he'd met Amber, he'd sat on a bench to wait and got so lost in his thoughts he hadn't seen her coming, so he thought this time he should try a bit harder to pay attention. The *Magazine* occupied a building in a pedestrian square dotted with small trees, raised flower beds and benches. It was really quite pleasant. There was a bench right opposite the entrance but, although it was bathed in warm sunshine, it was still wet from an earlier shower, so he decided to stand and wait, eyes glued to the entrance.

Focused on the doorway from behind his sunglasses, quite certain she'd appear at any moment, he was quite unprepared for the slender arm that slipped through his, or the thin body that was suddenly pressing against his left side. He turned quickly.

'Amber! What are you doing?'

'Just humour me.' She smiled, rising onto her toes to kiss him on the cheek.

He tried to brush her off, but she had a fierce grip on his arm.

'Please,' she said. 'It's not what you think. Just pretend until we get round the corner.'

He looked doubtfully at her and began to remove her arm from his.

'Please!' she insisted. 'Look pleased to see me and start walking.'

'This had better be good,' he warned, as he began to walk with her in the direction she was steering him.

'Trust me.' She smiled again. 'I'm not kiddin'. This is serious. And will you smile? Please?'

She marched him across the square, heading for the park where they had sat when he interviewed her before. As they walked, she spoke.

'What were you doing standing outside the building? I sent you a text telling you to meet me in the park.'

Slater had put his mobile on silent mode while he was travelling across to the *Magazine* and he'd forgotten to change it back, so he knew she probably had sent him a text and it was his fault he hadn't seen it.

'But why? What's going on? And why do I have to behave like your boyfriend?' he asked, the questions tumbling rapidly from his mouth.

'I've been told not to speak to you. She said I'd done my bit and if you asked to speak to me again I have to let her know and I'm not to talk to you. Not even on the phone. If she knows I'm meeting you she'll go potty.'

'You mean Camilla?'

'Yes. She called me into her office earlier this morning.'

'Was that what you meant about a crappy morning?' Slater asked.

'Yeah. It wasn't much fun being spoken to like I'm some sort of dim-witted schoolgirl.'

'So she doesn't know about meeting me now?'

'Course not. If she hadn't started nagging me about calling you, I might not have even remembered it.'

'Now look, I don't want to put you in any danger or cause you any trouble,' said Slater, anxiously.

'Are you kidding?' she said. 'This is more excitement than I've ever had in my life. Anyway, I think I'm alright as long as no one recognised you. That's why I thought I'd be your girlfriend. No one seeing me behave like that would think you're the policeman from out of town, would they? If anyone saw us they'd just think I finally pulled. I hope you don't mind.'

She smiled shyly at him.

'Actually, it was very quick thinking,' he admitted. 'I'm only sorry I didn't see your text, then we wouldn't have needed to act.'

'It's not that bad pretending to be my boyfriend, is it?' she said, looking glum.

'What?' said Slater. 'No. I didn't mean it like that. I just meant if I wasn't so careless I'd have checked my phone and seen your message, and then you wouldn't have needed to pretend. It was very clever of you to think of it.'

The compliment seemed to perk her up again, and she smiled happily. They were in the park now, heading for a small covered bandstand. Slater thought the time for acting was over, but Amber showed no inclination to take her hand from his arm or step away from his side. He patted her hand.

'I think we can probably stop this now, don't you?' he suggested.

'Better keep it up for now,' she assured him, beaming. 'Lots of people from the offices come here at lunchtime. You start getting all formal and someone might notice.'

Slater wasn't sure what to think now, and he was concerned it could get really awkward. He knew she had a crush on him, so he wondered, had she really been warned away, or had she invented this story just so she could con him into briefly being her boyfriend? He really didn't need this right now.

They had reached the far side of the bandstand now and she pointed to one of the benches under the overhanging roof.

'This one'll be dry,' she said.

She let go of him and sat down, patting the bench next to her. He looked doubtfully at the bench.

'Oh come on,' she said, sighing, 'I'm not going to bite. Is it really such a hardship to spend half an hour with a lonely girl who never has any fun? Perhaps I'm too ugly for you. Is that it?'

Now she was getting through to his softer side and he began to feel guilty about the whole situation. He heaved a heavy sigh and sat down, keeping enough space, but not too much, between them.

'Look, Amber,' he began, 'I happen to think you're very sweet, and you're certainly not ugly. But you have to understand I'm a police officer. I can't get involved with girls in situations like this. Besides, I'm old enough to be your father. And I have a girlfriend.'

The last bit was a lie. He didn't have a girlfriend, but he figured Amber wouldn't know that and it added a bit more weight to his argument.

'Yeah. I knew you'd say something like that.' She smiled sadly. 'I do understand, you know. But can you imagine what it's like being me? Everyone tells me how sweet I am, but d'you know what? I don't wanna be sweet. I wanna be like Ruth. She was beautiful and fun.' She seemed to choke on her words and he saw the tears in her eyes.

'You miss her, don't you?' he asked quietly.

'Yeah.' Amber nodded. 'She was good, a ray of sunshine. Now it's just like someone turned the light off, you know?'

Slater nodded. Yeah. Some people just seem to light up the world, and when they're gone the world seems a darker place. He knew exactly what she meant. He handed her a handkerchief kept for occasions like these.

'They didn't care, you know,' she said, suddenly. 'Those other coppers. They couldn't care less what happened to her. I thought that's what all coppers are like. And then you come along, and you want to find out what happened to her, and you listen to what I have to say . . .'

She stopped for a moment to wipe her eyes before continuing.

'And you're nice and you're kind,' she said, sniffing. 'And, well, you just seem to care.'

Slater didn't quite know what to say to that, so he chose to say nothing and wait for Amber to regain her composure. Eventually she held out his handkerchief.

'You'd better have this back. I'm sorry it's a bit snotty.'

'That's okay. You can keep it,' Slater said, smiling at her.

'Thanks,' she said, clutching it like the crown jewels. 'You're really nice, you are. You might be old enough to be my dad, but I can't talk to him like I can talk to you.'

She stared thoughtfully at her hands and then finally turned to look into his face.

'Why is the world such a shitty place?' she asked.

'That's just how it seems, Amber. It seems shitty while you're growing up because people are always telling you what you should do and what you shouldn't do, and then when you grow up it seems shitty because you realise it's no different. If anything, it seems worse, because you still have people trying to tell you what to do, and now you've got to start telling young people what to do as well.'

'That sounds pretty depressing,' she said. 'Makes you wonder if there's any point.'

'Oh it's not all bad.' Slater smiled. 'The thing is, you have to find enough good things to cancel out the crap. Find pleasures wherever you can and you'll be surprised how easy it is to forget about the shitty side of life. I mean, look at my job. I have to deal with crap almost all the time, but then I get to meet some really interesting people. And look at me today, getting paid to spend my lunch break with a pretty young girl. That's the sort of thing that makes it all worthwhile.'

A huge beam of pleasure crossed her face and then was replaced with a sudden look of alarm. She looked down at her wristwatch.

'Oh bum,' she said. 'Look at the time. I have to get back. There's the shitty side of life creeping up on me again, but I get what you said. I've also had the pleasure of spending *my* lunch break with a handsome policeman, so it's not all bad.'

She smiled happily at the idea.

'What did you want to tell me?' he asked, panicking slightly that she might disappear without telling him, and silently cursing for allowing himself to get so far off track.

'I found this,' she said, digging in her pocket. 'It was in Ruth's drawer. I was going to take it home and use it, but it's password protected.'

She handed Slater a memory stick.

'Obviously I haven't got a clue what's on it, and it might well be nothing, but you never know. If she went to the trouble of protecting it perhaps it's important.'

Slater looked at the memory stick in his hand. The possibilities made him feel slightly giddy.

'Amber, this could be really important. Well done! Does anyone else know about it?'

'No one's ever mentioned it, so I guess not. You and me are the only ones who know it exists,' she said, conspiratorially.

She stood and smiled at him.

'I suppose this is goodbye, then,' she said.

He stood up beside her awkwardly for a moment.

'A real boyfriend would kiss me goodbye,' she said with a twinkle in her eye. 'Even a pretend one would pretend to kiss me.'

He hesitated for just a moment then stepped forward, giving her a quick hug. She was a good deal shorter so he kissed the top of her head.

'Thank you for the best half hour of my life.' She smiled up at him.

'You're a lovely girl, Amber,' he said. 'But you need a much younger man than me.'

'You're probably right.' She sighed. 'But a girl can dream, can't she?'

Slater smiled at her as he stepped back.

'I promise you it'll get a lot better if you try to look for the little pleasures in amongst the crap,' he told her.

'I'm gonna try,' she said. 'Probably best if you head off in the other direction now, just in case, you know.'

She turned on her heel and headed resolutely back towards the *Magazine* and the shitty world that went with it.

Slater watched her as she walked away. He thought she really was a nice kid. If he was twenty years younger, he might even have thought about dating her . . .

He felt the memory stick in his fist. *Let's just hope this might prove to be useful,* he thought, slipping it into his pocket. Then he, too, turned on his heel and headed off to catch a train back to Tinton. If he was lucky he'd be early enough to miss the rush hour.

He fumbled his mobile phone from his pocket. No doubt Norman had nothing doing tonight. Perhaps they could meet down the pub and do some catching up.

But Norman wasn't keen on going to the pub. He had a much better idea.

'Why don't I come over to your place? I'll pick up a takeaway on the way over. Chinese or Indian? Your choice.'

Slater didn't think this was the best idea he'd ever heard, but as Norman pointed out, he had lots of paperwork to show Slater. He could hardly do that in a pub, now, could he?

'But at your place we can spread it out as much as we want and no one sees any of it except us. And I promise you, you will want to see it.'

Slater had finally agreed grudgingly. 'This had better be as good as you say it is.'

'Oh, you'll love it,' promised Norman.

CHAPTER FIFTEEN

Slater stared at the memory stick in frustration. At 64GB, it was big enough to hold plenty of information. Right now, it was plugged into his laptop, but it might just as well have been plugged into the microwave for all the good it was. Of course, there could be nothing on it at all, but he was convinced he had a key piece of evidence in his hands. However, without the password it was about as much good as the proverbial chocolate teapot.

This was so frustrating. How the bloody hell was he going to figure out the password? It could be anything.

* * *

'And just how long have you been swearing and cursing at it?' asked Norman, his amusement patently obvious.

'Ever since I got home and booted up my laptop,' said Slater, with a sigh.

'And that was when?'

'About five thirty.'

Norman made a grand gesture of looking at his watch.

'It's now coming up to eight thirty,' he announced. 'So that's, ooh, let me see, almost three hours wasted. I mean, people have spent years developing some very sophisticated software to work these things out, and yet here you are thinking you can crack a password just by swearing at it. Do you really think this is the best use of your time and brain?'

'I suppose you've got a better idea,' grumbled Slater.

'Well, I should hope so.' Norman laughed. 'The Anglo-Saxons weren't up to much when it comes to computers, so I doubt you'll find using their language is going to be very helpful. On the other hand, someone who speaks fluent computer code might just have a slightly better chance, don't you think?'

'That's a great idea, Einstein,' argued Slater, 'but we don't have access to anyone fluent in code at Tinton, and do you know how long the waiting list is for stuff like this?'

'Sometimes,' said Norman, patiently, 'the shortest distance between two places isn't necessarily the approved route.'

'If you don't start speaking in plain English,' warned Slater, 'there's going to be a lot more Anglo-Saxon flying around here.'

'Boy, oh boy. You are such a grouch this evening. And that's after you were given what could be a key piece of evidence. I'd hate to be around when your lunchtime totty fails to deliver.'

'Oh yes, you cheeky sod.' Slater smiled, warming to the argument. 'I'll have you know she was not, is not, and never will be, my "lunchtime totty". She's just a kid with a misguided crush, that's all.'

'Well, forgive me for touching a raw nerve,' said Norman. 'Anyway, did she have anything to tell you?'

'Not really. But she has been warned not to talk to me again,' said Slater.

'Who by?'

'Her boss, Camilla. But she was quite happy to talk to me before, and she was happy for me to talk to her staff too, so my feeling is that someone's leaning on her.'

'Now that's interesting,' said Norman, thoughtfully. 'It would be very helpful to find out who that was.'

'Yeah,' agreed Slater. 'I'm beginning to think we could do with another dozen pairs of hands.'

'Small teams make for better security,' Norman said, sagely. 'We'll just have to prioritise what we do.'

'What about this damned memory stick?' Slater sighed impatiently.

'Patience,' said Norman with an evil grin. 'You've told me about your day. Now it's my turn.'

Slater pointed to the bag containing their takeaway.

'That's going to get cold. Let's eat while you talk.'

'Sounds good to me.'

Norman began to unpack the bag, carefully laying the individual trays on the table. 'I hope you like curry.'

'No problem,' said Slater happily, lifting the lids from the containers. He licked sauce from his fingers. 'Like feeding a donkey on strawberries,' he said, sighing blissfully.

As they feasted, Norman gave a quick rundown on his day's findings. It turned out Mr Chan had several dodgy businesses.

'The kind,' said Norman, 'that the SCU should be very interested in. But even though he operates right under their very noses, they haven't so much as glanced in his direction.'

'Somehow I'm not surprised after what you told me this morning,' said Slater gloomily. 'Pity we can't get hold of that membership list.'

'Ahem.' Norman coughed theatrically. 'As it happens . . .'

'What?' Slater nearly sprayed curry everywhere. 'You mean you got it? But how?'

'It's probably better if you don't know that.'

'If it's iffy, Norm, we won't be able to use it. You know that.'

'Look,' said Norman. 'We needed to know who was on it, right? If we think we need it "officially" we can go through the proper channels to get it. Okay?'

'Yeah, but—'

'Never mind "yeah, but",' interrupted Norman. 'If this thing is as corrupt as it looks, do you think these guys are going to play fair with us?'

He let Slater think about that for a moment but continued before he could answer.

'They've already tried to push you under a bus, Dave. Do you think they're going to start playing fair now? Of course not. You said you wanted my experience and knowledge, didn't you? Well, my experience and knowledge says you gotta fight fire with fire. You just have to make sure you keep the dodgy stuff out of sight, that's all.'

Slater was still doubtful.

'Trust me,' said Norman. 'I'm a detective. How d'you think I've survived so long?'

He slid the list across to Slater. It was on a tatty piece of paper.

'Printed it off my own laptop,' explained Norman. 'It's not seen inside Tinton station, so don't worry about that.'

'I'd be a lot happier about this if I knew how you got it,' moaned Slater, unfolding the list.

He looked through it and whistled softly when he saw the first name Norman had underlined with a biro.

'Well, well. If it isn't my old mate Jimmy Jones. Now that is good news.'

He looked down a bit further.

'Who's the other guy you've marked?' he asked. 'Mark Clinton.'

'Jones' boss,' Norman reminded him.

'Oh, right. Of course. You told me about him before,' said Slater. A lot had happened since Norman had told him the story.

'Now do you think you'd rather not have this information?' asked Norman with a smile.

'But how?' repeated Slater. 'And where? And who?'

'D'you want the password for that memory stick?'

'Of course I do!'

'In that case, I'll take you to meet the how, the where, and the who. But you have to promise me you keep it to yourself. And no more questions about it.'

Norman's tone had changed now. There was no doubt he meant exactly what he said. This was no joke and he obviously intended to protect whoever was behind it. But Slater was pretty sure he could trust Norman so if that was the deal it was okay by him.

'When will you take me?'

'I need to make a phone call, but I should be able to set it up in a day or two, so let's see,' mumbled Norman. Slater could almost hear his brain whirring. 'It's Friday now, weekend coming up, but that shouldn't make too much difference. Give him time to get here and get settled in . . .' Then, turning to Slater, he asked, 'How about Monday morning?'

'Is that the soonest you can do?' sighed Slater, impatiently.

'Of course,' said Norman, sounding irritated with Slater's impatience. 'If you can get anything arranged sooner . . .'

Okay, okay,' agreed Slater. 'You're right. I can't do any better. We have a deal.'

They toasted each other with their half empty beer cans.

'Right then,' said Norman. 'As we're going to have the weekend off, how about we have a run-through, right from the start? It'll give us a chance to see if we've missed anything, and I find it seems to set my subconscious to work. You never know, after forty-eight hours not focusing on the case one of us might just come up with some idea that will move us forward.'

'Weekend off? Don't know what I'll do with a weekend off.' Slater hadn't even thought about having the weekend off, but Norman was right, a break was probably a good idea.

'Well, for a start you could phone that girl in the tea shop. Jelena, wasn't it?' suggested Norman.

Slater thought that might just be the best suggestion Norman had made so far. Or it could be a really bad one. He didn't know why, but something about that girl made him think twice.

* * *

An hour or so later, they were pretty sure they were both on the same page. In fact, they were in complete agreement. They agreed they had no idea what it was they were investigating.

The original inquiry into Ruth Thornhill's disappearance appeared to be changing into something quite different. Bizarrely, they seemed to have lots of suspects, but as yet, they had no specific crime. It could even be possible they had stumbled across several overlapping crimes. Or, then again, it could just be they had stumbled across lots of people behaving suspiciously.

'My head hurts from trying to figure this all out,' moaned Slater as he opened the door to let Norman out.

'And that,' said Norman, 'is exactly why you need to take a weekend off. Call Jelena. Have some fun. It'll do you good. I'll pick you up here on Monday morning.'

CHAPTER SIXTEEN

'Where are we going?' asked Slater, as they pulled away from his house on Monday morning.

'Oh, it's not far,' smiled Norman, knowingly.

'What is this? A magical mystery tour?'

'Well, it could be said that you're going to meet a magician, and what he does is certainly a mystery to me,' said Norman. 'But it's hardly going to be a tour. We'll be there in a few minutes.'

Slater looked across at Norman, but he continued to keep his eyes focused on the road ahead and refused to make eye contact.

'I'm guessing you've got access to some sort of tame computer hacker,' guessed Slater. 'But if you've spent all your life in London, how would you know one just a few minutes from Tinton?'

'I know,' agreed Norman, clearly enjoying himself hugely. 'It's yet another mystery, isn't it?'

'No one likes a smart-arse,' Slater said, smiling. 'Just remember that.'

'I'm the new boy in the area,' explained Norman. 'Of course I don't know anyone down here. But I do know people in London, and some of them owe me favours. The guy you're going to meet is one of them, okay?'

'We're not going up to London in this old heap, are we?'

'Hey! Don't talk about my car like that.' said Norman, in dismay. 'This car may not be the trendiest in town, but it does the job. And it's never let me down.'

'Norm,' Slater said, sighing, 'it lets you down all the time. Just by admitting you own it, it lets you down.'

'You're a philistine, Slater. This car is a tribute to style and design.'

Slater took a look around the battered, well-worn inside of the car.

'I think you're probably right. It is a tribute . . .' He paused before delivering his punchline. 'It's a tribute to bad style and poor design.'

This time Norman did take his eyes off the road long enough to glance disdainfully at Slater.

'Heathen,' was all he said.

Then he indicated left and turned off the road into the rather grand entrance to the Old House Hotel. Back in its heyday, it was an old manor house with an adjoining coach house, stables and numerous outbuildings. Now it was a luxurious, and rather exclusive, hotel.

'I hope you're not expecting to charge this to expenses,' said Slater in alarm. 'Bob Murray will have a fit.'

'Stop worrying,' Norman assured him. 'It's not costing us a penny.'

He pulled into a space at the far end of the car park and switched off the engine.

'Right,' he turned to Slater. 'There are some ground rules.'

'What?'

'I would imagine the guy you're about to meet is a little different from anyone you've ever met before. In my opinion, he's a genius. You won't think that when you first meet him, but trust me, he is. I get on with him, because he likes me and he knows me. He doesn't know you and he won't trust you just because I say he should. He'll decide for himself in his own time, so let me do the talking. Is that okay?'

'Sure,' agreed Slater. 'He's your man, you know how to deal with him. That's fine by me.'

'Okay, let's go,' said Norman, swinging his door open and easing himself from the car.

* * *

The reception area of the hotel was every bit as opulent as Slater had imagined it would be, and the well-groomed, immaculately made-up young lady who greeted them blended perfectly into her surroundings.

'Good morning, gentlemen,' she purred, her beaming smile almost dazzling them. 'What can I do for you?'

'We're here to see Mr Korda,' Norman told her.

'Ah, yes.' She looked down at her desk. 'He said you would be calling. He's in number eight. Just take the lift to the first floor and follow the passage to your left when you exit.'

'Thank you.' Norman smiled at her.

He led the way over to the lift and pressed the button. Slater took a look around as he waited. He felt distinctly under-dressed in jeans, but it was too late to do anything about it now. There was a gentle ping and the lift doors slid quietly open.

Number eight seemed to be all on its own, and the door seemed to be a long way down the hall. Slater figured it had to be more than just a room. It had to be a whole suite. He whistled quietly to himself and wondered just how much it must have cost to hire a whole suite in this hotel. He figured it had to be thousands.

Norman knocked.

A few seconds later, the door swung slowly open.

'Mister Norm! Long time no see. How you doin', guy?'

The voice came from a colourfully, and expensively, dressed black guy. Slater guessed he was in his early thirties.

His powder blue silk shirt would have cost more than Slater and Norman's clothes put together.

'How are you, Vinnie?' greeted Norman, extending his hand.

They shook hands, but then the black guy decided to ditch formality, stepped forward and gave Norman a hug. He stepped back and looked Norman up and down.

'I heard life had been a bitch to you, Mister Norm. Now I see it's true. You carryin' some weight there, guy, an' you look sorta smashed up, you know what I mean?'

Slater watched this exchange with interest. He thought Vinnie had summed Norman up pretty accurately. And then Vinnie seemed to notice him for the first time, and his eyes narrowed.

'Who's the stranger, Mister Norm? Is he friend or foe?'

'He's ok, Vinnie,' Norman assured him. 'This is Dave Slater. Like me, he's been crapped upon from on high, too.'

Slater held out his hand but Vinnie ignored it.

'Well, Dave Slater,' he said, 'you couldn't look more like the fuzz if you had it tattooed on your forehead, guy.'

Slater had never considered whether he looked like a policeman or not, and frankly he didn't care if he looked like one anyway, but he decided he wasn't enamoured with Vinnie's rather direct approach. He was offended that his proffered handshake had been ignored too. He felt he might find this guy difficult to work with.

'Well, come on in, guys,' said Vinnie leading the way into his suite. 'Make yourself at home. I got fresh coffee, but if you want tea I can have some sent up.'

Coffee was okay, they agreed, and helped themselves.

'Okay, Mister Norm,' began Vinnie. 'I don't see or hear from you in years, and then suddenly you call me twice out of the blue. I figure this can only mean you is in trouble and need the help of Vinnie the Geek. Am I right, or am I right?'

'Vinnie the Geek?' repeated Slater.

A look of alarm flashed across Norman's face.

'That's my alter-ego, guy. You have a problem with that?' snapped Vinnie.

'I don't know,' answered Slater, ready for an argument. 'Should I have a problem with that?'

'Only if you have a problem acknowledging genius,' said Vinnie, smugly.

'You're very sure of yourself,' said Slater.

Vinnie turned to Norman.

'What's with this guy, Mister Norm? Is he just here to fight, or what?'

'Now, cool it, please,' pleaded Norman, looking from one to the other. 'I think this is my fault. I probably didn't explain the situation properly to you, Dave, and Vinnie, I should have told you about Dave. I want you two to be friends. No, correct that, I need you two to be friends. Let's start again, can we? Please?'

Vinnie and Slater glared at each other. Neither one wanted to back down, but Slater knew he needed Vinnie's help, whether he liked the guy or not, so he was the one to break the ice.

'I apologise. I was out of order,' he said, stepping forward and offering Vinnie his hand.

Vinnie looked at the outstretched hand, then he took it and they shook hands.

'Alright, guy,' Vinnie said. 'It takes a big man to admit you're in the wrong. And if you're a friend of Mister Norm, I'm prepared to give you a second chance.'

Slater was suitably unimpressed that Vinnie thought it was all his fault, and was equally pissed at being given 'a second chance', but he chose to keep his opinion to himself. For now, anyway. He supposed anyone as arrogant as Vinnie wouldn't even begin to understand that his manner might just be a tad provocative.

Norman looked enquiringly at Vinnie.

'Is it okay if I tell him?' he asked.

'If you're sure he's on our side, then yeah, why not?' said Vinnie.

Norman turned to Slater.

'You're probably wondering how I come to know Vinnie. It all started about fifteen years ago, when I caught this skinny black kid breaking into a shop. Well, actually, he'd already broken in. I caught him as he was coming out. It was computer stuff he'd nicked, but he only had one of everything, just enough to set himself up at home. Well, anyway, instead of nicking him I persuaded him if he put all the stuff back I would buy him a computer—'

'Turned my life around, Mister Norm did,' interrupted Vinnie. 'I'da been in all sorts of trouble if it wasn't for him, like.'

Norman looked suitably embarrassed.

'Well, I don't know about that,' he said, blushing. 'I just thought you deserved a chance. It didn't work out too bad, did it?'

He turned to Slater.

'Vinnie makes a living online now. Selling stuff.'

'What? You mean like eBay?' asked Slater.

'Bit better'n that,' said Vinnie. 'When you get it sussed and know what you're doin' you can make megabucks. How do you think I can afford to stay in a place like this? Five K a night for this suite, guy!'

'So what are you then?' asked Slater. 'Some sort of hacker?'

Vinnie looked horrified at this suggestion. Norman looked aghast.

'Hacker?' said Vinnie indignantly. 'Hacker? I'll have you know I'm no hacker, guy. What I do to make a living is perfectly legit. There's thousands of people doing what I do. It's just that most of 'em aren't as good as me. There's only a very small few who's as good. Right?'

'It's true, Dave. What he does is perfectly legal,' agreed Norman. 'He even tried to teach me, but most of it went straight over my head.'

'Well, I don't understand this stuff either,' admitted Slater. 'But if you say it's for real I guess that's good enough for me. But how does that help us with this?' He fished the memory stick from his pocket.

'Ah!' cried Vinnie, addressing Norman. 'Is this the problem you want me to look at?'

'Yes. We think whatever's on there could help us with the case we're working on, but its password protected and we don't know where to start. I was hoping you might take a look.'

'For you, Mister Norm, no problem,' announced Vinnie. 'Is it something to do with that list I got you the other day?'

He reached out a hand and Slater passed him the stick. He walked to a door off the room they were in and into the next room.

Slater looked at Norman.

'So that's where you got that list from,' he hissed. 'This guy is a hacker!'

'It's not quite like that,' said Norman, quietly. 'Just trust me. And will you stop winding the guy up. He's our best hope to solve this and you keep pissing him off. It's not helping.'

'I'm geared up in here,' called Vinnie, from the adjoining room.

Slater and Norman followed into what would normally be a bedroom, but Vinnie had obviously arranged for the furniture to be replaced by two tables. On the first table there sat a solitary laptop. An empty chair awaited the operator. On the second table, immediately behind the first, was a huge music system.

'Is that it?' asked Slater. 'A laptop? We've got a laptop you could have used.'

Vinnie looked pityingly at Slater.

'This ain't just "a laptop", guy. This is state of the art equipment, built by yours truly, aka Vinnie the Geek. The software on this machine is also designed by yours truly. There ain't another one of these on the planet. This is a truly unique machine, trust me.'

'Ah! So that's what you do, build laptops,' said Slater, triumphantly. Now he thought he understood what Vinnie did to make his money.

'I already told you what I do,' snapped Vinnie. 'This stuff's just something to do in my spare time.'

'Dave,' warned Norman, 'why don't you give it a rest and let Vinnie do what he does best?'

'Sorry.' Slater was chastened. 'It's just I'm out of my depth with this stuff and I don't really understand—'

'Which is all the more reason to stop interferin' an' leave it to the expert, right?' interrupted Vinnie.

He settled in front of the laptop, inserted the memory stick and pressed a few keys. Looking over his shoulder, Slater could see this was certainly like no laptop he'd ever seen. The laptop buzzed and whirred for a few seconds, and then the screen lit up with a series of commands. Vinnie flexed his fingers and began to type. His fingers were a blur as he responded to questions scrolling across the screen. After a couple of minutes, he stopped typing and sat back.

'Where'd this come from?' he asked, scratching his head.

'A clerk who works in an office,' said Norman. 'It's nothing special. Is there a problem?'

'It's a bit more complicated than I was expectin'.' Vinnie said, sighing.

'Is it too complicated?' asked Slater, part of him hoping it would be.

'Guy,' said Vinnie arrogantly, 'nothin's too complicated for Vinnie the Geek. It'll just take a bit longer, that's all. Leave it with the king, Mister Norm, and I'll call you when I've cracked it.'

'If you're sure you don't mind,' said Norman apologetically.

'Its fine,' said Vinnie. 'I like a challenge. You two get off and do whatever it is you do. I jus' need more time. An' music.' He approached the huge sound system. 'I need music.' He pressed a button and the system boomed into life, blasting out Bob Marley. Vinnie began to ease into the rhythm, his body seemingly designed specifically to move to the reggae beat.

Slater liked Bob Marley, but not at this volume. He thought it was no surprise they'd put Vinnie in a suite well away from the other rooms. It seemed Norman was keen to avoid damage to his hearing as well and he led the retreat from Vinnie's room.

* * *

'Arrogant git, isn't he?' observed Slater, as they walked across the car park.

'Yes,' agreed Norman, 'he is, but it doesn't help when you keep sniping at him. He's also bloody good at what he does.'

'What? You mean hacking? That's how he got that list for you, wasn't it?'

'Alright. So he's a bit of a hacker. But he's not a malicious hacker. He doesn't set out to destroy things. He's more about righting wrongs.'

'You can see him as a modern-day Robin Hood if you want,' said Slater grimly. 'But if we get caught using him we're going to be in deep shit, you know that, don't you? And we can't use anything he finds in court.'

'Look.' Norman sighed. 'Vinnie's like a secret weapon. He can get in and out and no one ever knows he's been there. Like I said before, if you want to play by the rules we've got no chance. It'll be like entering the ring with your hands tied behind your back. Now, I don't know about you, but I reckon if we have an opportunity to level the odds just a little bit we should grab it with both hands, and Vinnie's the best opportunity we have.'

'Yeah. But—' began Slater.

'Sometimes,' interrupted Norman. 'The rules get in the way and stop us solving cases. It's not as if we're trying to fit someone up, is it? We know these guys are guilty.'

Slater had to concede Norman had a point. He could think of dozens of cases where the rules had prevented justice being served and someone had got off on a technicality. And they had been happy enough to try to push him under a bus . . .

'Alright,' Slater decided as they reached Norman's car. 'I'll stop worrying about using Vinnie. And I'll stop sniping at him. But I want something in exchange.'

'What's that?' asked Norman, unlocking the car.

'Tell him to stop calling me "guy". It's bloody annoying!'

As he slid into his seat, Norman started laughing.

'Is that it?' he said, chortling. 'Okay, guy, whatever you say.'

Slater glared at him. 'Ha, ha. Very funny. Just start this heap and drive us back.'

'Right.' Norman was clearly trying not to laugh. 'Whatever you say, guy.'

Slater's mobile phone was ringing.

'You really want to choose a better ringtone,' said Norman, as Slater's phone began to burble in his pocket. 'Because that really is annoying.'

'It's just how the phone came. I didn't choose it,' said Slater, wriggling around in his seat as he tried to ease the phone from his back pocket.

'It's because of the crappy, annoying ringtones these phones come with that the booming ringtone market was born,' said Norman. 'It's easy enough. Just change it. And it would be a lot easier to answer if you weren't sat on it.'

'Oh hush,' said Slater, finally managing to rescue his phone.

He didn't recognise the number calling him, but he could see it was from another mobile phone.

'I wonder who this is?'

'If you press that button and hold the phone to your ear you might find out,' suggested Norman.

Slater gave him a dirty look.

'Hello. Dave Slater.'

'Is that Sergeant Slater?' said a posh, business-like voice. 'This is Camilla Heywood from the *Magazine*.'

'Oh hi, Ms Heywood. I was going to call you.'

'Really?'

'Yeah. There are a couple of things I wanted to go over with you. I was going to ask if I could call in and see you, if that's convenient.'

He wondered why she would be using her mobile phone. It was mid-morning. Surely she would be in her office by now.

'No,' she said hastily, 'you can't do that!'

He sensed something wasn't right.

'Is there something wrong, Ms Heywood?'

'I can't talk right now,' she said nervously. 'But look, I'm going to a friend's wedding tomorrow, in Winchester. I'm travelling down later this afternoon and staying overnight at the Langton House Hotel just outside Winchester. Do you know it? You could meet me there.'

'That's not far from Starsholt College, isn't it?'

'Yes,' she said, 'that's right. Can you be there at about eight thirty? I really need to talk to you.'

'Yes, of course,' said Slater, puzzled that she wanted to talk to him but didn't want him to go to her office. 'I'll be there.'

Norman looked across at him as he ended the call.

'Problem?' he asked. 'Only you look confused.'

'That was Camilla Heywood from the *Magazine*. I was going to go up there and ask her why she told Amber not to talk to me. When I mentioned it, she said no, I can't go up there. So I'm thinking she doesn't want to talk to me. Then she asks me to meet her tonight in Winchester because she does want to talk to me. So, if I look confused, it's because I am confused . . .'

'Perhaps she fancies a bit of rough tonight,' joked Norman.

Slater didn't respond, he was thinking hard.

'Could be anything, couldn't it?' Norman said after a pause. 'We can speculate all day, but there's only one way to find out for sure.'

'Yep. You're right there,' agreed Slater. 'Are you doing anything tonight?'

'Yeah.' Norman sighed. 'Apparently I'm going to some fancy sounding hotel near Winchester to help interview someone called Camilla.'

CHAPTER SEVENTEEN

The Langton House Hotel was hidden away up a long winding driveway lined with silver birch trees on one side and neatly fenced paddocks on the other. A few horses looked up as they drove past.

'Jeez,' muttered Norman, closing his window. 'Is that horse shit I can smell?'

Slater looked at him in dismay, and then laughed out loud.

'Now who's the philistine?' he said. 'That, my friend, is the fresh air smell of the beautiful English countryside. People pay big bucks to stay here and soak up this atmosphere.'

'Yeah, yeah. Whatever,' said Norman. 'If you say so it must be true. But give me the big city anytime.'

'Really?' asked Slater, genuinely surprised. 'You prefer London to this?'

'I know you find that hard to believe, but I can't help it. It's true what they say, you can take the boy out of the city, but you can't take the city out of the boy. It works the other way, too. No one could ever take the country out of you. That's just how it is, see.'

Slater shook his head and smiled. He was enjoying working with Norman, whose take on things was often quite different from his own and made for some interesting conversations. Also, Norman was happy to exchange banter with him, and banter was something Slater really enjoyed.

The drive took a turn to the left and a large country house appeared ahead of them.

'Are all the hotels down here like this?' asked Norman. 'Don't you have anything with more than two floors? Whatever happened to high-rise?'

'You'd never get planning permission for a high-rise out here, would you?' Slater said. 'That's what planning laws are for — to stop people sticking damn great tower blocks all over the countryside and ruining it. Besides, there's no need. There are plenty of grand old houses like this that have become too expensive for one family to run. Turning them into luxury hotels makes good sense.'

'But they're so expensive,' argued Norman, pulling into a parking space.

'Excuse me?' said Slater. 'Have you booked a room in London recently? And here you get these beautiful surroundings.'

'I'm beginning to think you have shares in these hotels,' grumbled Norman. 'You certainly seem to like selling their virtues.'

'You can even ride horses here,' said Slater, swinging his door open.

'Oh, great! I can't wait,' said Norman under his breath. Then as he climbed from the car, he added a final comment. 'And there we are, very neatly back to the topic that started this conversation, the awful smell of horse shit.'

'Ha!' replied Slater, with a smile. 'Like I said, you're just a philistine with no appreciation for the good things in life.'

When Slater asked for Camilla, the receptionist pointed them in the direction of the bar where, she assured them, Ms Heywood was waiting for them. If anything, this hotel was even more luxurious than the one they had been to this morning to see Vinnie.

'Talk about how the other half live,' muttered Norman, walking alongside Slater. 'I couldn't afford a cup of tea in here, never mind stay for the night.'

'If you want to start getting bolshie and talking about how unfair the distribution of wealth is in this country, could you at least wait until after we've spoken to Camilla?' hissed Slater.

'I was just saying,' Norman said, apologetically.

'Well, just don't. At least, not now, alright?'

They walked through the open doorway into the hushed atmosphere of the bar.

'Like a morgue in here,' mumbled Norman. 'Not exactly a lively atmosphere, is it?'

'What were you expecting? Spit and sawdust on the floor, and a jukebox blaring away in the corner?'

'Well, no. But—'

'Look, this is just right to sit and chat, and that's what we're here for, isn't it?' said Slater. Then he added, 'There she is, over in the corner.'

He led the way over to a table where Camilla Heywood sat looking through what appeared to be a menu, a large glass of red wine before her on the table. She smiled a greeting as she saw them approaching and laid the menu down.

'Ms Heywood, this is DS Norman,' introduced Slater. 'He's working with me on this case.'

'How do you do, Sergeant?' she said. 'But please call me Camilla. Ms Heywood sounds far too formal. Please sit down.'

They took the two seats opposite her, and she signalled a waiter to come over. They exchanged pleasantries until their drinks arrived: tea for Norman, coffee for Slater.

'You said you needed to talk to me,' Slater began, once the waiter had gone.

'I've had a call,' she said. 'From one of your colleagues.'

Slater and Norman exchanged a quick glance, but it was enough for Camilla.

'Your faces are telling me this is news to you, but to be honest that's what I expected. I knew it was all wrong.'

'Why don't you tell us what happened?' suggested Norman.

'It was last Thursday afternoon. Everyone had finished for the day and I was the only one left in the office. I guess he must have known I would answer the phone myself if he called that late.'

'Who called?' prompted Slater.

'I think he said his name was DS Donovan, but I couldn't swear to it. But he told me you had been taken off the case, that you were no longer involved with the inquiry into Ruth's disappearance, and if you called again I shouldn't talk to you and I should call him.'

'Was there anything else?' asked Norman.

'Yes,' she said, and now she looked worried. 'He said if I did talk to you, and he found out, I could expect nothing but trouble, and lots of it.'

'Have you told anyone else about this?' asked Slater.

'I've told my staff that if they're asked to speak to the police to let me know first, but I've not mentioned it to anyone else.'

She studied their faces and took a sip of her wine.

'I don't like being threatened, especially by the police,' she said.

'You could report it and make a complaint,' suggested Norman. Slater hoped she wouldn't, because that would bring Professional Standards crawling all over their inquiry, which was the last thing he and Norman needed.

'That would be a waste of time, wouldn't it?' She shrugged. 'It's his word against mine and no evidence to back it up. I bet he made the call from a payphone too.'

'But you contacted me and invited me here,' Slater pointed out.

'That's because I trust you, and I want to know what's going on,' she said. 'I thought this was about finding out what happened to Ruth, so why would anyone want to stop us talking to you? You are still on this case, aren't you?'

'Yes I am, but you must understand I can't really discuss an active investigation with you,' said Slater.

'Yes, I understand that,' she said. 'But when I'm being threatened I have a right to know the bloody reason why, don't I? How do I know he's not watching my office, or my home?'

Slater could understand her frustration and indignation, and part of him agreed with her, but he was reluctant to share information that might actually drag her deeper into this situation. He was trying to figure out what to do for the best when Norman's voice interrupted his thoughts.

'You obviously believe you can trust Sergeant Slater, Camilla.'

'Well, yes I do,' she said. 'I wouldn't have invited you here if I didn't.'

'Well,' said Norman, 'I've been doing this for a long, long time. I believe we can trust you, so I think we can tell you a little about what's going on. But you have to understand, this has become a very complicated investigation so there's only so much we can share at this time. Of course, we may be able to share much more after we've finished.'

Slater turned towards him and was going to protest, but Norman kicked him under the table.

'It's okay, Dave. I think Camilla knows where I'm coming from.'

He raised his eyebrows at Camilla. She nodded.

'Yes,' she agreed. 'I think I do.'

'Ok, this is what we know so far . . .'

Norman gave her a very short briefing. He actually told her very little, and Slater marvelled as the man's ability to make it seem like he'd told her a lot more than he actually had. By the time he'd finished, all she knew was Ruth had disappeared and someone, somewhere within the police force, might be trying to slow down their inquiry.

Slater had to admit he was impressed. Norman had got him out of a hole there, and Camilla seemed happy enough with what he had told her. He was especially pleased Norman had steered clear of mentioning Amber and the memory stick. What she didn't know about couldn't hurt her.

They had got what they came for, so he thought now might be a good time to make a getaway.

'Right,' he said. 'Thank you for seeing us. And, don't worry, we won't turn up at your office. We won't even call your office. Is it alright if we call your mobile number if we need to speak to you again?'

'Yes, of course.'

'In that case we'll let you get back to your menu.'

They said their goodbyes and made their way back to the car.

As Norman pulled his keys from his right-hand jacket pocket, a tinny noise began in the opposite pocket.

'What the hell's that?' asked Slater.

'Listen,' said Norman, pulling the phone from his pocket and holding it towards Slater so he could hear it more clearly.

'That,' he announced, sounding proud, 'is a proper ringtone'.

Slater thought it just sounded like a jingly-jangly racket.

'You'd better answer it then if that's the only way we can stop the bloody thing,' he said.

'It's okay. That's my text notification. The actual ringtone's even better.'

The music stopped.

'What the hell is it?' asked Slater.

Norman looked horrified that Slater didn't know the song.

'Didn't you recognise it?'

'Maybe if you turned the volume down a bit so it's not so jangly I might be able to make something of it.'

'I'm supposed to be the old guy here,' complained Norman. 'But it's you that seems to be the grumpy one.'

'I'm not grumpy,' snapped Slater. 'It's just that my ears are attuned to decent music with bass, not tinny crap like that.'

'Hmmph,' grumbled Norman. He was in the car now, fumbling his way through his phone settings. As Slater climbed in alongside him, he pointed the phone at him.

'Listen up, Mr Oldbeforemytime.'

Now Slater could make out the tune. It was The Proclaimers, 'Letter from America'.

'Just right, don't you think? Letter from America, text message incoming,' explained Norman.

'Yes, okay. I get it. You don't need to explain. I'm not a complete idiot.'

Slater was slightly envious of Norman. He seemed to know far more about this stuff than he did. He thought maybe that was why Norman could connect with people like Vinnie and he couldn't.

'How come you know so much about this stuff anyway?' he asked grudgingly. 'Have you been on some training course we don't have access to down here?'

'D'you know,' Norman said, sighing and sounding sad, 'I wish that was the case, but it's not. When you suddenly find yourself on your own, hundreds of miles from home, you have to find some way of amusing yourself. I've lost count of the number of hours I've frittered away fiddling about with my mobile phone. I suppose some people would say it stops you going mad. Personally, I think it's a form of madness in itself.'

There was an uncomfortable silence. Silently, Slater cursed himself for allowing the conversation to go where it had gone and bringing Norman's mood down so low. He hadn't done it on purpose, of course, he just hadn't seen where it was going. Norman had been in good spirits for the last couple of days and now he was looking morose again.

'Can I ask you a question, Norm?' he asked, cautiously.

'Yeah, why not?'

'I understand why you get upset, right? I think I would too. So how come you've been in such good spirits these past couple of days.'

Norman stared at his hands for a few seconds.

'This is going to sound like a lecture, but I don't mean it to be. You're still young, but one day you'll meet someone, and for whatever reason you'll just know that this is the person you want to spend the rest of your days with. And when that happens, you'll discover you now have a genuine reason to get out of bed every day. Yeah, I know you do it now, but you know as well as I do, it's as much about habit as anything else. But when you meet "the one" you'll find that's the only reason you need for anything. She'll be your purpose.

'But what happens if that purpose is taken away? What if you're not one of these people who can just "get on with it" and carry on regardless? I'll tell you what happens. You wonder why you bother. You wonder "what's the point of anything?". And why? Because you've lost your purpose. I lost my purpose back then, and you know what? I just couldn't give a shit about anything.

'I only came down here because Bob Murray offered me a lifeline and I just couldn't stand it up there anymore. I still didn't give a shit, but I had somewhere else to not give a shit about.'

He shifted in his seat. Slater wasn't sure if he was supposed to speak. He guessed not.

'And then you came along,' said Norman suddenly, his voice much more upbeat. 'And you bring with you a possible chance to get even with the man who screwed up my life. Suddenly I have a purpose again. It's not the same, I'll grant you that, but it's good enough for now!'

Slater thought it was as if the switch that took him into a black mood had suddenly been reversed.

'I'm gonna get those bastards,' Norman said, 'If it's the last thing I do.'

Slater was a bit taken aback by the vehemence behind that statement.

'Steady on, Norm,' he said. 'Remember revenge can get in the way, you know.'

'Oh, I know that,' agreed Norman. 'But it can also be a bloody powerful motivator.'

Obviously realising he still had his phone in his hand, he opened the text he'd been sent.

'Ha!' he yelled. 'It's from Vinnie. He's cracked it! He's worked out the password.'

'What? Already?' asked Slater. 'When he said he needed time, I thought it was going to take days.'

'Didn't I tell you he was a genius?' said Norman. 'He says he's tired now and he's going to sleep, but if we go back in the morning he'll show us what he's found.'

'This could be a major step forward,' said Slater, happily. 'I can feel it in my water.'

'Let's get home so we can get some sleep too,' said Norman. 'I think you're right. Tomorrow's going to be a big day.'

He swung the car round and they headed back up the drive and on home to Tinton.

'So tell me,' asked Slater. 'What is your ringtone?'

'"Call Me" by Blondie.'

Slater looked puzzled. He didn't know the song.

'Don't you know any decent music?' asked Norman.

'It's before my time,' argued Slater.

'Is it bollocks!' Norman laughed. 'What? Are you telling me you're under thirty?'

'I'm thirty-eight,' said Slater indignantly.

'And you never heard of Blondie? Jesus, you must have been living in a cave or something. See, I said you were a heathen. I'll have to introduce you to some real music.'

And with that he was off, berating Slater for his poor taste in music all the way back to Tinton. But Slater didn't mind. In fact, he loved it. This was the Norm he was getting used to . . .

CHAPTER EIGHTEEN

'Is this it?' Slater was disappointed. He didn't really know what he was expecting, but this certainly wasn't it. He watched a few more seconds of the two bodies writhing around in the bed.

'It's just a porn video, and not a very good one. It's just two bodies under a blanket. It could be anyone.'

'Which is exactly the point, guy,' said Vinnie angrily. He stopped the video in disgust. 'Hey, Mister Norm.' Vinnie appealed to Norman. 'Can't you send Mister Very Negative here back where he came from so we can get on and do some real work? I can't do my thing proper wiv all this negative stuff in the room.'

'Yeah, Dave,' said Norman, turning to look at Slater. 'Give Vinnie a break, will you? If he reckons this is worthwhile you could at least wait and see.'

Slater spread his arms in appeal. 'Okay, okay. I'm sorry. I was just hoping for a big breakthrough, that's all, but we seem to have a not very good porn film.'

'Ha!' exclaimed Vinnie triumphantly. 'Well, that's where you're wrong. This is no porn film, guy. And I'm tellin' you it's a blindin' good film, made for a very specific purpose.'

He sat at his desk looking very smug. Then he realised that both Norman and Slater were looking at him in a strange way.

'Not that I know anythin' about this type of film, of course. I'm just guessin'.'

He was clearly trying to look innocent, but Slater wasn't fooled. Vinnie pressed play again and the video re-started. After another ten minutes, Slater was none the wiser.

'It's not exactly hardcore, is it?' he said. 'No one would pay for this stuff.'

'That's where you're wrong, Dave,' said Norman. 'There's one person who might pay a small fortune for this particular video.'

Slater didn't say anything. He was missing something obvious, but he couldn't see it. Norman could see it, and that bloody annoying Vinnie could see it, but he couldn't. It was Vinnie who decided to put him out of his misery.

'What if you was the geezer in the bed? What if someone told you afterwards that there was a video of you performing like a stallion wiv some chick that wasn't your wife, and it was about to be featured on YouTube?'

'Of course!' exclaimed Slater, the penny dropping for him with a loud clang. 'The guy in the video. This has been made to blackmail him.'

'It could well be,' agreed Norman. 'And if that's Ruth in the bed with him that would be one awfully powerful motive for getting rid of her. We need to find out who this guy is.'

'That's a blonde,' said Slater. 'Ruby had dark hair.'

'Ever heard of a thing called a wig?' asked Norman.

He turned to Vinnie. 'Can you get a good image of his face?'

'No problem,' said Vinnie. 'Towards the end there's so many shots of his face, this has to be a blackmail video. I've got a great one of the two faces together, all hot and steamy. And a beauty of him just as he's spillin' his beans, like. I tried enhancing that one so it's nice and clear, but his face was all screwed up like he's crappin' hisself so that was no good. But I found something else that might help.'

'What's that?' chorused the other two.

'Well,' explained Vinnie, 'I thought it might get a bit exciting so I watched it all the way through.'

He briefly looked guilty, but then turned defiant.

'But there's no decent action, alright? He's obviously giving her one, but there's no money shot.'

'Money shot?' said a puzzled Slater.

'What sort of detective are you?' asked Vinnie. 'Don't you know nuffin' about this stuff? The money shot's the one where they show a close-up of her bits. When the captain's unloading the cargo from his ship, as it were.'

'Oh. Right.' Slater blushed. 'I see what you mean. Sorry if I seem a bit dim, but I don't get involved with Vice, and on a personal level I don't need this stuff.'

'Yeah. Whatever,' said Vinnie, sounding bored. 'Anyway, as I was sayin', I picked out the interestin' bits and made stills. I'll show you the faces in a minute, but first I wanna show you this. I think you'll find it worth a look.'

An image appeared on the TV screen in place of the video.

'See it?' asked Vinnie.

'See what?' Slater couldn't see anything of interest, and from the look on Norman's face, he couldn't either.

'An' you guys are trained observers? I don't fink so,' said Vinnie in disgust. 'Come on, guys, open your eyes. See that mirror in the background? Look in it. Off to the right. See? There's a jacket hanging on the back of a chair. Look familiar to you?'

'Jesus!' exclaimed Slater. 'That's a police uniform.'

'Yeah. That's what I thought.' Vinnie laughed. 'That should narrow the search a bit, don't you think?'

'Is there a clear view of his face anywhere in that film?'

'Of course there is,' said Vinnie. 'If you're gonna make a video to blackmail someone, you have to make sure there's no doubt who it is, right?'

'Can you make a copy?'

'Already done. I'm way ahead of the game, guy.'

Vinnie's cockiness could be annoying at times, but Slater had to admit, the man knew what he was doing.

'Well, let's see it then,' said Norman impatiently.

'Hey, stay cool, Mister Norm. I'm jus' gettin' to that bit, ok?'

He handed two glossy photos to Norman.

'So this is the babe in the bed,' said Vinnie. 'An' I'm tellin' you, guy, this is one foxy chick.'

'That's her alright,' said Norman, keeping one photo and passing the other copy across to Slater.

'Hot stuff, right?' said Vinnie, approvingly.

Slater looked at the photo. It was clearly Ruth/Ruby, even with the blonde wig.

'She's disappeared,' he said, still looking at the photo. 'Vanished into thin air. This video might be the reason why.'

'Oh shit, guy,' said Vinnie, looking horrified. 'Now I'm right out of order, sayin' those things about her.'

'She was a high-class hooker, Vinnie,' explained Norman. 'It was her job to make guys feel horny and want to give her one. And anyway, you weren't to know.'

Vinnie looked suitably chastened. At least that was something Slater could approve of.

'Let's have a look at the other photo then,' said Slater. 'Let's see who we've got.'

'Ah, yeah. The lucky shagnasty,' said Vinnie, producing another two photos. 'Who just might also be a killer.'

This time he reached across and passed them one photo each.

'That's just a possibility at this stage,' advised Norman. 'All this proves is he had sex with her, and there's no law against that.'

Slater looked at the photo. It was a good one, nice and clear. It wasn't anyone he could put a name to, but it shouldn't be too difficult to find out who he was. Meanwhile, Norman was staring at the photo. He looked at Slater, then at Vinnie, then back at the photo. A broad grin threatened to split his face in half.

'Vinnie,' he announced, 'have I ever told you that you're wonderful?'

'Ha! Thanks, Mister Norm, but I already know that, guy.'

'No. I mean it,' insisted Norman. 'This is the best thing you've ever done for me.'

Vinnie smiled, looking happy. Slater could tell he was fond of the policeman.

'D'you know this guy, Norm?' asked Slater.

'Do I know this guy?' repeated Norman, grinning like a Cheshire Cat. 'Oh yes, I know him. You could say we're quite well connected.'

In that moment, Slater knew who it was too.

'His name's Mark Clinton,' said Norman. 'That's Detective Chief Inspector Mark Clinton of the Serious Crime Unit. You're connected too. He's Jimmy Jones' boss.'

Norman turned to Vinnie.

'Vinnie, I owe you big time. You've made Christmas come early this year.'

'You owe me nuffink, Mister Norm,' replied Vinnie. 'I'm still payin' back what I owe you, an' I reckon I always will be.'

While Norm and Vinnie were having their little private love-in, Slater was considering the implications of what they had discovered and realising this could well turn out to be the biggest case he'd ever been involved in. And they were still just a two-man team. Surely Bob Murray would have to give them some help now.

* * *

Slater watched as Bob Murray put his head in his hands, and then very slowly ran his fingers through what was left of his hair. Without looking at either of them, Murray heaved a massive sigh, pushed his chair back and then very slowly and deliberately stood up. Then he walked across to his window, turned his back on them, placed his hands behind his back, and gazed out at the world.

Norman looked uncertainly across at Slater. Slater put a finger to his lips to indicate Norman should keep quiet. He knew this was Murray's thinking pose, and he also knew it was best to leave Murray alone when he was thinking. They'd just briefed their boss on progress so far, finishing with the video of Mark Clinton and Ruth Thornhill, aka Ruby Rider, so he had plenty to think about.

After what seemed an eternity, Murray turned away from the window and began to pace up and down.

'You're quite sure this is what it appears to be?' he asked. 'It's not some clever hoax, created with fancy software?'

'As far as we can tell, boss,' Slater assured him.

'And no one else knows it exists?'

'Can't be sure, but it looks that way,' said Norman.

'And this girl had it all the time? Surely she's seen it?'

'I don't think she has.' Slater hadn't mentioned the password protection or how they'd managed to get access to the video. 'She just took it to use to back up stuff on her PC at home, but she never actually used it. She found it in the bottom of her handbag.'

Slater was feeling just a tad uncomfortable. He told himself he wasn't exactly lying to his boss so much as avoiding the truth, but he hoped Murray wasn't going to pursue this point too much longer or guilt might just get the better of him.

Norman seemed to read Slater's guilty thoughts.

'The thing is, boss,' he said, 'we were wondering how Chief Inspector Clinton might react if we tried to arrange an interview. Me and Dave aren't exactly on top of his Christmas card list, are we? If he starts a shitstorm against us we'd have no choice but to get Professional Standards involved and then we'd have to hand the whole lot over.'

'You both know that, officially, that's what we should do, don't you?' asked Murray.

Slater knew alright, and he was pretty sure Norman did too. He also knew the pair of them would lose their chance to set the record straight if that happened. He watched Murray pace up and down, and then go back to the window. What was he going to do? Slater wondered. And then, finally, he walked back to his desk and sat down.

'This is actually a bit more complicated than you think,' he began. 'What I'm going to tell you goes no further than these four walls. Do you understand?'

They both nodded.

'As you know,' Murray continued, 'the Home Secretary got involved in the decision to re-investigate this inquiry. One of the reasons he was keen for it to be handled by a force outside the Met, and not by Professional Standards, is because he has a suspicion things have got far too cosy between them — in particular between Professional Standards and the Serious Crime Unit.

'He's also aware that several very good officers, and that includes both of you, have suffered as a result of the SCU's inability to accept responsibility for their own cock-ups. They'd much rather blame the nearest DS who's gone out on a limb to help them with local knowledge. In their view, nothing's ever their fault. The Home Secretary believes this has gone on for far too long now, and if he has his way, the SCU will be dismantled, but what he needs is some hard evidence to prove it's reached its sell-by date.'

'And that's where we come in,' said Slater. 'Now I see why you wanted me to keep to myself as much as possible.'

'Is that why I'm here too?' asked Norman. 'To make up a revenge squad?'

'You're here, Norman,' said Murray, 'because I know you're a damned good officer. I asked for you to come here before all this came together because I wanted someone with years of experience that I could rely on. I've got some really good officers here, but they're young and inexperienced. I want you to pass on your experience to help polish my rough diamonds into real gems.'

Slater thought that was some compliment. He looked across at Norman, who seemed to suddenly be sitting taller and straighter as he filled with pride.

'It just so happened,' Murray went on, 'that this case came along almost as soon as you arrived. I believe it's what's known as karma. What goes around, comes around.'

Slater was impressed to think the old man knew what karma was. Maybe he's not so old fashioned after all, he thought.

'Now we're getting off the point,' said Murray. 'I appreciate you could do with some help so I've assigned DC Biddeford to join you from tomorrow, but I'd prefer it if you just used him for research rather than sticking him in the firing line.'

'Is that it?' said Slater. 'Just one body?'

'I'm afraid so, for all sorts of reasons,' said Murray.

'That'll be fine,' Norman assured Slater. 'Keep it small. We already agreed the more staff we have the more potential there is for leaks. We can handle it. Besides, if we're going to carry on working from that tiny little house of yours, we couldn't fit any more in. One's gonna be a squeeze.'

He looked innocently at Slater and winked.

'Okay,' agreed Slater. 'One's better than none, I guess. But we still have the problem of getting to speak to Mark Clinton. We were rather hoping you might arrange it, sir.'

Murray pursed his lips.

'He can easily make life difficult for us lower ranks,' Norman reminded him, 'but you're on the same level. And you have the Home Secretary on your side.'

'We don't want Clinton to know that,' warned Murray. 'And I don't want you charging in there looking for revenge. I'll phone him and suggest it might be a good idea if he has an informal chat with a couple of my officers because his name has come up in an inquiry. I'll play it down as much as I can to get him in a room with you, but once you get him in there, you hit him with that video. Let the bugger know he's in some deep shit and then see what happens.'

'That's all we need,' said Slater. 'If you can get us in a room with him we can do the rest.'

CHAPTER NINETEEN

It had taken all Bob Murray's guile to persuade Mark Clinton it would be in his best interests to meet up with one of his officers for an informal chat. His initial hostility to the idea had been overcome by Murray's assertion that he was quite sure it was some sort of misunderstanding and that he was equally sure Clinton could very easily and quickly put their minds at rest.

'I like to think we can sort these things out without the need for paperwork. I'm sure you know what I mean,' Murray had said. 'It'll be much quicker than the official route.'

His assertion that a meeting should take place in a neutral venue seemed to convince Clinton he had nothing to worry about.

'Police stations are very good places for rumours to start, don't you think?' Murray had suggested. 'I'll tell Detective Sergeant Salter you'll meet him then, shall I?'

* * *

At seven thirty a.m. on Wednesday morning, Dave Slater approached a man sat on his own at Heston Services on the

M4. He was at a corner table, far away from the busy end of the cafeteria, reading a newspaper and sipping a cup of scalding hot liquid that was supposed to be coffee.

'Chief Inspector Clinton?' asked Slater politely.

Clinton looked up at him. His face made it quite clear what he thought about this whole situation, but Slater could handle a bit of hostility. It went with the job most of the time.

'I want to see your warrant card,' said Clinton.

Slater handed his card over. Clinton studied it, and then looked up.

'Murray told me I was meeting Detective Sergeant Salter,' he said warily.

'Ah!' said Slater with a cheeky grin. 'He's always getting my name wrong. It's his dyslexia.'

Clinton looked hard at him and Slater could tell he wasn't amused. He wondered if Clinton had recognised his name.

'I'm a busy man, Slater,' he warned, his voice full of his own importance. 'So you'd better make this quick.'

'Oh, I don't think it'll take long. Is it alright if I sit down?'

'Help yourself.'

Clinton pointed at the empty chairs opposite him. Slater dragged one out and made a big deal out of getting comfortable. He couldn't use his rank to intimidate Clinton, but he could certainly annoy the hell out of him.

'Right, Sergeant,' snapped Clinton. 'You can stop with the "aggravating and incompetent" act, and get to the point. I'm only here as a favour to Chief Inspector Murray. I hope you realise that.'

'Oh yes, of course, sir. And I'm very, very grateful,' Slater gushed. He thought about doffing an imaginary cap, but decided that might be going just a bit too far.

'Well, come on, man. Get on with it.' Clinton's fuse was getting shorter by the minute, which was good for Slater, but he knew if he pushed it too far, he might lose this chance.

'Well, I've been investigating this case,' he began, 'and your name's come up. Naturally I don't want to bring your name into it if it can be avoided—'

'Yes, yes,' snapped Clinton. 'I know all that.'

'Do you know someone called Ruth Thornhill?' asked Slater.

'I don't believe I do,' said Clinton confidently. 'It's not ringing any bells for me. I've never heard that name before.'

'Oh,' Slater sounded disappointed. 'Well, that answers that, then.'

'Is that it?' asked Clinton, red-faced with anger. 'You got me all the way out here just to ask me that?' He started to fold his newspaper in disgust. 'Bloody Toytown coppers, wasting my time. I'm going to be making a complaint about this. Do you understand?'

Slater looked suitably embarrassed.

'Right,' said Clinton pushing his chair back. 'If that's all?'

'How about Ruby Rider?' said Slater, quietly. 'Does that name ring any bells?'

Slater wished he'd had a camera with him, just so he could prove that the colour really does drain from people's faces. But Clinton was pretty good, and once he got over the initial shock he was red-faced again in no time.

'What is this? Twenty bloody questions? Have you got any more names you want to throw at me?'

'That depends,' said Slater calmly. 'How many other hookers have you been seeing?'

'You're making a big mistake here, Slater. You're going to regret making that accusation.'

'No, I don't think I am.' He slid a photograph across to Clinton. 'Recognise her now?'

Clinton looked at the photograph. Slater could see Clinton's eyes widen as he recognised her, but still he kept up his denial.

'What is this? Some sort of set-up? I don't care what anyone tells you. I've never seen this woman before. And I've certainly not had sex with any hooker.'

‘You must have a double, then,’ said Norman, who had crept up unnoticed by Clinton. ‘’Cos this sure looks like you having fun with her, don’t you think?’

He slid another photo across the table as he sat down next to Slater. This one clearly showed Ruby and Clinton having what might be described as ‘fun’.

Clinton looked at the photo, horror etched across his face.

‘You!’ he said, looking up at the new arrival. ‘But I thought—’

‘Yeah,’ interrupted Norman, an evil grin on his face. ‘You thought you’d never see me again, huh?’

‘Wait a minute.’ Clinton turned to Slater. ‘I know who you are now. I thought the name was familiar. You’re another failure, aren’t you? What’s Murray doing down there in Toytown? Creating a lame duck squad? By the time I’ve finished with him he’s going to be a lame duck himself.’

‘That’s very good,’ said Norman. ‘But do you really think you’re in a position to start using intimidation and threats? That’s not going to get you out of it this time.’

‘I know people,’ said Clinton. ‘One word from me and they’ll be more than happy to drum you out of the police force for trying to frame a senior officer with these trumped-up charges.’

He glared at Norman and then at Slater, clearly expecting them to back down under his threats, but all he got in return were two smiling faces. Slater was enjoying Norman’s performance. He was happy to play second fiddle — he knew Norman had waited a long, long time for a chance like this.

‘You’re full of shit, Clinton,’ countered Norman. ‘Do you really think I give a toss what you do next? You’ve already ruined my life. What more could you possibly do to hurt me?’

‘I’ll make sure you lose your pension,’ said Clinton, not sounding quite so sure of himself now.

‘Fine,’ said Norman. ‘I’ve got no one to share it with now, thanks to you, so I really don’t care. You’re the one who's finished. Not me, not Slater here, and not Bob Murray. We have a video.'

The news about the video was their nuclear option, and it worked. Those four little words had an amazing effect on Clinton. First, his face filled with disbelief, and then, once again, the colour drained from his face, only this time it stayed a ghostly white. He gulped, fish-like, as he tried to form the words of denial.

'You're lying,' he finally managed to say.

Slater and Norman shook their heads. Norman produced some more photos.

'These are stills taken from it.' He smiled. 'D'you still reckon we're lying?'

'Where did you get this? How dare you video me?' Clinton sounded desperate now.

'You know damned well we didn't make the video,' said Slater. 'Ruby made it. We reckon she was going to use it to blackmail you.'

'Or perhaps she was already blackmailing you and that's why you killed her,' added Norman.

Slater sat, watching Clinton closely. He could tell the man was wrestling with whether to tell the truth or not.

'Alright,' conceded Clinton eventually, 'I did know her. But I didn't pay her for sex, and you can't prove I did. I certainly didn't kill her, and I didn't know she had videoed me. She may well have been intending to blackmail me, but I can assure you she hadn't started. So if you think you've discovered a motive that makes me a suspect, you're wrong. And anyway, how do you know she's dead? Do you have a body? I thought she'd just disappeared.'

'So you know the findings of the investigation into her disappearance? That's very interesting. After all, it was just a runaway, wasn't it? That's hardly a case for your Serious Crime Unit, is it?' asked Slater.

Clinton stared at him defiantly. 'What investigation? I don't know what you're talking about.'

Slater shrugged his shoulders. 'Whatever,' he said. 'I didn't expect you to admit that anyway.'

Then he turned to Norman.

'I think we're done here, don't you?'

'I reckon so,' agreed Norman. 'It'll do, for now.'

They climbed to their feet, making a point of ignoring Clinton. Then, just as they were about to leave, Slater bent his head down towards him.

'And for your information,' he said quietly, 'we can prove you paid her for sex. She videoed the transaction. Very thorough, young Ruby, don't you think?'

Clinton was staring right through him. Slater wondered what he must be thinking right now. Maybe in his mind's eye he was seeing his career going down the toilet. He hoped so anyway.

As he straightened back up, and they began to walk away, Norman spoke. 'Did you tell him we've got the proof?'

'I did.'

'That should have been my line really.'

'But you had all the good lines in the first part.'

Norman seemed to consider this as they walked. 'I suppose you're right,' he said. 'It went alright, didn't it?'

'It was great, Norm, just great,' Slater assured him. 'So how d'you feel now?'

'Right now, I feel pretty good. Best I've felt in a long time.'

Slater clapped him on the back. 'That's good, Norm. I'm happy for you.'

'Yeah. Thanks,' said Norman.

They carried on walking without looking back, all the way out through the shopping area. Slater stopped to buy two takeaway coffees, and then they made their way out to the car. Bright, warm, morning sunshine bathed the car, so Slater and Norman chose to sit on the bonnet to drink their coffee.

'What d'you think he'll do now?' asked Slater.

'If he wants to shoot himself, I'll happily supply the gun,' joked Norman. 'In fact, I'd even pull the trigger, make sure he doesn't miss.'

'But seriously,' insisted Slater, 'what next for him?'

'If there was any decency about him, he'd resign,' said Norman. 'But we both know that's unlikely. My guess is he'll be calling in all the favours he can to try and save his arse.'

'I guess it's a case of "watch this space", and see what happens,' agreed Slater.

They sipped in silence for few minutes, enjoying the warmth of the sun. Finally, they finished their coffees. Norman took the empty cups and ambled across to the nearest bin. Slater looked at his wristwatch. It was nine a.m.

'You know,' said Norman, as he climbed into the car to join the waiting Slater. 'We make a pretty good team.'

'Yeah,' agreed Slater. 'And we have a bit of fun, too.'

'Yeah, we do.' Norman reached for his seat belt. 'I just wanted to say thank you.'

'For what?'

Norman was fumbling with his seat belt, trying to click it into place.

'Just thank you for being you, and for getting me to be more like the old me. I can't remember the last time I was really like that, you know?' He continued fighting with his seat belt.

'Here', said Slater finally, 'for God's sake let me do it. We can't sit here all day while you fart around like this. If I'd known the "old you" was incapable of doing up a simple seat belt I would have left you how you were.'

'I am not farting around,' said Norman indignantly. 'The bloody thing's too short.'

'I think maybe,' Slater pointed out, tugging on the seat belt, 'it's not a case of the seat belt being too short, but your waist being a little too large.'

'How dare you!' said Norman, his voice heavy with mock indignation.

There was a click and Slater sat back.

'There,' he sighed. 'Now, can we get going? We have work to do.'

'Are you trying to pull rank on me now?' asked Norman, starting the car.

In a matter of a few days, they had forged the sort of easy friendship that meant they could keep this sort of banter going for hours.

Norman started to pull out of the parking space and then stopped and tutted, as Slater's mobile began to trill.

'That awful ringtone,' he muttered. He really wished Slater would change it to something a bit more modern. He listened with interest to the conversation, although he could only hear Slater's side of the discussion.

'Dave Slater . . . Hi Steve, how are you? . . . Yeah, that's right. You've read the notes? . . . Okay. What I need you to do right now, is find out all you can about Detective Chief Inspector Mark Clinton of the SCU. You got that? . . . Good lad. Meet us over at my place at two p.m. . . . Knocker Norman?' Slater looked sideways at Norman. 'Yeah, that's right . . . Yeah, he is a pain in the arse, but what can you do?' Norman glanced at Slater and saw he was grinning. 'Yeah, totally useless. You'll meet him later and you'll see what I mean. Okay mate, see you later.'

Slater ended the call, still grinning broadly, but staring forward so Norman couldn't see his face.

Now Norman was grinning too.

'I think that's grossly unfair,' he complained.

'What?' asked Slater, trying to look innocent.

'Talking about me like that, while I'm sat here listening.'

'My mum would have said that's what you get for listening in on other people's conversations,' said Slater.

Norman took three attempts before he finally crunched his way into reverse gear and manoeuvred them out of their parking spot. He responded to Slater's jibe that 'there must be a reverse gear in there somewhere' with a disdainful look.

'Well,' he said, 'if I'm going to have to work with a guy who's just been told I'm a "totally useless pain in the arse", the least you could do is give me the lowdown on him. So, come on, in just a few words, what's he like?'

Slater seemed to consider this for a few moments before he spoke.

'Young, good-looking, honest, no, make that painfully honest, inexperienced, naive, keen to learn, keen to make a difference, brave, prepared to take responsibility for his own actions. Oh, and he's fast, like a greyhound on steroids. Should I go on?'

'So basically he's everything I'm not, right?'

'Yeah, more or less.' Slater nodded.

'Adding him to the team fills in all the gaps that I leave?'

'Most definitely,' agreed Slater.

'And you like him, right?'

'Yeah,' said Slater, 'I do. And so will you.'

'Then he sounds perfect for the job. I look forward to meeting him.'

'But I should tell you,' warned Slater, 'he can be even more of a stickler for following correct procedure than I am, and that can get seriously annoying at times, even for me, so I would imagine it will drive you mad.'

'I don't know what you mean,' said Norman innocently. 'I always follow procedure.'

'Yeah. Right,' said Slater. 'You mean like Vinnie?'

'Ah. Yes. Well, you have to have exceptions to illustrate the need for rules,' explained Norman.

'Do you have a degree in bullshit?' laughed Slater. 'You have an answer for everything, don't you?'

'I have a degree in survival, my friend,' Norman assured him, with a knowing smile. 'And let me assure you bullshit is one of the survivor's greatest tools.'

CHAPTER TWENTY

Slater knew that viewed on a map, it was a relatively simple journey from Heston services to Tinton. A short stretch of the M4, followed by a quick dash along the M25, and then slip onto the M3 down into Hampshire. That's less than forty miles on the motorways, plus a further ten miles on a decent dual carriageway, so they should have been back in an hour.

But the M25 is notorious for hold-ups that often reduce traffic to a snail's pace, and this morning was no exception. In fact, Slater would have been happy if they *had* been crawling along at a snail's pace. At least then they would have been moving.

Unfortunately, as they found out on the radio, just a mile ahead of them, a car travelling in the centre lane had suffered a burst tyre, causing the driver to lose control. A grain lorry, carrying thirty-eight tons of oats, and a milk tanker, fully laden with fresh milk collected that very morning, had been following closely behind the car. Both swerved to avoid colliding with the out-of-control car, instead colliding with each other, causing both vehicles to overturn, and spilling their respective loads across the carriageway.

The resulting sea of congealing porridge had turned the entire anticlockwise carriageway into a sticky, slippery mess.

The motorway had been closed for almost three hours, trapping all the traffic behind the accident where they had to stay until the mess was cleared.

As a result, it was close to one o'clock by the time they neared Tinton, so they decided to stop at a quiet pub outside town to grab some lunch. It was while they were enjoying their food, in the pub's beer garden, that Slater's phone began to ring. He would have preferred to leave the call until later, but the way things were developing, he didn't want to leave anything to chance.

'Slater.'

'It's Mark Clinton.'

Slater was so surprised he almost dropped the phone. Clinton was the last person he was expecting to hear from. He put his hand over the phone.

'It's Clinton,' he hissed to Norman.

Norman's mouth dropped open. Slater thought it wasn't the prettiest sight he'd ever seen, especially as Norman had a mouthful of coleslaw.

'I won't pretend I'm not surprised to hear from you, sir,' he said down the phone. 'But if you've just called to offer more threats, we're not listening.'

'This isn't easy for me, Slater. Don't make it more difficult or I might change my mind.'

There was a steeliness about Clinton's voice, but it was lacking the aggressive tone of earlier that morning.

'Fair enough,' said Slater. 'If you have something to say, I'd like to hear it.'

There was a pause. He could hear Clinton breathing, almost as though he was struggling to find the right words to say.

'It's about Ruby,' Clinton said. 'I met her at a health spa I belong to. I'd been going through a rough time at home, and she took an interest in me, you know?'

Slater thought it was amazing how people always found a reason to justify their behaviour, no matter how much in the wrong they were, but he chose to keep quiet and let Clinton speak.

'I didn't know she was a hooker, but she knew who I was. Like a fool, I told her I could protect her and keep her out of trouble and we ended up having sex. But it was just a one-night stand.'

'You mean you took advantage of your position to have sex with her,' sneered Slater.

'It wasn't like that,' Clinton said. 'You don't understand. She came on to me. She was like a drug, and I was the addict.'

There was another silence. This time Slater did speak.

'I'm not sure I understand why you're telling me this, sir. It's not really helping us, or you, at the moment.'

'Just listen to me,' snapped Clinton. 'I swear to you I did not kill that girl. I was worried when I found she'd gone missing. But she was a hooker, I couldn't afford to show a lot of interest, could I? Believe me, if I could have done something without arousing a lot of curiosity I would have. And now you tell me you think she's been murdered. I've done some things I regret, Sergeant, but I am not a killer.'

'Is that it?' said Slater, unimpressed by Clinton's speech. 'Only my lunch is getting cold here.'

'There was a letter,' blurted Clinton. 'It was sent to me a couple of weeks before Ruby disappeared. It said that the writer knew about me and Ruth and that if I didn't pay up they would make a lot of trouble for me.'

'A blackmail letter?' asked Slater.

'Yes. But it mentioned Ruth. I didn't know anyone called Ruth.'

'Did it mention a video? Did he threaten to send the video to your wife?' asked Slater.

'There was no mention of any video, and no specific threat. I thought it was from some sort of religious nut. It used a lot of biblical phrases and kept on about some girl called Ruth. I thought she was from the Bible too. I didn't make the connection between Ruth and Ruby because I didn't know they were the same person. I swear, on my children's lives, this is the truth.'

'But surely you did know they were the same person. That's why you were checking up on the investigation and making sure it concluded she was a simple runaway.'

'Why do you keep on about this investigation?' said Clinton angrily. 'I don't know anything about an investigation?'

'Missing person. Ruth Thornhill. Investigating officer DS Declan Donovan,' said Slater.

'Do you really thing a case like that would cross my desk?' asked Clinton. 'Do you seriously think I have time to check out every case that's going on in the Met? Come on, Sergeant. Get real! And if I started to ask questions, don't you think people would want to know why? I don't know where you've got that information from, but it's all wrong. I repeat, I know nothing about any investigation into a missing person called Ruth Thornhill. And I've never heard of DS Declan Donovan.'

'Have you still got the letter?' asked Slater.

'I'm afraid not. I kept it for a couple of weeks, but when there was no follow-up I just assumed it was a crank and I threw it away.'

* * *

'So what did he have to say?' asked Norman when Slater closed the call.

'He says he doesn't know Declan Donovan, or an investigation into Ruth Thornhill.'

'Yeah, well. He would say that, wouldn't he?' said Norman cynically. 'People like Clinton only have a passing acquaintance with the truth. What else?'

'He says he met Ruby at a health spa, he didn't know she was a hooker, but she knew who he was. He says he promised to keep her out of trouble if she had sex with him, but it was a one-night stand. Reckons he's done some bad things, but he's no killer.'

'Well, that certainly sounds like true love, doesn't it?' said Norman, becoming even more cynical. 'I think that's called abusing your position, don't you? Do you think it was a one-off, or was he hooked by the hooker? Do you believe him?'

'I don't know,' said Slater slowly. 'I'd have a better idea if I could have seen his face. It's always easier to tell lies over the phone. And there's more. He claims to have been sent a blackmail letter telling him if didn't pay up there was going to be trouble.'

'So someone knew he was seeing Ruby,' concluded Norman. 'And that someone had a copy of the video. Ruby had an accomplice.'

'No. The letter was all about him seeing a girl called Ruth. He claims he didn't make the connection because he didn't know anyone called Ruth. And there was no mention of a video.'

Norman looked as puzzled as Slater felt.

'So what happened next?' asked Norman.

'Nothing,' said Slater. 'He says there were no more letters so he threw the first one away. He put it down to the work of some religious crank because it was full of biblical passages and kept on about someone called Ruth.'

'So let me get this straight.' Norman sighed. 'He expects us to believe he knew nothing, saw nothing and did nothing, right? Oh, and by coincidence, some religious nut sent him a biblical blackmail letter just around the time she disappeared. Do you buy all that shit? 'Cos I don't.'

'I know where you're coming from, Norm, and I tend to agree with you. But let's assume he is telling the truth for a minute.'

'That's going to be difficult for me,' admitted Norman.

'I understand that,' said Slater, sympathetically. 'But just for a few moments, let's suppose he is. So, he didn't know Ruby was Ruth, and he didn't know Donovan was running an investigation.'

'You're quite sure the SCU is involved?' asked Norman.

'Donovan told me I didn't want to cross the people at "the Unit". That's what they call the SCU up there, isn't it?'

Norman nodded his head. 'That's right,' he confirmed. 'So, if Clinton's for real, someone else in the SCU must have known Ruth was Ruby.'

'Great.' Slater sighed. 'Just what we need. Another bloody suspect. I'm beginning to find it difficult to keep all these balls up in the air, you know?'

'That's only if Clinton's telling the truth,' Norman reminded him. 'But what about this blackmail letter? Biblical references, using Ruth's name. Is it just me, or does this point to someone we know?'

'Ruth's boyfriend, Tony Warwick,' said Slater. 'Of course. He's a Bible basher. I bet he could find biblical quotations for any situation.'

'I've not had the pleasure.' Norman grinned. 'But you've met him. Does he seem capable of blackmail?'

'The guy's quite intense, and he has some pretty extreme views on what's right and wrong, and how it should be punished. I think he's capable of just about anything.'

'Okay. Just let me finish my lunch,' said Norman. 'Then we'll go ask him.'

* * *

They found Steve Biddeford hopping up and down on Slater's doorstep and after Slater had introduced him to Norman, they made the short journey into town to speak to Tony Warwick.

On the way, Norman began the process of making friends with Biddeford. He was keen to recruit him as an ally in the ongoing banter with Slater.

'So, tell me, Steve,' he asked. 'Does DS Slater criticise your driving like he does mine?'

'Oh yes,' answered Biddeford. 'He always complains I'm going too slowly. He even once persuaded me to take a shortcut across a village green that was like a swamp. And then he let me get the bollocking when the car sank up to its axles and had to be towed back to the station.'

'Oh, did he now?' Norman smiled.

'The car is always the responsibility of the driver,' said Slater.

'But it was your idea to take the shortcut,' protested Biddeford. 'I just followed orders.'

'We were in pursuit,' argued Slater. 'And anyhow, how was I supposed to know we would sink?'

'Well,' said Norman. 'It sounds to me like the senior officer made the error of judgement and then left the junior to take the blame.' He looked at Biddeford in the mirror. 'Am I right, Steve?'

'Right!' said Slater. 'That's enough "let's gang up on Dave Slater" for now. I can see I'm going to get the blame for everything from here on in.'

'It's tough, right?' said Norman, with glee. 'But that's how it is. With high office, comes great responsibility. Didn't you know that?'

The dirty look from Slater suggested that maybe it was time he should keep quiet.

* * *

Warwick's small, shabby home was in Fenn Street, a narrow, cobbled street lined with old terraced houses on either side. Warwick lived in number fifty-two, almost exactly halfway down. Slater knew a narrow lane ran along the back of the houses so he instructed Norman to drop Biddeford at one end so he could walk along the lane and cover the back of the house.

They parked just short of Warwick's house and climbed from the car. Slater knocked on the rickety door and it shook alarmingly.

'Don't knock too hard, it'll fall apart,' suggested Norman. The door opened as far as the chain inside would allow. It was just enough for Warwick to peer around at them.

'Yes,' he snapped.

'Mr Warwick. D'you remember me? DS Slater? I'd like to ask you a few more questions about Ruth if I may.'

'I've told you all I know,' said Warwick, trying to push the door closed. But, out of habit, Slater already had his foot against it.

'I particularly wanted to ask you about the letter you sent to Detective Chief Inspector Mark Clinton.'

Suddenly Warwick was gone, sprinting back through the house towards the back door. Slater looked round at Norman.

'The bugger's done a runner.' He tried to push the door open but the chain did its job.

'Looks like you hit the jackpot with that one,' said Norman behind him. 'Here, stand aside.'

He manoeuvred Slater to one side and then smashed his bulk into the door, which seemed to sag slightly and then sort of explode into a shower of pieces of wood and dust, as if someone had thrown a bomb at it.

'Woodworm,' explained Norman, standing back to let Slater through.

Slater rushed through what was left of the door, which was now just a narrow piece of splintered wood hanging uselessly from its hinges. The house was small enough that he could see all the way through the back door and out into the back garden, where he caught a glimpse of Warwick disappearing through the gate and heading off to the right. He knew Biddeford was coming from the left, but he didn't know if he'd got there yet.

There was a loud shout of: 'Oi, you! Come back here,' which told him Biddeford hadn't got there in time.

'Quick,' Slater shouted over his shoulder to Norman, as he took off. 'He's gone right.'

'Yeah, so he has,' said Norman to himself, watching Slater charge through the house. 'But I don't do running, remember? And anyway there are already two of you.'

He strolled back to the car, climbed in and started the engine. Humming quietly to himself, he put it in gear and began to drive down the street. He could see where the lane emerged onto the street up ahead.

In the lane at the back of the row of houses, Slater panted heavily as he tried to catch up with the fleeing Warwick. The man was sprinting for all he was worth, hotly pursued by the faster, fitter Steve Biddeford, but Slater was lagging behind in third place He was definitely not the bookies' favourite to win.

Ahead of them, where the lane took a sharp turn to the right, Slater noticed a dustbin had been left on the corner. Biddeford was getting very close now and he was getting ready to bring Warwick to the ground as he slowed for the corner. But, just as he was about to leap, Warwick stuck out a hand and managed to pull the dustbin over as he passed. There was a loud clang as the bin fell across Biddeford's path, followed by the sound of a body falling heavily as he crashed into it. Slater grimaced, sure that Warwick was now going to get away. Where the hell was Norman, anyway?

As Slater tried in vain to catch up, he saw a car drive onto the pavement at the end of the lane. Wait, wasn't that Norman's car? He winced at the thump as Warwick crashed into the side of the car as it blocked the exit of the lane. He watched as the runner's legs were taken from under him, causing him to smash face down onto the bonnet.

Luckily for Warwick, he managed to bring his hands up to protect his face, but the impact was enough to knock the wind from him and leave him close to unconscious, by the looks of things. Slater watched as he seemed to bounce back upright. For a moment, he wondered if Warwick was going to carry on running, but then he slowly dropped to his knees and slumped forward against the car.

Norman climbed from the car, and Slater saw him slowly walk round to where Warwick had collapsed. He had just begun to inspect the side of his car when Slater and Biddeford arrived breathlessly behind him.

'Jesus,' said Slater, breathing heavily. 'What did you do to him?'

'Never mind that,' wailed Norman. 'Look what he's done to my car? He's put a dent in the wing.'

Slater looked at Warwick with some concern. 'Bloody hell, Norm, you could have killed him.'

'Oh rubbish. He's fine,' said Norman. 'I just parked my car, right? And then this maniac came along and attacked it. He kicked the wing and tried to head-butt the bonnet. It's criminal damage, at the very least.'

'You could have put him in hospital.' Slater sighed.

'Look, I told you before, I don't do running, I use my head. I stopped him, didn't I? That's more than you two were going to do.'

'I suppose you have a point,' conceded Slater. 'But how are we going to talk to him if he's unconscious?'

'Let's take him back home,' said Norman. 'He'll be alright in a few minutes, you'll see.'

* * *

'I'll sue you for this.' Warwick had been raging at them ever since he'd come to his senses. 'There must be a law against this sort of treatment.'

'I'm sure you're right,' agreed Norman. 'There's also one against resisting arrest, and there's another one against criminal damage.'

'What criminal damage?' asked Warwick, indignantly.

'You kicked my car. There's a great big dent in the side.'

'You tried to run me over. That's the truth of the matter. You could have killed me.'

'We've already been over this,' sighed Norman patiently. 'You can't run someone over sideways. You would have to be in front, or behind, for me to run you over. But you came at me from the side.'

'Right,' said Slater. He'd had enough of the fun and games. 'Now let's talk about a real crime, shall we, Tony? How about blackmail?'

'What about blackmail?'

'How about if I mention the name Mark Clinton and a letter you sent him?'

'I don't know what you mean,' said Warwick, but his voice, and his face, told Slater he clearly did know exactly what they meant.

'DCI Clinton kept the letter, Tony,' lied Slater. 'It's on the way down here now. We know it's from you because you're the only one we've met in this investigation who uses biblical terms. I'm sure when it gets here we'll be able to get our handwriting expert to confirm you wrote it.'

'It would be so much better for you if you told us about it now,' added Norman. 'It might get you a lesser sentence. You could even avoid going to prison.'

At the mention of prison, all Warwick's bravado seemed to melt away.

'Alright,' he said. 'Yes. I wrote him that letter, but only because Ruth asked me to.'

Slater and Norman exchanged a look.

'Ruth told you to?' echoed Norman.

'Yes.'

'So you're telling me Ruth made the video and you were going to use it to blackmail Clinton. I guess you thought he'd pay a small fortune to keep a video like that quiet.'

'Video?' asked Warwick, sounding genuinely surprised. 'What video? I don't know anything about any video.'

'Come on, Tony, don't play games with us,' said Norman, clearly getting irritated. 'The video of Ruth, or Ruby, or whatever you want to call her, having sex with Clinton. You know the one.'

'I don't know what you're talking about,' said Warwick, a look of surprise and horror on his face. 'Ruth wouldn't have sex with that man. She hated him. And who's this Ruby? Where does she come into all this?'

Slater looked at Norman. This wasn't right. Warwick seemed genuine enough, yet he seemed to know nothing. Something didn't add up here.

'Alright, Tony,' he said, 'you tell us why you sent the letter.'

'Ruth told me she'd met Clinton at work and for some reason he'd taken a shine to her. He kept calling her at work suggesting she should have a relationship with him. She told me he wouldn't take no for an answer, so I wrote to him telling him that if he didn't leave her alone I'd make trouble for him.'

'How much money were you going to ask for? And what trouble were you intending to make?'

'I didn't want money. Don't you understand? I hadn't even thought about what I was going to do next. I just wanted to make him stop for Ruth's sake.'

'And you don't know who Ruby Rider is?' asked Norman.

'I've never heard of her.'

Norman produced a photograph and laid it on the table before Warwick.

'Take a good look at this photo. Does it remind you of anyone?'

Warwick studied the photo and Slater watched him closely. He thought perhaps Warwick found something familiar in the photo, but he looked confused. Norman then placed one of the photos of Ruth next to it. Warwick obviously *did* recognise this one. He looked again at the other photo, and then from one to the other several times. Then finally, Slater saw the penny drop, and he knew Warwick wasn't bluffing.

'That looks just like Ruth!' he cried. 'But she never wears make-up, or dresses like that.'

'I don't know how to tell you this, Mr Warwick,' said Norman, 'but that is Ruth. Or at least, that's Ruth as her other self. When she was up in London, she called herself Ruby Rider. She was a high-class hooker. Mark Clinton was one of her clients.'

'No. You must be mistaken. Ruth wasn't like that. She wasn't a hooker. And he was a pest, not a client. You've got this all wrong.'

'I'm sorry, Mr Warwick, but we even have a video Ruby made of her and Clinton together. We believe that she, along with an accomplice, intended to blackmail Mark Clinton.'

'No,' insisted Warwick. 'You're making this up.'

'Now why would we do that?' said Slater. 'We can show you the video if you don't believe us.'

'You disgust me,' said Warwick. 'You come in here making accusations about Ruth leading some sort of double life, and now you want to show me some cheap pornography. How dare you!'

'Well, there's a possible scenario I have to consider, Tony, and it's why we're here right now asking you these questions. Let's suppose you knew what Ruth was doing. Let's suppose you knew she was Ruby Rider. Let's suppose it was your idea to make the video of her and Clinton, and blackmail him. And then, let's suppose you watched the video and you got jealous, and having got jealous you decided you had to stop her, so you killed her.'

'I told you I knew nothing about any of that. I just wrote the letter to stop him calling her.' He was crying now, and in Slater's heart he knew whatever Tony Warwick might be, he wasn't their killer.

* * *

'This case is beginning to drive me mad,' said Norman gloomily, back at Slater's house. 'How many more red herrings are we going to find? Every time we find a likely suspect, or line of enquiry, it turns out to lead up a blind alley.'

'We still don't have a crime, don't forget,' Slater said, sighing. 'I thought we might be onto something with Warwick, but all we have is speculation and suspicion. We can't even prove he was trying to blackmail Clinton without the letter.' He looked morosely into his empty teacup. 'But we get paid for wading through all this crap to find the truth, so I suppose it's no good getting downbeat about it.'

He made a conscious decision that he'd had enough doom and gloom for now. It was time to be a bit more positive, time to move forward.

'Well, you've heard about our crappy day, Steve,' he said to Biddeford. 'Now it's your turn. What did you learn about Clinton?'

Biddeford dragged a notebook from his pocket and thumbed through to the relevant pages. 'Nothing of any great note so far,' he began. 'Basically he's a high flyer with the SCU, heading for great things. Like I said, there doesn't seem to be anything dark in his past. Although, reading between the lines, it seems to me he's made his way up the ladder by using other people to step on.'

'That's for sure,' agreed Norman.

'He seems almost untouchable,' added Biddeford. 'It's like he has a charmed life and everybody loves him.'

He looked up at them, and Slater knew he was unsure if he had done a good job or not.

'More like he's got something on everybody so they have to love him,' corrected Norman.

'I tell you what I have found,' said Biddeford. 'And maybe it's one of the reasons he's untouchable. He knows a lot of people within the legal system. He's even related to some fancy barrister who has connections in very high places. He married her sister. Now what's her name?' He looked through his notes again. 'Ah! Here it is,' he said. 'Her name's Jenny Radstock. She's his sister-in-law, and her family are friends with the Home Secretary, no less.'

Slater sucked in a breath, making a loud hissing sound. Both Norman and Biddeford turned to look at him, and Slater felt his face redden.

'Well, well,' said Norman. 'I get the feeling there's something here we should all know, but right now only you know. So come on, do tell. What's the thing with Jenny Radstock?'

'This is a bit embarrassing,' Slater began, looking guiltily at Norman. 'Jenny Radstock is the barrister who latched onto Beverley Green's complaint about the original investigation and took it up with the local MP and the Home Secretary. She came to see me when I was first given the case. She's the one who persuaded me to take it on.'

'Is that it?' asked Norman.

'I didn't know she had a connection with Mark Clinton. I didn't even know Mark Clinton was involved back then,' pleaded Slater.

'And have you spoken to her since?' asked Norman.

'Only to tell her I'd got started.'

'And do you plan to speak to her again?'

'Well, she's asked me to keep her informed, but so far I haven't.'

He was feeling distinctly uncomfortable now as the implications began to jump into his head. He looked anxiously at Norman. 'Shit, Norm,' he said. 'What the hell's going on here? What have we got into?'

'Whoa! Just hold on now,' said Norman soothingly. 'We don't know if this changes anything yet, do we? I can see three possible scenarios. One, it's just a coincidence. Two, she's trying to help Clinton save his arse. Or three, she wants to bury Clinton and she's using you to do it. Of course, there could be a fourth option, although I haven't got a bloody clue what that might be. But with this case nothing would surprise me.'

'But I should have known,' said Slater.

'How could you have known?' said Norman. 'Clinton wasn't even on the field of play when you started.'

'So how do we figure out what she's up to?' asked Slater.

'If she really is covering up the cover-up, you need to play along for now. Maybe it's time you met up with her and gave her an update,' suggested Norman. 'We'll just have to edit the news a bit and tone some of it down, that's all. We'll make sure you tell her enough, without telling her much, if you see what I mean.'

'But what if Beverley Green's already told her what we know?' said Slater, unhappily.

'Even if that has happened,' said Norman, clearly trying to keep Slater calm, 'she's still way behind where we are now, right?'

'I suppose so,' agreed Slater unhappily.

'But there's an upside to that scenario too. If she knows about Ruth being Ruby, she's not passing that information on to Clinton. If he had known he would have been better prepared for us, don't you think?'

Norman looked at his watch. 'Good lord, is that the time? No wonder my stomach's rumbling. It's dinner time. How about a takeaway while we work out what you're going to report to Miss Radstock?'

CHAPTER TWENTY-ONE

'Oh my God! What happened to you?' Jenny Radstock looked shocked at the sight of Slater's arm, heavily bandaged and supported by a sling. She stepped back to let Slater into her house.

'You'd better come in,' she said.

'Err, yes. I had a bit of an accident. I'm sorry I've not called sooner, but it's rather slowed things down,' said Slater, stretching the truth to fit the scenario he had dreamed up with Norman and Biddeford.

They had decided it wouldn't be wise to tell her everything they knew because it was just possible she was planning to feed this information back to Clinton. Then again, they had to make sure he gave her enough information to satisfy her curiosity. It was Norman who had come up with the bright idea of exaggerating the situation with Slater's damaged wrist and using that as an excuse.

In reality, the lightweight cast he now wore barely interfered with his activities and certainly didn't stop him working. However, for the sake of the story Norman had sent Biddeford into town to buy bandages and a sling. The addition of those bandages and the supporting sling made it almost impossible for him to do anything with the offending arm. It would be easy for anyone who didn't know the truth to assume he would find it a struggle to do most things at the moment.

From the way she was dressed, Jenny had obviously anticipated an opportunity to satisfy some of her curiosity about Slater during the course of the evening. Her short silk kimono showed off her long legs to great effect, and the front was open just far enough to show tantalising glimpses of what was inside every time she moved. He couldn't be sure, but he thought the expression on her face when she saw his arm was more an expression of disappointment than one of concern.

She led him through to a sumptuous lounge. The pile on the carpet was so deep he was surprised he could still see his feet when he looked down.

'Sit down,' she said, waving across at a two-seater settee while she busied herself at a small bar in one corner. 'Gin and tonic?'

'Please,' he said as he sank down onto the settee.

'So,' she asked solicitously, 'what happened?'

'Accident,' he explained. 'Silly, really. I slipped and fell. It's made life pretty difficult and certainly slowed me down a lot.'

She walked across and handed him his drink, then she walked back across the room and curled into the armchair opposite him, drawing those long, slender legs up underneath her. She moved slowly and sensuously. She reminded Slater of a cat, and right now he felt a bit like the mouse who was about to be devoured.

'Now, tell me how you're getting on.'

So he told her about his meetings with Beverley Green and Tony Warwick, and then about his visit to the *Magazine*, carefully omitting anything of any great importance.

'So you haven't really got far at all?' she said finally.

'I'm afraid not, no. I lost a couple of days when I had my accident, so it's taken a lot longer than I would have hoped.'

'How incapacitated are you?' she asked.

'Oh, I can do most things,' he said, wondering what she really meant. 'I just have to be a bit careful not to bang it against anything or put any weight on it.'

'And I suppose you have to make sure you don't get it all wet.'

'Err, yes, that's right,' he said, beginning to see where this was going.

'Are you up to doing a little job for me?' she asked.

'Err, what sort of job?' he said suspiciously.

'Something I can't manage,' she said teasingly, sipping at her drink. 'But I'm sure you'll make a good job of it. It's upstairs in the bathroom.'

Ah! Now he could see where this was going.

'Mustn't get my arm wet,' he reminded her.

'Oh, I'm sure you can manage just fine with the one hand.' She smiled at him.

Now Dave Slater wasn't averse to an encounter of this sort with an attractive woman, and Jenny Radstock was a very attractive woman. Indeed, five years ago he'd have seen this as a great offer, and he'd have been in there like a rat up a drainpipe, but over the last couple of years he'd begun to tire of such things. He was beginning to realise that what he really wanted was a proper, meaningful relationship, not this easy come, easy go, sort of thing.

He was considering how he was going to play the situation and what to do next when she decided it for him.

'So,' she said, easing her legs from beneath her and stretching them forward so the kimono rode upwards. 'How about if I go up and run the bath while you finish your drink? Then perhaps you could come up and scrub my back.'

'Perhaps I will,' replied Slater with a reluctant smile, knowing that he wouldn't.

'Do I frighten you, Sergeant Dave?' she asked, picking up on his reluctance.

'No,' he said.

'Perhaps you don't find me attractive.'

'I think you're very attractive,' he answered diplomatically. 'And you know you are.'

'But I get the feeling you're not very keen.' She sighed, sounding disappointed.

'I'm just not sure it would help our working relationship.'

'Oh, I can assure you that wouldn't be a problem,' she said. 'Or at least it never has been before. I know how to keep work and fun separate. But, of course, if you can't handle it . . .'

She left the sentence unfinished and looked meaningfully at him, confident in her ability to seduce. Then slowly she rose from her chair, the kimono falling open just long enough to reveal a lack of underwear that proved she was a true redhead.

'Oops! Clumsy me,' she said, biting her lip as she hastily pulled it back together. 'Well, I'm going up for a bath. Perhaps you'll join me in a few minutes. I do hope so.'

She walked her sensuous, cat-like walk across the room. Slater couldn't stop himself from watching, and admiring, the gentle sway of her hips as she walked away from him. He knew it had been a close-run thing. She was sex-on-legs, but despite all her seductive charms, it had been the lip-biting that had nearly swayed him. If she had done that a bit more, he doubted he would have been able to resist.

He could hear the bath running upstairs. It was time to make a discreet withdrawal. If she came down and started biting her lip again he'd have no chance.

He climbed quietly to his feet and headed for the front door. There was a well-scuffed handbag lying on a small table just inside the front door. He couldn't resist stopping to peep inside. He was surprised to find there wasn't much in there. Most of the women he knew could easily fill a small suitcase with the contents of their handbags.

There was a small pocket on the inside, just right for holding a few business cards. He guessed they must be her own cards, and as he'd spilt tea all over the one she had given him, he helped himself to a new one.

He glanced at it and realised it wasn't hers at all. It was for an escort agency called Beautiful Ladies. He picked out a second. It was the same. He put the second card back, but curiosity made him keep the first one and he slipped it into his pocket.

Then he eased the front door open and crept quietly out of the house, making sure the door had locked behind him.

CHAPTER TWENTY-TWO

When they gathered at Slater's next morning he gave them a quick rundown on the previous evening's events. He didn't tell them about Ms Radstock's failed attempt at seducing him; he didn't think they needed to know. But he did show them the Beautiful Ladies Escort Agency business card.

Norman looked at it with interest and passed it over to Biddeford. He turned to Slater.

'Where d'you pick that up?'

'She had a handful of them in her bag. I didn't think she'd miss one.'

'D'you think it's relevant, or are you getting desperate for company?'

'What do you think?'

'I think you probably couldn't afford it,' Norman said, grinning at Slater.

'So how does this fit in?' asked Biddeford, turning to his laptop.

'I'm not sure it does,' Slater answered. 'Perhaps I'm just nosey, but I got to wondering why a lady barrister would be carrying around a bunch of escort agency business cards.'

'Perhaps it's a sideline,' suggested Norman. 'Everyone should have a hobby. Or maybe she hands them out to judges to keep them sweet.'

'It's a posh-looking website,' Biddeford interrupted. 'It certainly looks high-class.'

'I hope there are no naughty pictures on there that are going to embarrass you,' teased Norman.

'Nothing smutty here, Norm,' Biddeford said, as he navigated his way through the site. 'Like I said, posh and classy.'

'Anything that might interest us?' asked Slater.

'Not yet,' answered Biddeford, clearly distracted. 'Lots of waffle, nice looking girls. Beautiful Ladies is exactly what I'm seeing. Really nice photos actually. Oh . . .'

'What?' chorused Slater and Norman.

'What's up?' insisted Slater.

'You'd better take a look at this,' said Biddeford. 'I think you could say this is relevant.'

They moved across to look at the laptop over his shoulders.

'Bingo!' said Norman. 'It looks like Jenny Radstock might have a bit more invested in this case than you thought.'

'Oh crap!' was all Slater could think to say.

They were looking at a photograph of one of the 'Beautiful Ladies'. They all knew her of course, but if there had been any doubt, the caption underneath told them her name was Ruby.

'That bloody Jenny Radstock's just using me, isn't she?' said Slater, animated with rage. 'Bloody cow. I'm going to see her and find out what the hell she thinks she's playing at!'

'Whoa! Just hold on there,' cried Norman. He placed his hands on Slater's shoulders and held on tight. 'Let's just think about this for a moment before you fly off and do anything hasty.'

Slater was tempted to push him aside and storm off, but one look told him Norman would have none of that.

'Just sit down and let's talk about this, Dave. You'll regret it if you storm over there in this mood. You could blow the whole thing.'

Slater glared at him but he had to admit, Norman had a point.

'You know I'm right, Dave. Come on now. Let's talk about this. Please?'

Slater relaxed a little and nodded his head. 'Okay,' he agreed.

'You sit down here while I make us some tea, and then we'll talk.'

Slater let himself be eased into a chair. Norman turned to Biddeford.

'See if you can find out who owns that site and where we can get hold of them, can you, Steve?'

* * *

Five minutes later, Slater had calmed down enough to start thinking again.

'Now let's think about this,' said Norman. 'I know it looks bad, but there could be a simple explanation.'

'Oh yeah? Like what?' scoffed Slater.

'Well, let's see,' began Norman. 'It could be she found them somewhere. Or maybe she really does hand them out to people. It could even be that you're right and she's involved in whatever it is we've stumbled across.'

'So why don't we go and ask her?' said Slater.

'If that's what you really want to do, and you think that will solve this case, then go ahead and do it,' said Norman. 'But if you want my opinion, that would be a big mistake.'

Slater was unconvinced.

'She even tried to seduce me to keep me sweet and get more information out of me,' he explained, as if that was enough to prove he was right.

'Has it occurred to you that she might just fancy you?' said Norman.

Slater looked sceptical.

'Oh come on!' said Norman. 'You're a good-looking guy. Don't tell me it's never happened before.'

Slater wasn't a vain man, but he knew Norman had a point. And he had allowed himself to be seduced in the past, on more than one occasion.

'So what do you suggest?' he said, much more calm now.

'I suggest we let our whizz kid over there find out what he can about this escort agency. If we get lucky we might even find out who owns it, and that could lead to a very interesting conversation. For a start, we might be able to confirm if Clinton's telling the truth about Ruby being a one-night stand.'

'You think he was a regular customer?'

'You've seen her. Do you think a guy like Clinton would be satisfied with a one-night stand when he could come back for more? If he was prepared to offer her protection for a one-off, maybe he was prepared to offer the owner of the agency protection for a regular slot.'

'You may have a point there,' Slater agreed.

'We can decide what to do about Jenny Radstock after we've spoken to the owner. Alright?'

'Okay. I suppose you're right,' admitted Slater.

'Of course I am.' Norman beamed. 'That's why you like working with me so much.'

It didn't take long for Biddeford to come up with the information Norman was hoping to find.

'Her name's Lucinda DeLove,' he told them. 'Thirty-eight years old, lives in Hampton. As far as I can tell, she runs the website from home. I've got the address here.'

He handed Norman a sheet of paper.

'Lucinda DeLove? Good name for someone who owns an escort agency,' said Norman appreciatively, looking at the address. 'I wonder what her real name is. Oh, Spring Gardens. I think I know where this is. Posh area.'

'Probably,' agreed Biddeford. 'And the name looks genuine. Her parents have money. She was privately educated. And get this, she went to the same school as Jenny Radstock. They even studied law together, but Lucinda gave it all up before she qualified. Sorry, but that's about all I've got.'

'Sorry?' Slater was surprised. 'Jeez, Steve, you don't need to apologise. You've done really well. We've got plenty to be going on with here.'

'Oh, right,' said Biddeford, looking slightly embarrassed. 'Do you want me to carry on with this, or what?'

'Actually I've got something a bit juicier for you. I need you to go over to see Bob Murray and make sure we've got the warrant I asked for him to arrange this morning. And then, when you've got it, come back here and start looking into Mark Clinton's financial affairs.'

'Wow! Murray okayed that?' asked Norman, sounding surprised.

'He wasn't happy about it, but he agreed with me that it had to be done.'

Slater clapped his hands together.

'Right,' he said. 'Maybe now we can start getting some answers.'

'It would be a lot easier if we knew which questions to ask,' said Norman. 'But then we can always do what I usually do.'

'What's that?'

'Make it up as I go along. It works every time!'

* * *

As Norman had so rightly pointed out earlier, Spring Gardens, in Hampton, was indeed what might be called a posh area. Exclusive would be just one of the words an estate agent might use.

'Are you sure it wouldn't have been a better idea to call first and make an appointment?' asked Slater, as they climbed from Norman's car.

'Would you have preferred it if we'd given her a chance to contact Jenny Radstock before we got here? This way no one knows we're coming, so we have the advantage of surprise.'

'I hope you're right,' warned Slater. 'Otherwise we'll have wasted a whole afternoon by the time we get back.'

'Will you stop being so negative?' Norman sighed. 'Vinnie was right. All this negative stuff you give off doesn't help anyone.'

'Negative?' said Slater. 'I'm not being negative. It's just that if she's not—'

'Can't you hear yourself?' asked Norman. 'You're looking at what might happen to stop our progress. How about, just for a change, you start looking at what might happen in our favour? Is that too much to ask?'

That shut Slater up. He had never thought of himself as being negative, but now two people had suggested he was. Surely they must be wrong. Mustn't they?

'Am I really negative?' he asked.

'Not always, but you do have a tendency,' Norman replied.

'I do?'

'Afraid so.'

'Hmmppphh.'

'Come on,' said Norman. 'Let's go see. She'll be at home, I'm telling you.'

He led the way towards number ten.

* * *

The door was opened by an elegantly tall, good-looking woman with thick dark hair that tumbled over her shoulders. She smiled expectantly at the two detectives.

'Can I help you?'

The cultured tones told Slater this must be who they were looking for.

'We're looking for Miss Lucinda DeLove,' said Norman.

'Well, your search is over. You've found her,' she replied.

They showed their warrant cards and Norman made the introductions.

'We'd like to talk to you if you could spare a few minutes,' he said.

'Goodness! How exciting,' she said. 'Have I done something wrong?'

She had the confident air that comes from money and a private education. Slater thought she was a bit too 'jolly hockey sticks' for his liking, and he hoped she wasn't going to start saying 'Okay, yah!' at the end of every sentence. He couldn't decide if she really was pleased to see them, or if she was taking the piss, but he chose to follow the agreed plan and keep quiet. Norman was taking the lead here, and he certainly didn't look phased by her.

'Could we come in?' asked Norman.

'Oh, of course. How rude of me. I am sorry,' she gushed. 'Do come in.' She stepped back and opened the door wider to reveal a thick-piled, white carpet.

'Do go through.' She waved them towards a door across the hallway.

'We'd better take our shoes off,' said Norman, indicating the carpet.

'Oh don't worry,' she said, smiling. 'Just make sure you don't walk any dog poo in and it'll be fine.'

Obediently they checked the soles of their shoes, just in case.

As they had expected, the decor oozed class, and must have cost a small fortune.

'Do sit down,' she insisted. 'Can I offer you tea? Or coffee?'

'Err, no, we're fine, thank you, Miss DeLove.'

'Call me Lucinda, please,' she said. 'Miss DeLove is so formal, don't you think? Or are you not allowed to be informal? Am I in trouble?'

Slater decided no, she wasn't taking the piss, this was the real her.

'It's about Beautiful Ladies,' said Norman.

'Oh! Is there a problem? It's not illegal you know. I've made sure of that.'

'You have photos of your escorts on the site,' Norman continued. 'We're interested in one of them. Her name's Ruby.'

'Goodness, Ruby hasn't been with us for some time now,' said Lucinda, looking concerned. 'I told them to remove her page and picture months ago. Honestly, you pay a small fortune to have someone look after your website and they can't do the simplest job.'

'What can you tell us about Ruby?' asked Norman, ignoring her comment.

'She left about six months ago. I was quite pleased really because she was getting to be quite difficult.'

'In what way?' prompted Norman.

'When she first joined us she was wonderful. She was very popular, always in demand. She would have made a fortune if she'd been prepared to work weekends. For a year she was brilliant, but then she started to become a bit awkward. First, she wanted to pick and choose who she saw, and then she didn't want to work Wednesdays. Then she'd sometimes call at the last minute to tell me she was unavailable on a Tuesday, or a Thursday. It wouldn't have been so bad, but it meant I had to come out of retirement to fill in. So when she left I think it was for the best, you know?'

'Do you think she was cheating on you? Stealing your clients?'

'Heavens, no. I don't work like that, Sergeant. I run an escort agency, I'm not some sort of pimp. If a client wants to see one of the girls without asking me first, that's fine by me. I have a constant stream of new clients. I make a nice steady income whatever. And the girls appreciate the fact that I'm so easy-going. It makes for great working relationships, I can tell you.'

Slater thought it was interesting Lucinda didn't see herself as a pimp. He thought that was exactly what she was. No matter how she might dress it up, it was money for sex at the end of the day, wasn't it?

'I know what you're thinking,' she said. 'But they're all adults. They pay for an introduction and for the company. If it goes any further that's nothing to do with me.'

Slater found it slightly unnerving that she had read his mind so accurately. He wondered if they learned that at private school.

'Did Ruby let you know she was leaving?' Norman clearly had no intention of getting into the 'is this just a posh brothel' argument.

'No, she didn't. I suppose that just goes to show how far apart we'd become.'

'And you didn't try to contact her to find out?'

'Goodness, no.' She looked appalled. 'As I said, she had become more and more difficult. To be honest I was quite relieved.'

'The thing is,' said Norman, 'we believe something may have happened to her. She seems to have just disappeared off the face of the earth. She even left all her things at her flat.'

'Oh my God! How awful. Poor girl. What do you think happened?'

As the observer, Slater thought she certainly looked and sounded genuine.

'That's what we're trying to figure out. So, if there's anything you can think of that might help us . . .' Norman said, encouragingly.

'I feel terrible now,' said Lucinda quietly. 'Perhaps if I'd made an effort to talk to her . . .' The sentence fizzled out to silence.

Norman paused for a moment before continuing on a different thread.

'Was a DCI Mark Clinton one of your clients?'

Lucinda looked visibly shaken at the mention of Clinton's name.

'Why yes,' she blurted. 'But that's supposed to be confidential information. How do you know about it?'

'His name has come up in our enquiries,' admitted Norman, and Slater knew he had been playing a hunch. 'Naturally we want to keep that as quiet as we can.'

'Ah. Yes, I see,' said Lucinda conspiratorially. 'You know about that. I suppose you have to go through the motions in a case like this.'

Slater had to fight hard to keep his relaxed pose and stop himself snapping to attention.

'Just to make sure we're on the same side.' Norman smiled. 'Can you just confirm the situation for us?'

'Mark and Ruby. I made sure he always got her, he made sure I never got any hassle. That was it.'

'So he was a regular, paying client?'

'Regular, yes. Paying? Heavens, no. Complimentary service, so to speak.'

'Oh yeah,' lied Norman. 'That's the word he used. Complimentary. And I bet he's never let you down.'

'You're the first visit I've ever had,' she said, nodding.

'Do you know Jennifer Radstock, the barrister?' asked Norman.

Slater was poised ready to pounce as soon as she denied all knowledge.

'Jenny? Good lord, yes. I've known her for as long as I can remember. We went through school together. Even went to college together, but we sort of drifted apart after that. She was brilliant. Law suited her like a duck to water, but I struggled with it for a couple of years, then realised I was never going to make it so I dropped out and did this instead.'

She seemed to lose herself in reminiscence for a moment before suspicion took over.

'Why do you want to know about Jenny? I haven't seen her for ages. Surely she's got nothing to do with this?'

'Well, we found a bunch of your business cards in her possession, so we got to wondering how come? So you see, we have to think maybe she is involved or maybe it's just a coincidence. Perhaps you could help us out with that.'

'Wait a minute,' cried Lucinda. 'You think you've discovered some sort of conspiracy here, don't you? Surely you don't think Mark has anything to do with Ruby going missing? You're totally wrong if you do. He adored her. And as for Jenny, I'm sure she doesn't even know Mark uses the agency. She would be appalled to think he was cheating on her sister like that. She certainly wouldn't be helping him.'

'Well, I'll be honest with you, Lucinda,' said Norman. 'Right now we're not sure what to think. Solving a case like this is a bit like building a jigsaw. We have all these different pieces and we're trying to figure out where they all fit in. We have a piece called Ruby, a piece called Mark, a piece called

Lucinda and a piece called Jennifer. Right now, they're all connected by your agency.

'So I'm sure you can see our problem. We can guess how they're all connected, and maybe we'll get it all wrong. Or we can ask someone who knows, and then we'll get it right. So far you've told us about Ruby, and about Mark. All that's left is Jennifer. All we want to know is why she's carrying your business cards.'

Lucinda looked hard at Norman and then at Slater. She was obviously struggling to make a decision. For the first time since they had arrived, she looked just a tad worried. Finally, she seemed to make her mind up.

'Look. Do you promise me this won't go any further? Jen's done really well for herself, and I wouldn't want to be the one who brought the house tumbling down.' She looked anxiously at them.

'Anything you say here is just between the three of us,' promised Norman.

'It had jolly well better be, or I'm dead,' she said, grimly.

'I know secrets about plenty of people and they still have their careers,' Norman assured her.

'Discretion is all part of our job,' agreed Slater.

'God, I hope I don't regret this,' muttered Lucinda. 'Back in the days when we started at college,' she began, finally, 'it came as a bit of a shock to find we had to pay our own way. We were used to spending what we wanted, when we wanted, and suddenly we had no cash. So we had this bright idea of creating an escort agency. I mean, why not? We were two attractive girls, we knew how to behave, how to make intelligent conversation. We were the business. And we soon found we could make very good money working just a couple of nights a week.'

Slater looked at Lucinda, and thought about Jenny Radstock. They weren't sisters, but anyone could see they came from the same mould. It was easy to imagine how popular these two would be if someone wanted some company for the night.

'So you're partners?' asked Norman.

'Were partners,' she corrected him. 'When it became clear Jen had a flair for the law and putting her case, she chose to step away from the agency. It wouldn't have done much for her career, would it? And that was the same time I was thinking of dropping out, so it all worked out rather well. She focused on the law and I focused on Beautiful Ladies. It all worked out rather nicely for both of us, actually. The only downside was we drifted apart. It's a pity really; we used to have so much fun.'

'How long ago was this?' asked Norman.

'Gosh! Ages. I haven't been to college for something like fifteen years,' she said.

'So why would she have your business cards?'

'I have no idea,' she said. Then, as an afterthought, she asked, 'Do you have one with you?'

Slater fished in his pocket and handed her the card.

'Good lord.' She laughed. 'This is so old! These must be the cards we were using back in college. They've been updated several times since then. Look, we don't even include a website on here, because we didn't have one back then.'

She handed the card back to Slater.

'She must be keeping these for old time's sake, that's all I can think.'

* * *

'So what do you think?' asked Slater when they were back in the car.

'I think we now know Clinton's a liar. He was seeing Ruby on a regular basis. Maybe that's why Ruby started to become a problem. Maybe she didn't like his company. Perhaps she made the video to blackmail him into keeping away?'

'Yeah. That would make sense,' agreed Slater. 'But what about Lucinda DeLove. Do you think she's for real, or is she bullshitting us? Maybe she was in on this with Ruby. Perhaps it was a joint venture to get him out of both their lives.'

'Well, that's a possibility, but I didn't hear anything that didn't add up, did you? And if she's acting she ought to go to Hollywood, she's that good. What did you think?'

'I've got to be honest,' answered Slater. 'I actually liked her. I didn't think I would at first, but she came across as genuine. Her reactions all seemed real enough, so I agree with you. I think she's telling the truth. But I still don't understand why Jenny would have those business cards in her bag, especially as they're so old.'

'You realise you're going to have to speak to her now, don't you?' Norman grinned. 'We have to find out for sure that what Lucinda's just told us about the early days of the agency is true.'

'Ah, yeah,' said Slater. 'I'm really looking forward to that. It's going to be a seriously uncomfortable conversation. I can just see it now: "Hello Ms Radstock, is it true you used to be a high-class hooker before you became a barrister?"'

'Can I come with you? I've just got to see how you handle this.'

'I think you'd better. I may need protection,' said Slater, grimly.

'There's no avoiding it, you know. We have to know whose side she's on.' Norman was obviously enjoying this so much he just couldn't keep the grin off his face. 'Maybe we could ask for some body armour,' he suggested.

'Just drive, and stop enjoying my discomfort quite so much, could you?'

'I'll try.' Norman smiled, starting the car and pulling away. 'But I'm not sure I can.'

CHAPTER TWENTY-THREE

'Dave Slater,' he said into the phone.

'Detective Sergeant Slater. How dare you go looking into my past without my permission?'

Oh shit. Jenny Radstock. How did she find out so quickly?

'I've just had a call from my old friend Lucinda DeLove. And, do you know, at first I thought how wonderful to hear from her for the first time in ages, but then she told me she'd been visited by two bloody policemen who were asking questions about my past.'

'Er, yes. It wasn't quite like that. I can explain,' he said, wondering how exactly he was going to handle this.

'Oh good. I do hope so for your sake. How could what I was doing fifteen years ago have anything to do with Ruth Thornhill's disappearance?'

'Well, it's funny you should mention that—'

'Funny!' she stormed. 'I'm glad you think it's funny, but I'm sorry, I don't seem to get the joke. Perhaps you'd like to explain it to me? While you're at it perhaps you'd also like to explain how you came to make this quantum leap.'

'Now look, Jenny, I understand why you're angry, but just calm down, will you? If you'll just let me explain, you'll understand why we had to go and see Lucinda.'

'Oh yes, please,' she snapped. 'Go ahead. I can't wait to hear it.'

'I can't do this over the phone.'

'You'd better get your backside in gear and get over here, then.'

'This has become part of our investigation now. I have to have another officer with me when I speak to you.'

'What?' she shrieked. 'Are you going to question me? What am I, some sort of suspect? If any of this comes out it could destroy my career.'

'No, you're not a suspect, not at all. We weren't looking into your past to see if we could dig up some dirt, and what we found out won't go any further. I promise. Let us come over in the morning and talk to you. I'm sure you'll understand.'

'I'm not very bloody happy about this.'

'I think you've made that quite clear.' Slater sighed, unhappily. 'Are you at home? Where I came last time?'

'Yes, but I have to be away by ten o'clock, so you'd better get here early. Be here at eight, and don't be late.'

'Right. We'll be there. Eight o'clock. On the dot.'

He heard a click as she put the phone down on him.

He dialled another number.

'Hi, Norm. She knows. Lucinda phoned and told her.'

'Oh crap! How did she take it?'

'Incandescent. She wants my balls as a paperweight.'

'That good, huh?'

'We have been summoned to her place in the morning so I can explain. Eight o'clock sharp.'

'Do I need armour too?'

'You will if we're late.'

'I'll be round for breakfast at seven.'

* * *

Slater had described Jenny Radstock to Norman as an attractive redhead with intense green eyes. As the door swung open, Slater reflected that he should perhaps amend one or two adjectives in that description. She looked furious, and he thought 'aggressive' and 'fierce' were perhaps more appropriate. This could get messy.

'Good morning,' he began, optimistically.

'Is it?' She gave him a withering look.

Norman took a step back, slightly behind his colleague. She glared at him.

'Who's this?' she demanded, looking Norman up and down.

'Err, this is Detective Sergeant Norman,' explained Slater. 'He's working with me on this case.'

'Norman,' she repeated. 'Didn't you get sent up north?'

'Why, yes,' answered Norman, sounding surprised. 'How did you know about that?'

'You're one of half a dozen I know about,' she said shortly. 'Along with Sergeant Sneaky, here.'

Slater looked horrified. He saw Norman look away, but had seen the grin cross his face. This really wasn't supposed to be funny.

'Well don't just stand there,' she snapped. 'My neighbours will think there are tramps in the neighbourhood. Through here.'

She led the way into the house and pointed at two chairs in the living room. 'Right, Detective Sergeant Slater,' she said curtly, when they were all seated. 'Talk to me. Let's start with your accident. Tell me again what happened.'

'I just slipped and fell, that's all.'

'Oh, really,' she said. 'I heard someone tried to push you under a bus.'

'Ah!' said Slater. Caught in the lie, he sat there red-faced like the naughty schoolboy caught telling fibs.

There was an uncomfortable silence, finally broken by Jenny Radstock.

'This relationship won't work if you're going to lie to me, Sergeant.'

'I didn't know we were in a relationship,' countered Slater. 'And I didn't know you were checking up on me.'

‘I told you I was involved,’ she said.

‘But you didn’t tell me whose side you were on.’

‘What the hell is that supposed to mean?’ she demanded.

Slater thought it had started about as well as could be expected in the circumstances. At least she hadn’t physically attacked him, yet. But being called Sergeant Sneaky had certainly hurt.

‘Right. Hold on. Let me explain what’s going on,’ he began nervously. ‘It’s like this: during our investigations, we discovered Ruth was leading a double life. Up in town she was a high-class escort called Ruby Rider, and we believe she was taking things a stage further and charging for sex.’

‘Are you sure? Does her sister know? You didn’t mention any of this the other night, did you?’

‘I’ll get to why in a minute,’ said Slater patiently. ‘We then found a link between DCI Mark Clinton and Ruby Rider, aka Ruth Thornhill.’

‘Mark?’ she interrupted. ‘You didn’t tell me this the other night either.’

‘I had my reasons.’

‘Like what?’ she snapped.

‘Like, you’re related to him by marriage.’

‘What difference does that make?’

‘It makes a lot of difference to us,’ explained Slater. ‘We know there’s some sort of cover-up going on, and we had reason to believe it may involve the Serious Crime Unit. Then we discover Mark Clinton, who’s close to the top of the SCU, is involved with Ruby.’

‘What? And you think that means I’m involved in this as well?’ she said indignantly. ‘Do you go around suspecting everyone?’

Slater and Norman exchanged glances. Slater sighed heavily.

‘Unfortunately, due to the nature of what we do, we can’t afford to assume everyone’s innocent.’

‘Oh. So we’re all suspects then. Whatever happened to “innocent until proven guilty”,’ she quoted. ‘That’s the law of the land, isn’t it?’

'If you don't mind me saying,' interrupted Norman. 'For someone in your position that's a very naive attitude.'

She glared at him as if he was infectious.

'Actually, yes, I do mind you saying,' she snapped.

'Alright,' said Slater, beginning to get annoyed. 'Let's say we do it your way, and we assume everyone's innocent. So I would have come around here the other night, told you everything I know, including what we now know about Mark Clinton, and if you weren't innocent you would have gone straight back to him and told him what we know. With his connections he could pull all sorts of strings and all our work goes down the drain.'

'But I wouldn't have told him,' she said. 'Believe me, I wouldn't throw him a rope if he was drowning, so I certainly wouldn't want to get him off your hook.'

'Fine,' said Slater. 'But I didn't know that, did I? Having found the family connection between you, I couldn't take that risk until I'd checked you out. It's the job. It's what we do. I'm sorry if that offends you, but it's how we solve crimes. We couldn't do that if we assumed everyone was innocent, now could we?'

She seemed to take on board what he had said, and Slater thought her rage faded just a tad.

'Yes, but why did you have to involve Lucinda and go looking into what happened years ago?'

'We have a link between an escort and a police officer,' explained Slater, patiently. 'Then we find a link between that police officer and you. Then I spot a business card for an escort agency in your handbag.'

'So you put two and two together and come up with five,' she argued. 'It's all very circumstantial. It certainly wouldn't hold up in court.'

'Which is exactly why we have to check it out,' Norman jumped in. 'If there's a possible link, we have to check and see where it leads. I understand how you must feel about what we've done, but how else could we build a case?'

'But if this gets out . . .' she began. 'It costs enough to keep it quiet as it is.'

'It won't get out,' said Norman emphatically. 'Not from us. You have my word on that.'

Slater could see she was still feeling decidedly unhappy about the whole thing, but she was also an intelligent woman. Much as she may feel like a victim, Slater felt she could see their side as well. After a few moments, she spoke again.

'So, what were you doing poking around in my handbag? I'm sure I didn't leave it laying around where you could see it.'

'It was open on that little table in the hall. The business cards were poking out of the inside pocket. I only took it because I thought it was yours, with your number. Then I realised what it was and thought it might be significant.'

'That wasn't my handbag,' she said. 'That's an old bag I haven't used in years. I'm having a clear out — it's bound for the local charity shop.'

'I didn't think there was much in it,' he admitted. 'But at least now we know whose side you're on.'

'I hardly think I would have been urging you to investigate if I wasn't on your side.'

Slater could see the anger was still there, bubbling away just under the surface, but he was beginning to feel a degree of righteous indignation of his own now. He was just doing his job, and he didn't feel inclined to keep on apologising for doing it. If she didn't like it she'd just have to get on with it.

'You'd be surprised how many people would do exactly that,' said Norman. 'It's supposed to make us think they couldn't possibly be guilty of anything. But we're not quite as stupid as people think.'

'Alright,' Ms Radstock said finally, 'you had your reasons. We'll have to agree to disagree about whether you were right or not. But you said there's a connection between Mark Clinton and Ruth, or Ruby, or whatever her name is now.'

'I can't tell you what that is, right now.' Slater knew this would probably make her annoyed again.

'I think you bloody well can,' she snapped.

'I prefer not to.'

'What do you mean, you prefer not to?'

'You just told us you don't like the guy. How do we know you won't confront him? Then he'll know we're on to him,' Norman cut in.

'Have you interviewed him yet?'

'Not yet.'

Slater glanced at Norman, surprised at the lie. Although, he supposed, it hadn't technically been a formal interview, had it?

'So what makes you think I'll confront him?'

The two detectives exchanged an uncomfortable look. She seemed to read it perfectly.

'Oh my God!' she cried. 'He was screwing her, wasn't he? The bastard. He's been cheating on my sister with a high-class whore. I'll bloody well kill him when I get hold of him.'

'Whoa! Calm down,' said Slater. 'That's exactly what you mustn't do. If he's alerted to what we know anything might happen. It certainly won't do our case any good, will it? This is exactly why we didn't want you to know.'

'But this is my sister we're talking about.'

'I think maybe now you're beginning to get a feel for just how difficult our job can be,' said Norman. 'It's often a case of making a compromise between what we should do and what we have to do.'

She looked at them and Slater thought he detected a note of sympathy on her face. Perhaps she hadn't ever considered what it was like to do their job before.

'But you can't expect me to just say nothing,' she said. 'It's my sister. I have to.'

'We're asking you to wait,' said Slater. 'We think we're on the brink of proving your brother-in-law has done a whole lot more than commit adultery.'

He just hoped that would be enough to make her think twice about speaking to her sister.

'Can I ask you a question?' asked Norman.

'Go on,' she said.

'A few minutes ago you said, "it costs enough to keep it quiet". Is someone blackmailing you?'

Her hesitation was momentary, but it was enough.

'How preposterous!' she said. 'Of course not.'

'Miss Radstock. I hate to say this, but you're not a very good liar. We weren't born yesterday. If someone is blackmailing you, we can help. But only if you tell us who it is.'

For a moment, it looked as though she was going to make a big deal out of Norman suggesting she was a liar, but then the fight seemed to drain from her.

'Is it Mark Clinton?' asked Slater.

'Good heavens no,' she said. 'I don't think he knows anything about my connection to Beautiful Ladies. I don't know for sure who it is, but I have my suspicions.'

'Who?'

'Well, that apology for a police officer, DI Jones, is the most likely candidate. He knows I'm gunning for him, and he would certainly know how to dig into my past.'

'How much is it costing you?' asked Norman.

'Five hundred a month,' she said. 'If he finds out I've told you he'll tell the world. I know he will.'

'Now, just calm down,' coaxed Norman. 'We're not going to rush in and start shooting just yet. Can you keep paying him for now?'

'I don't have much choice, do I?' she said unhappily.

'We can sort this,' Slater assured her. 'Trust me. This is all part of something bigger, I'm sure of that now.'

He looked sharply at her. 'Is there anything else we should know?' he asked.

She shook her head. 'No. Not that I can think of. Oh God, look at the time! I'm going to have to go. I have to be up in London this afternoon.'

'Well, I think we're done for now,' said Slater. 'But promise me you'll get in touch if you think of anything else, please?'

'Alright,' she agreed. 'But I want to know what's going on. No more keeping me in the dark.'

* * *

'Well, you've still got your wedding tackle,' said Norman on the way back, 'but it was a close thing. I'd hate to get on the wrong side of her without a good reason.'

'She's pretty fierce, isn't she?' agreed Slater.

'Nice looking though,' said Norman. 'Once she calmed down. All that aggression did nothing for her, but I guess that's redheads for you. Fiery.'

Slater said nothing and they drove on in silence for a while. Norman kept glancing in Slater's direction. Finally, Slater could stand it no more.

'What?'

'Did she really try to seduce you?' asked Norman.

'It's no big deal,' said Slater.

'Are you kidding? She's gorgeous!'

'Yeah,' agreed Slater. 'She is. But I'd just be another notch in the bedpost, you know?'

'You turned her down?'

'She was a possible suspect, Norm. And I'm a professional.'

'Wow! If you turned her down, that was truly professional.'

They drove on a bit further. Slater could see Norman was itching to speak.

'What is it now?' he said, becoming slightly irritated.

'I bet there was a time when you would have jumped at the chance, right?'

'A few years ago,' Slater conceded.

'But now you feel different?'

'Yeah. Now you come to mention it,' agreed Slater, wondering where this conversation was going.

'Have you called Jelena yet?'

'Do we have to discuss my private life?'

'You haven't, have you?' said Norman with surprise. 'What's the matter with you? She's beautiful, she wants you to take her out and you want to be with her. All you have to do is pick the phone up.'

At the mention of Jelena's name, Slater began to feel distinctly uncomfortable. He wondered why he hadn't called her. He wanted to, but for some reason he just hadn't. Why?

'Shall I tell you why you haven't called her?' asked Norman.

'Since when did I ask for your advice?' Slater was getting really irritated now.

'I'll tell you anyway,' said Norman, ignoring Slater's irritation. 'You're frightened of her.'

'Don't give up your day job to become an agony aunt.' Slater said, laughing. 'What a load of old bollocks. Why would I be frightened of her?'

'Because you want a different sort of relationship, that's why. Part of you wants to find out if she's the one, and part of you is terrified she is and would prefer not to find out. At the moment, the terrified part is winning.'

'You think so, do you?'

'I know so,' said Norman, sounding certain. 'You need to tell the terrified part of you the only way to know for sure is to make that call. Just do it, please. For me, huh?'

'Well, Deidre, thank you so much for your advice, but can we stop this conversation? Right now?' said Slater with finality.

'I'm done anyway.' Norman smiled, and Slater knew his fellow officer found it great fun getting under his skin. 'Anyway,' Norman said, changing the subject, 'what do you think about what Ms Radstock had to say this morning?'

'I think she's telling the truth. I just hope she doesn't go and tell her sister what Clinton's been up to behind her back.'

'Actually, I don't know if that would be such a bad thing,' said Norman, thoughtfully. 'If she stirs him up it might just work to our advantage. It could force him to make a move of some sort.'

'I suppose it might,' conceded Slater. 'What about that arsehole Jones? Blackmailing her like that? Do you really think we should let it run?'

'For now, yeah. I'm sure it's all linked together. If we rush in now we might catch the one link but then lose the rest of the chain. What about the video of Clinton? Do you think Ruby did it all on her own?'

'I'm beginning to think it's more and more unlikely, but it's anyone's guess who's in it with her,' said Slater gloomily.

'How many suspects do we have for that right now? Is it three, or four? And they all have a motive of some sort. It's like bloody mastermind, isn't it? Every question we ask seems to lead to more questions. When are we going to start finding some sodding answers?'

'I've been thinking about Ruby's partner in crime,' Norman said, thoughtfully. 'We thought it was the boyfriend, but I don't fancy him. Lucinda's a possibility, but she doesn't seem right to me. I'm no expert on these things, but in my experience there's usually only one blackmailer.'

'You mean Jones?' Now Slater was a bit more excited. 'But we've found no link between him and Ruby.'

'That doesn't mean there isn't one.'

'Maybe it's time we asked Bob Murray for another warrant. I think perhaps it's time we had a look at Jimmy Jones' financials,' said Slater.

'Now there's a coincidence,' Norman said, grinning. 'That's exactly what I was thinking.'

* * *

'How bad was it?' asked Biddeford when they got back. He looked Slater up and down. 'I don't see any flesh wounds, and I see you can still walk.'

'Let's just say it ended better than it started,' said Norman with a grin. 'She'd already had breakfast.'

'She did see our point.' Slater smiled. 'Albeit somewhat reluctantly. But I'm not so sure she's capable of keeping her promise not to tell her sister and drop Clinton in the shit.'

'We'll have to deal with that if it happens,' said Norman. 'But at least we're still all on the same side.'

'As you're so good at doing this financial research,' Slater told Biddeford, 'we've got another one for you to look into.' He dropped the search warrant onto the table Biddeford was using as a desk.

'Oh great! You're just too kind.' Biddeford grimaced. 'I'd much rather be out with you guys, you know.'

'Yes, I know that, Steve,' said Slater, sympathetically. 'But the boss wants us to keep you out of the firing line, and on this occasion I think he's right. Besides, there's not much more room on this tightrope, and we need someone we can rely on back here in the engine room.'

Biddeford accepted the compliment in silence as he looked at the new warrant.

'When do you want this done?' he asked. 'Right now?'

'As soon as you can, mate, please.'

'I'm still working on Clinton's. Do you want me to stop?'

Slater thought for a moment, and then turned to Norman. 'What d'you think, Norm? Put Clinton on the back burner and focus on Jones first?'

'I'm beginning to think Jones is definitely the bigger crook,' Norman said, nodding his head. He turned to Biddeford. 'Is that alright with you, Steve?'

'It makes no difference to me, but before I start on Jones, there's something I want to show you.'

He had a pile of printouts on the table. He handed Slater the top one.

'I've been going through Clinton's bank account. It would be nice if I could find a direct debit to A. Blackmailer, but there's nothing major that stands out straightaway.'

'So no big, one-off payments, or regular cash withdrawals?' asked Norman.

'No big ones, no,' Biddeford said. 'But, then I got to thinking, suppose I wanted to hide a big monthly cash payment. How would I do it?'

'Go ahead, Steve, we're listening,' Slater said.

'I thought one way would be to make lots of smaller withdrawals,' continued Biddeford. 'So I looked for just that, and sure enough, there is one regular withdrawal that fits the bill. It happens at the same place, and more or less the same time, every week. And it's always for the same amount. The only time he misses is when there's a five-week month.'

'So he's withdrawing the same amount every time?' asked Slater.

'Yep,' agreed Biddeford. 'One hundred and twenty-five quid, four times a month.'

'Five hundred a month,' chorused Slater and Norman.

'It's not megabucks, but it looks like a regular payment,' said Norman.

'The thing is, he seems to pay for everything with his credit cards, so I can't see any other way he can be spending that cash,' said Biddeford. 'And the same amount every time?'

'Good work, Steve,' said Norman. 'Dave's right, you have a gift for this stuff.'

'Flattery won't make me enjoy it more.' But Biddeford smiled.

'I know,' agreed Norman. 'It's a crap job. But someone's gotta do it, right?'

'Okay. Point taken,' Biddeford said, sighing. 'Now let me take a look at Jones. Let's see what skeletons I can rattle in his cupboard.'

As Biddeford settled into his latest task, Slater's phone began to make strange noises.

'You have to change that ringtone, please!' Norman said, holding out his hands in a pleading gesture.

'If it'll stop you complaining, perhaps I will.' Slater grinned and reached for the phone.

'Slater.'

'It's DCI Clinton here.'

'Oh! DCI Clinton,' said Slater, loud enough to alert Norman and Biddeford. 'What can I do for you, sir?'

'I need to arrange to talk to you,' said Clinton, curtly.

'About anything in particular, sir?' asked Slater, trying his hardest to sound innocent.

'What the hell do you think I want to talk to you about? If I were you I'd stop trying to be clever and grab this opportunity with both hands.'

'Oh! Er, right. Yessir,' said Slater, surprised by Clinton's vehemence.

'Where we met last time,' snapped Clinton. 'How soon can you get there?'

'We can leave now,' said an excited Slater, looking at his watch. 'We should be there by one o'clock, traffic permitting.'

'I'll be there at one thirty,' said Clinton. 'I'll walk in and buy a coffee then walk back to my car. It'll be an unmarked Volvo. You'll be able to spot me easily enough, but don't approach the car until you're sure I've not been followed. If I think I have been followed I'll just get back in my car and drive off. I don't want anyone to know about this meeting, do you understand?'

'Yes, sir. You think you might be followed. I understand, don't worry.'

The phone was dead before he finished speaking.

'What was all that about?' asked Norman.

'He wants to meet,' Slater said, mulling the conversation over.

'That's a bit sudden, isn't it?'

'He sounds worried, says he needs to talk to us urgently.'

'Really?' Norman sounded surprised. 'How urgent?'

'Like "get your coat we're going now" urgent,' said Slater.

'Wow! D'you think maybe Jenny Radstock couldn't resist telling her sister about him and Ruby already?'

'He didn't say,' said Slater. 'But something has certainly rung his alarm bell.'

'I did say it might work to our advantage if she shook his tree, but I didn't expect her to do it just yet,' said Norman thoughtfully, getting to his feet. 'But if she has, let's hope something nice and juicy is going to fall out.'

'Let's go see,' Slater said.

* * *

Mark Clinton was an easy spot for Norman sitting in Slater's car, as he walked slowly from his car, across the car park, towards the coffee shop. It was a face Norman wished he'd never met, but it was for that very reason he knew he'd never forget it. As Clinton walked, Norman scanned the car park looking for anyone who seemed to be taking an interest in Clinton, but he saw nothing to cause concern.

Inside the building Slater sat in the corner of the coffee shop slowly sipping his drink and glancing at the newspaper before him. He watched over the newspaper as Clinton entered the shop and looked around. Their eyes met briefly, but each ignored the other. Slater watched carefully as Clinton ordered, paid for his coffee, and then very deliberately retraced his steps. He gave his man a few seconds' start and then followed his path. Just like Norman, he saw no cause for concern.

They reached Clinton's car at the same time, each arriving from a different direction. They slid into the back seats behind Clinton and quietly clicked the doors closed. He didn't even turn round to acknowledge their arrival.

'So, the Keystone Cops have arrived at last,' he said, sighing.

Slater and Norman had expected hostility from Clinton, so they were neither surprised nor annoyed by his attitude.

'You asked to speak to us, if I recall correctly,' said Slater, adding, 'sir,' as an afterthought.

'Which one of you bastards went to see my wife?' Clinton snarled.

'Much as we would have enjoyed being the ones to rub your nose in that particular pile of shit,' said Norman, smiling, 'I'm afraid someone has beaten us to it.'

'If it wasn't you two, who the hell else could it have been?' Clinton said, turning around to glare at them.

'Maybe your blackmailer got tired of playing the game,' Slater said. 'Or maybe you didn't do as you were told.'

'I already told you I don't have a bloody blackmailer!'

'So why do you draw out the same amount of cash every Thursday?' asked Norman. 'We worked it out. Five hundred a month. It's not a fortune but it's a regular income for a blackmailer who's not too greedy, don't you think?'

Clinton shrugged his shoulders, but said nothing.

'It might not have been Ruby,' insisted Norman. 'Maybe that was a coincidence, or maybe she disappeared before she could put her plan into action, but someone is using you as a cash cow right now, aren't they?'

'You think you've got it all worked out, don't you?' said Clinton. 'But you're way off the mark. You really don't have a clue.'

'So why not fill in the bits we're missing?' said Slater. 'You're right. We don't know it all yet, but you know we're on to you, and you know we're not going to give up until we find it all out and bring the whole damned thing crashing down around your ears, so why not do us all a favour and get it over with right now? Why not start by telling us what happened to Ruby? Did you kill her because she was trying to blackmail you?'

'Kill her?' said Clinton, and he sounded appalled at the suggestion. 'I didn't kill her. I could never have hurt her. I loved her.'

Slater knew from experience that now would be a good time to keep quiet and let Clinton talk, and a quick glance at Norman told him his fellow officer knew so too. They waited in silence, and eventually Clinton began to tell his side of the story.

'That first night I met her, I thought she was the most beautiful person I had ever met,' he began. 'She had it all, and when she showed an interest in me, well, I couldn't resist, and after that first night I just had to see her again, and again.'

'And were you paying her?' asked Slater.

'Oh yes,' said Clinton. 'I had to, you see. I just had to keep seeing her.'

'Did she use the video to blackmail you?'

'I didn't know anything about that video until you came along. I swear she wasn't blackmailing me.'

'So who is then?' asked Norman.

'Can't you work it out?' asked Clinton. 'You should be able to, Slater. You were one of his victims.'

'You mean Jimmy Jones?' asked Slater. 'My, my, he is a bad boy. So that's why you cover his arse all the time. And he costs you five hundred a month?'

'I wish he was that cheap,' said Clinton. 'That's not even the half of it. I have to take backhanders so I can keep up my repayments.'

'Jeez,' said Norman, 'this hole you're in is getting deeper and deeper.'

'Look,' said Clinton, suddenly, 'I know I'm in it right up to my neck, but I owe that bastard Jones. I'm quite happy to tell you a whole lot more, but what's in it for me?'

'Oh, look, everybody,' Norman spoke in a jeering tone of voice, 'the ship's starting to sink and here comes the first rat looking for a way to escape.'

'Do you want my help, or not?' Clinton said. 'Look, I know I'm finished. Like you said, the whole thing's going to come crashing down now. I just want to make sure I take him down with me, that's all.'

'You know how this works, and you know we can't make any promises,' said Slater. 'That's up to the powers above. But any help you give us is going to work in your favour, right? But you need to give us a bit more than we have right now.'

'I'll tell you what I know,' said Clinton, and for the next half hour he did exactly that.

* * *

'D'you think he'll keep to his side of the deal?' asked Norman as they headed back to Tinton.

'He'll have to if he wants us to get Jones,' said Slater. 'I don't think he knows Jenny Radstock has a similar problem with Jones, so right now he thinks all we've got is his word. I think if he keeps Jones sweet for a few more days, we'll have enough evidence to take them both down.'

'It's strange though,' Norman said, shaking his head. 'We're still no nearer to finding out what happened to Ruby.'

Slater knew he was right. They seemed to have uncovered a serious case of corruption, quite by accident, but they still had no real evidence to suggest what might have happened to Ruth Thornhill.

CHAPTER TWENTY-FOUR

'So let me get this right,' said Norman, trying to put the pieces together. 'You're telling us that Jones transfers the whole of his salary into a savings account every month, and that he keeps nothing back to live on. Are you sure about that?'

Biddeford looked somewhat affronted that Norman should suggest that maybe he hadn't checked his facts properly, but he didn't say as much.

'Absolutely sure,' he said, nodding. 'Just look at the printout. You can see for yourself. Every single penny goes straight into his savings account.'

Norman took the hint.

'I didn't mean that to sound like I think you got it wrong,' he said, apologetically. 'It was more a case of "is he really that stupid he would make it so easy for us"?'

'He's arrogant and overconfident,' said Slater. 'He thinks he's so clever he's untouchable. What else have you got, Steve?'

When they had returned from seeing Clinton, Biddeford had already prepared a set of printouts for each of them.

'He could maybe argue that he doesn't need to do any food shopping, but if you look at the second sheet you'll see he has a Nectar account. Visits Sainsbury's every week to buy his groceries and collects the points. He also gets points when he buys his fuel.'

'How does he pay for them?' asked Slater.

'Credit card,' said Biddeford. 'But, he pays off his credit card with cash.'

'So he's getting cash from somewhere.' Norman rubbed his chin thoughtfully. 'Any idea how much?'

'Well, his credit card bill is usually over three grand,' Biddeford said, looking at the printouts in front of him. 'And it's possible he's spending cash on other stuff too.'

'That means he's almost certainly got more victims than the two we know about.' Slater shook his head. 'He must spend all his time collecting cash.'

'We've got more than enough here to put him away,' said Norman. 'As long as Jenny Radstock and Clinton are prepared to give evidence, he's got no chance.'

'This is very good work, Steve.' Slater clapped the younger man on the back. 'I'd like you to go with Norm and put it in front of Bob Murray. It's high time we dragged Jimmy Jones in for a chat, don't you guys agree?'

'Me?' said Biddeford in surprise. 'You want me to go and see Bob Murray?'

'Yeah. Why not?' said Norman, agreeing with Slater. 'You've done a lot of donkey work here, so it's only right you should get the credit for it.'

Then he turned to Slater. 'And what about you? Where will you be while we're with the big chief?'

'I'm going to ask Jenny Radstock why she couldn't wait to tell Clinton's wife. After all, we did ask her to wait.'

'But it's worked out rather well for us, hasn't it?' asked Norman.

'Yes, but she doesn't know that, does she?'

'Oh, I see,' said Norman, nodding his understanding. 'You want to get your own back for the bollocking she gave you the other day. I can't say I blame you.'

'I know it's a bit unnecessary,' Slater said, smiling ruefully. 'But it won't do her any harm to see things from our side. And she did ask me to keep her informed, didn't she?'

'Jenny Radstock.'

'Hello Ms Radstock. It's DS Slater here.'

'Ah!' she said, sounding rather uncomfortable. 'I guess, by the formal tone, you're not calling to congratulate me.'

'Correct,' said Slater, doing his best to sound stern. 'I'm rather disappointed.'

'Life's quite often like that, don't you agree?' she said.

Slater got the distinct impression she was trying to deflect the criticism he was about to throw at her.

'I would have preferred it if you had resisted the temptation to tell your sister.'

'I did try, honestly. But how could I possibly have just carried on as if nothing had happened when I knew what you had told me? She is my sister, for goodness' sake.'

Slater decided to say nothing and let her stew for a minute.

'Look, I'm really, really sorry,' she said, sounding truly apologetic. 'I tried so hard, but I just couldn't do it. Not to my own sister. I'll make it up to you, I promise.'

'Actually,' said Slater, deciding to let her off the hook before she made a fool of herself, 'it's worked out quite well. Now Clinton's world seems to be tumbling down around him, he's decided to talk to us. It turns out you're not the only one Jones has been blackmailing.'

'Really? Good heavens. Is that why Jones seems to be untouchable?'

'Yeah. If Clinton didn't watch his back, and pay up every month, Jones was going to spill the beans to his wife, to senior officers, and to anyone else he chose.'

'Gosh! Does Mark know it was me?' Ms Radstock asked.

'He thinks it was us at the moment. It suits us for now, but I don't know how long it will last. Can you make sure your sister doesn't tell him it was you?'

'I'm sure she won't, but I'll call her. So what happens now?'

'We've got enough evidence to charge Clinton and Jones. Norman's with Bob Murray now. I would imagine he'll want to bring them in as soon as he can. He'll be asking the questions when they do get here.'

'Does that mean he gets all the credit for the work you've done?'

'These are high-ranking officers. It needs an equal, or higher rank to interview them. I'm okay with that anyway. There's plenty more for us to do.'

'You've done very well, you know,' said Jenny, admiringly. 'I knew if we could get you on the case you could prove Mark Clinton was a wrong 'un. Getting Jones as well is like icing on the cake.'

Slater was a bit taken aback by this.

'The thing is, I haven't done it yet, have I?' he said. 'We still haven't found out what happened to Ruth.'

'And perhaps we never will,' she said, quietly. 'But does that matter? Look on the bright side. At least we've got my brother-in-law. That's who we were really after.'

Slater said nothing. So he was right. She had been using him to get at her brother-in-law all along. He began to wonder just how much she really did know about all this before they'd even got started.

'So, DS Slater,' she said, in a sultry tone, 'I suppose this must mean we're friends again. Why don't you come over tonight and help me celebrate?'

'Sorry, Ms Radstock. I don't think so. I prefer clear water that runs deep, not the shallow murky stuff. I find there's usually something unpleasant just below the surface.'

There was a shocked silence from the other end of the phone.

'Besides,' he added. 'I have a missing person to find.'

There was still no reply, but he could feel a deep, silent animosity coming down the line at him.

'DC Biddeford will be in touch to arrange for you to come in and give your statement,' he finished. 'Thank you so much for your help.'

He cut the call.

Almost straightaway, the phone began to ring. He checked the incoming number. If it was Jenny Radstock, he was going to ignore it. But it wasn't her number.

'DS Slater.'

'Ah, good. I'm so glad I caught you. It's Lucinda DeLove here.'

'What can I do for you, Ms DeLove?'

'Since this all blew up, Jenny and I have had a chance to catch up. She suggested I need to talk to you.'

* * *

Norman arrived back just as Slater was thanking Lucinda DeLove and saying goodbye.

'We've got an even stronger case against Jones now,' Slater told him. 'It seems he's been stinging Ms DeLove for five hundred pounds a month too, and she's more than willing to make a statement. Even if Clinton changes his mind now, it won't matter.'

'Game, set and match to us, then.' Norman grinned.

'Now you sound like Jenny bloody Radstock,' snapped Slater.

'What have I done now?' said Norman, confused. 'All I said was "well done us".'

'I'm sorry,' said Slater. 'It's just that bloody woman has got to me. All she cares about is getting Clinton. When I pointed out we still hadn't found out what happened to Ruth, she told me it didn't matter.'

'Well, don't put me in the same box as her,' said Norman, irritated himself now. 'I'm not trying to suggest for one minute that we forget about Ruth. Maybe now we've cleared some of the rubbish out of the way we can see where we're going and start making some progress.'

Slater looked suitably embarrassed, and Norman knew he had regretted snapping.

'What's happening with Murray?' he asked.

'He's having the Likely Lads arrested as we speak. They're going to be chauffeur-driven down here and invited to sample our hospitality in adjoining cells overnight. He's going to start questioning them in the morning. He's got another DCI joining him, and he's going to keep Biddeford with him.'

'He says we're welcome to join them, but I think I'd rather keep away. There are some steep steps down to those cells. I'm not sure I could stop Clinton falling down them. If you see what I mean.'

'And I'd probably help push him if I was there,' Slater said, smiling. 'I think I'd rather keep looking for Ruby, don't you?'

'That sounds perfect to me.' Norman nodded enthusiastically. 'I think now we've got Laurel and Hardy in custody, we need Bob Murray to ask them some questions about Ruby and that video, so how about we have a little conference and go through what we know in light of the two arrests?'

'Now you're talking, partner,' Slater said. 'Where shall we start?'

Norman considered this for a few moments, his hands cradling his overlarge stomach. Finally, he came to a decision. 'I think we should start by ordering a takeaway. You know I can't think properly on an empty stomach.'

CHAPTER TWENTY-FIVE

It was a rather bleary-eyed Dave Slater who took an early call next morning from his boss, Bob Murray. It turned out DI Jimmy Jones wasn't made of very stern stuff. In order to try to save his own skin, he had demanded to see Murray as soon as he'd arrived at Tinton.

But Murray had no intention of pandering to Jones' demands and he'd been made to wait until Murray arrived at seven a.m., whereupon he'd presented Murray with a list of names. These were all people, he assured them, who were paying backhanders to Clinton.

'I don't mind telling you,' Murray said, shaking his head, 'I find this extremely distasteful. The man's a coward, trying to save his own neck by incriminating Clinton.'

'They sound as bad as each other,' Slater said.

'I haven't checked out these names yet, but I'm going to email you a copy of the list,' continued Murray. 'In case there are any names that might help your inquiry.'

A few minutes later when Slater fired up his laptop, there was the email as promised. He scanned quickly down the list, not really expecting to see any familiar names, but to his surprise, there was one that immediately grabbed his attention.

* * *

It was nearing nine a.m. when Norman finally arrived, looking even more untidy than usual. His usually unruly mop of curly hair seemed to have been ironed on one side, making his whole head look rather lopsided.

'What happened to you?' asked Slater, looking him up and down disapprovingly.

'What d'you mean?' asked Norman.

'Has your style guru gone on strike?' Slater indicated his clothes. 'And what have you done to your hair? Did you sleep on a board?'

'For some reason I have no water or electricity in my flat this morning. So I have no shower, and no means of ironing my clothes.'

'You own an iron?' said a surprised Slater. 'You've certainly kept that a secret up until now.'

'What's that supposed to mean?'

'Well, come on, Norm,' Slater said, laughing. 'You normally look like you're auditioning for Mr Crumply, the new Mister Man.'

'So, I have a style all of my own,' said Norman, with dignity. 'But the thing is this: if people look at me and think I look like a village idiot that's fine by me, because it means they won't be prepared for the razor sharp mind that's on the inside.'

'You always have an answer, don't you?' Slater smiled.

'Which kinda proves my point about the razor sharp mind, don't you think?'

'Yeah. Right.' Slater passed across the printed list of names. 'So what does your razor sharp mind make of this? It's a list of names Clinton is supposed to be collecting payments from.'

Norman spotted it straightaway.

'Oh my. Now there's a name I've seen before. What a coincidence,' he said.

'Guess where we're going this morning?' said Slater.

'Sounds good,' agreed Norman. 'But could I use your shower first?'

'And the iron?' asked Slater, optimistically.

'Change my style and spoil my image?' Norman laughed. 'I don't think so.'

* * *

'Are you sure Mr Chan's even going to be here?' asked Norman as they walked towards Mistral Court. He was intrigued to meet the man after hearing Slater talk about him.

'This is where he's based,' Slater said. 'He tried to pretend it isn't, but he's always here. He'll be here now. Trust me.'

To Norman's great surprise, Mr Chan was not only on the premises, he even agreed to see them. Of course, he thought, if Chan was willing to talk to them it probably meant they weren't going to get much from him. He then went on to chide himself for being pessimistic, and decided it could just be the case that he was getting more cynical in his old age. But experience told him he was probably right.

As usual, Mr Chan was very polite and courteous, the smile never wavering for a moment. His young henchman Mr Ling was also present, looking suitably hostile and unimpressed by them.

'We understand you have been placed in a situation whereby a senior officer has coerced you into making payments,' Slater said.

'When you say "you understand",' asked Chan, 'what exactly does that mean?'

'It means we have information,' explained Slater. 'We've been told, by a source.'

'Ah!' Chan's smile widened. 'A source. That means someone has told you something but you have no proof. Am I right?'

'Err, well,' Slater began. 'It's come to our attention during our enquiries—'

'Why do police always speak like that?' asked Chan. 'Why not speak in words people can easily understand? What you really mean, I think,' he continued, 'is someone has told you I make payments to someone else. Is that correct?'

'Err, yes. I suppose so,' agreed Slater reluctantly.

'The thing is,' said Norman, trying to help Slater out, 'if what we've been told is true, it would mean you have the motive to seek revenge.'

'First you suggest,' said Chan, the smile fading slightly, 'and now you accuse.'

'No one's accusing you of anything, Mr Chan,' said Slater hastily. 'We're just trying to establish whether you were being blackmailed or not.'

'You obviously have no proof of this blackmail,' said Chan. 'So you have no reason to jump to conclusions about me seeking revenge. The fact is, you have nothing to link me to any crime either as the victim or the perpetrator. Is this what you might call a "fishing trip"? If so, please see yourselves out. I am a busy man.'

'It concerns an old tenant of yours,' said Slater, Norman smiling at his colleague's persistence. 'You know, the girl who went missing. Ruby Rider.'

'I have already told you all I know about Miss Rider,' said Chan.

'But you didn't tell me she was a hooker, did you?'

'She must have been very discreet,' said Mr Chan after the briefest of pauses. 'I know nothing about that.'

'She selected a senior police officer,' said Slater. 'And seduced him into becoming a regular client. He thought she liked him, but she was setting up a honey trap. A video was made of him in a very compromising situation with her.'

'And why should this be of interest to me?' asked Chan.

'Because,' Norman joined in, 'if that was the police officer you were having to pay off, getting Ruby to be the bait to help you set the guy up would give you the means to turn the tables on him. You might even have been able to get him to pay you to keep it quiet.'

By the time he had finished, Chan was laughing quietly. Even Ling's face broke into something approaching a smile.

'Forgive me.' Chan smiled. 'I should not laugh, but you have such fertile imaginations. This is an excellent theory, gentlemen, but for one or two little problems.'

Norman felt uncomfortable, and one glance at Slater told him his colleague felt the same.

'First,' began Chan, 'you have no proof. If you had, you surely would arrest me. Am I right?' He looked from one to the other. 'I thought so.' Chan sighed, sadly. 'Second,' he continued, 'I can assure you I have never seen this "video" you claim I am supposed to have arranged to have made.'

For the first time, Ling was actually smiling at their collective discomfort.

'But I like to see imagination at work. It makes for great entertainment. You could perhaps turn your theory into a film script,' Chan suggested, brightening again. 'Let's consider how you might develop the story,' he continued. 'Of course you could now assume I have something to do with Miss Rider's disappearance because she double-crossed me over the video.'

He studied their faces, and then broke into an even broader smile. 'Ah! So you have already considered this possibility. This is good, very good indeed.'

He clasped his hands together and considered them for a moment.

'You have told me an interesting and imaginative story, gentlemen. Now it's my turn. My story is about a fisherman who struggles, every day, to find enough fish to feed his family. Then one day, right under his nose, he stumbles upon the perfect bait to catch nice big fish. Now he knows he will still need to fish every day, but he will never have to worry again about finding enough fish to feed his family.

'Sometimes the bait is a little difficult to handle, and tests his patience, but because it works so well he feels it's worth being tested occasionally. And then one day, our fisherman sees the biggest fish he has ever seen, swimming towards him. To his delight, as soon as this big fish sees the bait it seems unable to resist and is caught without a fight. On that day, the fisherman finally understands he no longer needs to go out fishing every day because he now has the power to catch the biggest of fish anytime he wants. All he has to do is look after his precious bait.'

He studied both faces again.

'You understand my point, gentlemen. If you were the fisherman, would you really consider destroying the bait that was guaranteed to land the biggest, most golden fish?'

He stood up and bowed slightly. Ling stood alongside him glowering. Out of politeness, Slater and Norman stood also.

'Thank you, gentlemen,' said Chan. 'I think we're finished here. If you would like to talk again, please do me the courtesy of calling to arrange an appointment first.'

He nodded once more and walked from the room, Ling obediently scurrying along behind.

'Are we going to accept that?' asked Norman.

'Do we have a choice?' replied Slater, and Norman knew he was annoyed that Mr Chan had got the better of him again. 'Come on, let's get out of here.'

* * *

'Did you buy all that crap about the fisherman?' asked Norman, as they walked back down the road away from Mistral Court.

'You mean do I think Chan got rid of Ruby? If there really was a bigger fish, and he saw her as a useful asset, he would have plenty of reason to look after her. But then again, maybe the whole fish thing is just another red herring.'

Norman looked hard at Slater and groaned loudly.

'Do you have to think hard to come up with such crappy puns? Whatever you do, don't give up your day job for comedy.'

They walked on in silence for a while, until Norman spoke again. 'So who is the bigger fish?'

'That's what I'm wondering, too,' Slater said, looking thoughtful.

A couple more minutes passed.

'Do you think he'll testify against Clinton?'

'Nah!' said Slater. 'Not a chance.'

'Me neither,' agreed Norman. 'It wouldn't do anything for his credibility in the community, would it?'

* * *

After the successes of the last few days, Slater and Norman had every reason to be celebrating, but Slater felt strangely subdued, and he got the impression Norman did too. Even the usual, easy rapport they had developed seemed to elude them, so it was a quiet journey back home.

Being so brilliantly stone-walled by Mr Chan hadn't really surprised Slater. He knew that characters like Chan don't survive in their murky little worlds without learning how to be obstructive and uncooperative, so the fact he had told them so little wasn't the problem.

Slater knew the reason they were both quietly brooding was their complete lack of progress in finding out what had happened to Ruby, or Ruth, or whichever of the two was the real her. People don't just walk out, leave everything behind, and simply disappear. There had to be an answer, but they were no nearer to finding it now than when their inquiry had first started.

Slater's unspoken thought, that he was sure Norman shared, was that the reason they hadn't found an answer yet was simply because they had allowed their desire to catch Jones and Clinton become the focus of their enquiries. Perhaps a vital clue had been right under their noses all the time, but because they both had revenge in mind they'd missed it.

They were guilty of letting Ruth/Ruby down. Slater suggested they should have a weekend off to clear their heads, and Norman agreed. They would start again with renewed vigour on Monday morning.

CHAPTER TWENTY-SIX

Slater knew that sometimes the best thing to do when you have a problem on your mind and you're making no progress is to step away from it for a day or two and focus on something completely different. That's often the time that you make the most progress because you allow your subconscious to work unhindered.

However, if you take a weekend off and just carry on focusing on it anyway, you often get nowhere and can even begin to question everything you've done so far and start going backwards.

Shared guilt had caused Slater to do nothing but think about what he and Norman might have missed. One look at Norman on Monday morning confirmed to Slater that they had both had unhappy weekends and, instead of coming back refreshed on Monday morning, Slater thought the pair of them were, if anything, even more jaded.

It was probably fortunate they had Steve Biddeford as the third member of the team, Slater thought. At least he was bright and cheerful. Or at least he was trying to be. After half an hour of listening to the other two complaining about how they were letting everyone down, Slater could see even he was beginning to falter.

'I know I'm the junior partner in this team,' he said, finally. 'And it's probably not my place to say, but don't you two think you might achieve more if you were to adopt a more positive attitude?'

'What?' said Slater, glaring at Biddeford. Norman was looking his way too, but Slater was surprised when he offered some encouragement instead.

'Go on,' he said. 'You are a member of this team, and you are allowed a voice. So go ahead, say what you think.'

'Well,' began Biddeford, sounding uncomfortable, 'I have a lot of respect for you two guys, but have you heard yourselves today? I came in this morning, happy and refreshed, raring to go, and all I've done is listen to you two prattle on about how bad you feel and how you should have done better. You're beginning to depress me. Isn't this an inquiry about a missing girl? Or is it all about you two and how you feel?'

Before he could say any more, his phone began to ring. *Saved by the bell*, thought Slater, knowing his face was like thunder.

'I'll just take this,' Biddeford said, indicating his mobile phone, stepping away and turning his back on them.

'He's got a point, you know,' said Norman to Slater, as Biddeford took his call. 'We're not exactly setting a great example, are we?'

Slater was struggling to come to terms with yet another person suggesting he was being negative. But the more he thought about it, the more he realised Biddeford was right. Here he was with a missing person to find and all he could do was feel sorry for himself.

'Yeah,' he agreed, reluctantly. 'He is right. But I don't understand why I've become so negative all of a sudden. What's happening to me?'

'Now that,' explained Norman, 'is what can happen to you when the world seems to turn against you.'

Slater was sceptical.

'You got suspended and nearly lost your job for something that wasn't your fault,' explained Norman. 'That's the world turning against you. Trust me. I've been there as well, remember? And I can tell you it made me pretty negative too.'

Their conversation was interrupted by a sudden excitement in Biddeford's voice as he continued his phone call.

'You have? Really? Where? Are you sure? How sure? Eighty-five percent sounds pretty sure to me. Let me get a pen.' He rushed back to find his notebook and pen. 'Okay. Go ahead. How do you spell that? Okay. Got it!'

He looked at Slater and Norman, who were now fully tuned into his excitement.

'Later today I should think,' he continued into the phone. 'Give me your number and I'll call you back as soon as I know. Fabulous news. I'll get back to you shortly. Promise. Thank you.'

He cut the call, looking immensely pleased with himself. Slater looked at him expectantly.

'Well?' said Slater. 'It must be good. You look as if you're going to burst.'

'I've got some good news, and I've got some bad news,' said Biddeford, almost shaking with excitement. 'The good news is, I think we might have found Ruth. The bad news is, if it is her, she's dead.'

Slater didn't know how to feel, and neither did Norman, going by the look on his face. He was torn between delight and dismay.

'I don't understand,' said Slater, confused.

'Well, I hope you don't object,' said Biddeford, 'but you two were getting so caught up with following the trail after Jones and Clinton, I wondered what I could do, from behind my desk, to keep trying to find Ruth. It occurred to me that the original investigation might never have circulated a description to the UK mortuary database, and even if they had, they probably only circulated her original photo and description.

'Now we know from Mrs Webster, the nosey lady in the flat opposite Mistral Court, that Ruby likes to change her hair colour quite often. I don't know much about hair, but I do know you can't keep bleaching it without doing it a lot of damage. But suppose she wears a wig? That way she could change her hair colour every day if she wanted and still there'd be no damage.

'But then I thought if she was in a mortuary, on a slab, there might not be any wig at all. So I figured it wouldn't do any harm to circulate a doctored photo showing Ruth as Ruby with short hair and see if there was an unclaimed body out there somewhere.'

There was a short, stunned silence, finally broken by Norman.

'Wow! How good are you?' he said. 'I'd take my hat off to you, if I was wearing one.'

'Steve,' said Slater, with true gratitude, 'd'you really think we're going to object to you using your initiative like that?' Then, turning to Norman, he said, 'See. I told you he was good.'

Biddeford beamed with obvious delight, and Slater let him bask in glory for a couple of seconds before he interrupted. 'Okay. So, you go to the top of the class, but this information's only good if you share it with us.'

'Oh, er, right. Yes, of course.' Biddeford thumbed through his notebook.

'That was a guy called Sid Murgatroyd. He's a pathologist in the mortuary at Gravesend in Kent. Apparently they have a female body that washed ashore a week ago. They've done a post-mortem and everything, but the local police have got nowhere because this person has never been reported missing, and with no ID they have no idea who she is, or where she's from. Another couple of weeks and she would probably have been put on the back burner and forgotten about.'

'We need to get down there and see if it's her,' said Slater. 'Call your friend Sid back and tell him we're on the way. All three of us.'

'What, me too?' asked Biddeford. 'I thought I was desk duties only.'

'It looks like you're the only one here with the brains to keep this inquiry moving,' said Slater. 'We can't afford to leave you here today. We need you with us.'

CHAPTER TWENTY-SEVEN

Sid Murgatroyd was in his late thirties, although his youthful good looks and thick dark hair, which seemed to flop in his eyes at every opportunity, made him look a whole lot younger. He greeted them rather formally, and for the first couple of minutes, Slater thought he was going to be hard work. But once Murgatroyd seemed to realise he had a captive audience who really wanted to hear what he had to say, he relaxed into an easy style that Slater thought probably made him a joy to work with.

'So, here she is,' said Murgatroyd, sliding the long, refrigerated drawer out of the wall. 'I'm glad somebody's interested in finding her. I hate it when we can't even give them their rightful name. It just doesn't seem right, you know?'

He unzipped the bag to reveal her face. It could be Ruby, thought Slater. But it was difficult to be really sure.

'So I can finally put a name to her,' said the pathologist. 'But is it Ruth or Ruby? I'm confused.'

Slater gave him the short version of the story behind this mysterious girl with two names.

'So which is this? Ruth or Ruby?'

'This is Ruth,' confirmed Slater. 'But in this guise, definitely appearing as Ruby. If you see what I mean.'

'Are you sure that's her?' asked Norman.

'I wasn't sure when I called first thing, but dental records confirmed it, while you were en route,' said Murgatroyd.

'Why's her face all blotchy? And why is the end of her nose black?' asked Biddeford.

'I'll get to that in a minute,' said Murgatroyd mysteriously.

'And you say she was fished out of the river a week ago?' asked Slater. 'She disappeared six months ago. Surely if she'd been in the water for six months there would have been a lot more decomposition?'

'That's correct,' agreed Murgatroyd. 'And that's one of the reasons I find this case so interesting, and why I'd love to help you guys get to the bottom of what happened to her.'

'You're making this sound like quite a mystery,' said Norman. 'Why the puzzle?'

'If you've seen enough here,' said Murgatroyd. 'I'll put her back to bed and we can go to my office where I can explain much better.'

'Yeah. I think so,' said Slater. 'There's not much we can do for her here.'

* * *

Back in his office, Murgatroyd settled his guests and then began to explain just why this body was so interesting.

'She washed ashore a week ago,' he began. 'There's nothing special in that, I'm afraid. All around the mouth of the estuary bodies come bobbing ashore. Mostly they're people who have drowned trying to cross the Channel and sneak ashore illegally, but we do get the odd one washed downstream too. I suspect this one came downstream from London.'

'Does that mean you think she drowned?' asked Slater.

'She definitely didn't drown,' said Murgatroyd. 'There was no water in the lungs. But there are suspicious circumstances that make me wonder what really happened.'

'Go on then, Doc,' said Norman, intrigued. 'Explain these suspicious circumstances.'

'You said Ruth, or Ruby, disappeared six months ago. So, if it is her, I'm sure you must be wondering where she had been for the intervening six months?'

'She was involved in the sort of activity that can get a girl into some serious trouble,' said Slater. 'She could have been on the run, or incarcerated. I only wish we knew.'

'How about she was in a freezer?' asked Murgatroyd.

'Jeez.' Norman sighed, shaking his head. 'Are you serious?'

'The blotchy face. The blackened end to her nose. It's freezer burn,' the young pathologist explained. 'You should see her toes and fingers.'

'Yeah. But—' began Slater.

'And she was still frozen deep inside when we pulled her out of the water,' finished Murgatroyd.

'Shit!' said Norman.

'I'm afraid I can't tell you exactly how long she had been in the freezer, but my guess is six months wouldn't be out of the question.'

'What else can you tell us?' asked Slater.

'She'd had sex shortly before she died. We found traces of frozen semen inside her. And she was pregnant, about ten weeks or so.'

'The fact she'd had sex doesn't surprise me,' said Slater. 'She was a hooker, after all.'

'Pregnant?' said Norman. 'That would be a tad careless for a hooker, wouldn't it?'

'So what did she actually die of?' asked Slater, finally.

'Anaphylactic shock,' said Murgatroyd. 'Her airways closed and she suffocated.'

'You mean like an allergic reaction to a bee sting?' asked Biddeford.

'There are all sorts of triggers,' explained Murgatroyd. 'It can be anything from an insect bite, or sting, through to eating the wrong sort of nut.'

'Do you know what caused hers?' asked Slater.

Murgatroyd smiled. 'It just so happens, anaphylaxis is something I'm very interested in,' he explained. 'So when I get one to deal with I tend to look into it as closely as I can. After doing a detailed analysis of her blood, I can tell you quite definitely, she was allergic to, and sent into shock by, Brazil nuts.'

'Brazil nuts?' echoed Norman and Biddeford together.

'So this is just a tragic accident?' asked Slater, disappointed by the findings. It seemed an anti-climax, somehow.

'In normal circumstances, with a body that's recently deceased, I'd say yes,' agreed Murgatroyd. 'But in this case all I can tell you is yes, she was killed by her allergy to Brazil nuts. Can I confirm it was an accident? No way. As far as I'm concerned, the very fact she was kept deep-frozen for six months makes it a suspicious death. But that's what you guys have to prove.'

There was silence in the room as Murgatroyd finished giving his report. Slater felt stunned, and it looked like Norman and Biddeford were too.

Eventually he spoke. 'Can we have a copy of that report?' he asked.

'Of course you can,' said Murgatroyd. 'It's been ready and waiting for someone to pick it up and run with it. Now I've got a name for her, I'd like to find out why she ended up in here as an unknown. I'll do anything I can to help.'

'How about a DNA profile from that semen sample?' asked Slater.

'I was hoping you wouldn't ask that,' replied Murgatroyd, sounding rueful. 'Every time I do one of them it cats a huge hole in a small budget.'

Then, more optimistically, he added, 'But I can find out what the blood type is without breaking the bank, and it won't take long to do.'

'Thank you. That would definitely be a start,' said Slater. 'I'm sure we'll need to talk again.'

'No problem. You've got my mobile number. Call anytime.'

* * *

'Have we gone forward here, or taken several steps back?' asked Norman on the drive back. He wasn't sure what to make of this latest discovery.

'It's going to be a bit of a disappointment if it turns out to be an accident,' said Biddeford, sounding gloomy for the first time.

'If it was an accident, why put her in a deep freeze?' said Slater. 'It doesn't make sense. Even if you were a client who didn't want to risk getting exposed to a scandal you could just run. The body might not have been found for days, but at least it would have eventually. No, putting her in a freezer just isn't right. I can't believe we're dealing with an accident.'

'If you had an allergy like that you'd probably know, wouldn't you?' asked Biddeford.

'How do you mean?' asked Slater.

'She was in her twenties,' explained Biddeford. 'She must, surely, have eaten a Brazil nut at some time in those twenty years and found out she was allergic. And if she did, she would know not to eat another one. You have to be careful when you have an allergy that might kill you.'

'Suppose someone gave her some food with Brazil nuts as an ingredient?' asked Slater.

'I dunno. I suppose that could have happened,' conceded Biddeford. 'But then we'd have to determine if it was done on purpose or accidently, wouldn't we?'

'Is it just me,' Norman interrupted, bored of the to-ing and fro-ing about nuts, 'or does it seem like an amazing coincidence that her body should suddenly appear just as we've locked away Jones and Clinton? Just suppose you were an outsider watching us. You might think now we've got what we wanted, we're about to forget about Ruth. If you were that outsider, could you think of a better way of rekindling our interest?'

Nobody said anything to this, so after giving them what he considered ample time to respond, Norman continued. 'Okay. So maybe it is just me.'

'It's not that I disagree with you, Norm,' said Slater. 'But if it is murder, and the body was hidden in a deep freeze, it's reasonable to assume only the murderer knew where it was. So why release it now?'

'Maybe they have to empty the freezer for some reason,' said Biddeford. 'Or perhaps they were so confident we'd stop looking now, they thought they were in the clear.'

'So why not do it three or four months ago when it was obvious the original investigation didn't care? They would have been in the clear then.'

There was a frustrated silence, and Norman knew they were all wrestling with the possibilities.

'There's another thing I have a problem with,' said Slater. 'Why would a high-class hooker have sex without using a condom? I thought they all used them nowadays what with the risk of infection. And surely getting pregnant isn't part of the plan.'

'Can a hooker have a boyfriend?' asked Biddeford.

'Hundreds,' said Norman. 'That's what they do.'

'No, that's not what I mean.' Biddeford shook his head. 'What if she meets someone she actually likes and falls in love with? I mean sex with all the other guys is the job, right? They pay, she obliges. It's just a business deal and it means nothing. But suppose there's a guy she likes. He doesn't pay, and she doesn't do it for the money. It's for love. It's special to them both so they don't use condoms. Maybe it becomes so special she wants to settle down with him. And because she doesn't use the condoms she gets pregnant. Could that happen?'

'It would certainly explain the sex without a condom, and the pregnancy,' agreed Slater. 'But then what about the video she made? Where does that come into it?'

'Well,' Norman joined in, enthused about this new thread of discussion, 'here's another boyfriend scenario. Suppose she got pregnant to try to trap this boyfriend? Maybe he was stringing her along for free sex, and then suddenly he finds she's sprung the baby trap. For some guys, that could be enough to kill a woman.'

'Another murder suspect to add to the list,' said Slater gloomily. 'We've already got Mark Clinton, Jimmy Jones, and Mr Chan as front runners, and then in reserve we have

Tony Warwick and Lucinda DeLove. And now we've got the possibility of a mystery man we've not come across before.'

For the next five minutes, a depressed silence began to settle in the car.

'Can you stop the car, please?' asked Norman. His stomach was gurgling.

'Why?'

'We could all do with a break. And my stomach says it's lunchtime. Let's stop somewhere and eat. And can we stop getting so gloomy? We've just had the biggest breakthrough yet in this case. We're gonna solve it. Trust me. I'm a policeman.'

'You're right,' agreed Slater. 'It's not a problem. It's just a challenge.'

'Oooh!' said Norman, glad that Slater seemed to have rediscovered his optimism. 'Welcome home, Mr Positive. Boy, am I glad to see you!'

* * *

It was a nice day so they found a pub with a garden, and tables outside, and ordered lunch.

'OK,' said Slater. 'I think we're all more or less in agreement that what we're dealing with here is a murder, and not some kind of accident.' He looked from Norman to Biddeford but there was no dissent so far.

'So, while we're waiting, how about we take a run-through our list of suspects? We need to put them in some sort of order and start eliminating them one by one. Agreed?'

Norman nodded his agreement, and saw Biddeford do the same. Over the next hour and a half, they discussed, argued and hypothesised over the relative merits of Tony Warwick, Mark Clinton, Jimmy Jones, Mr Chan and Lucinda DeLove as potential murder suspects.

They quickly demoted Tony Warwick to the position of rank outsider on the grounds he just didn't have it in him. 'No bottle' was Norman's decisive assessment, and no one argued with him.

Lucinda was similarly pushed to the back of the field, not because they thought she was incapable, but because they thought she didn't have a strong enough motive.

They also thought Jimmy Jones was unlikely to be the villain in this case. They were all in agreement he was a particularly unsavoury character, and that he had known of Clinton's affair with Ruby, but they had yet to prove he was connected to Ruby in any other way.

So that left two. Both Clinton and Chan had good motives, Clinton as the blackmail victim, and Chan as the double-crossed blackmailer. However, both Slater and Norman felt Mr Chan's story about the fisherman seemed likely to be telling them the truth. Norman definitely favoured Mark Clinton as chief suspect, but he knew Slater felt inclined to believe what Clinton had told them, and one thing Norman had to concede was if they couldn't prove Ruby had started to blackmail him, he had no motive.

'So if it's not Clinton,' said Norman, feeling slightly disappointed, 'and we've eliminated everyone else, all we've got left is this mystery boyfriend who maybe didn't like the idea of getting caught in a baby trap.'

'We definitely have to find this boyfriend,' agreed Slater. 'But I can't help feeling we've missed something, somewhere along the line. Maybe we need to take a closer look at some of the people on the periphery of this inquiry.'

'You think some people aren't telling us all they know?' asked Norman.

'I could be totally wrong,' said Slater. 'But my gut's telling me there's something not right about all this. I get the feeling there's a lot of smoke and mirrors in use.'

'You should always follow your gut.' Norman was a strong believer in following his instincts. 'And I agree with you. I still think it's very convenient the body turns up as soon as Clinton and Jones have been locked up.'

'I think we need to use your expertise with the shovel again, Steve,' said Slater, turning to Biddeford.

'Sorry?' Biddeford looked confused. 'With a shovel?'

'He means digging.' Norman laughed at the look on his young colleague's face.

'Oh, right. You have anyone particular in mind?' asked Biddeford.

'I think you should start with Jenny Radstock,' said Slater, quietly.

'Really? But I thought she was on our side?' said Biddeford, sounding surprised.

'She used all that fake outrage about Ruth's disappearance to get us involved and then led us to Clinton and Jones,' said Norman. 'You're right. She couldn't give a damn about Ruth.'

'Okay,' said Biddeford. 'I'll get on it as soon as we get back.'

He looked thoughtful for a moment, then he spoke again. 'While we're on the subject of things not being quite right,' he said, 'does anyone else think it's a little odd we've not heard anything from Ruth's sister? I mean she made all that fuss about the original investigation, then she went to great lengths to get it re-investigated, and now it seems she's not interested in how we're getting on.'

'Maybe she's busy,' said Norman. 'Or maybe she just trusts us to come up with the right result.'

'Yeah, maybe. I just think it's a bit strange, that's all.'

'Now you come to mention it,' said Slater, 'it does seem to be out of character. But we've got the delightful job of telling her we've found a body tomorrow morning. Maybe we'll learn a bit more about her when we do that. Don't you agree, Norm?'

'Am I being volunteered to go with you? I really don't mind if young Steve here wants to go.' Telling people about the death of a loved one was a part of the job they'd all rather not have to do, and it was something Norman particularly hated.

'Young Steve here will be busy with a shovel,' Slater reminded Norman.

'Oh. Right,' said Norman, reluctantly. 'So that's a definite booking then. Gee, thanks.'

CHAPTER TWENTY-EIGHT

Slater thought Tuesday morning wasn't a good time to be telling someone their missing sister had just been found in a mortuary. Actually, he knew it really wouldn't have mattered what morning it was. The fact is, there's never a good time to do this part of the job. He knew he wasn't alone in feeling this way — it was the one part of the job you could never enjoy. Everyone really detested doing it, but, like the national anthem, it was one of those things that had to be endured.

Beverley Green's eyes sparkled with pleasure when she opened the door and saw Slater standing there. Dressed in her tennis outfit, she looked tanned and fit, and there was nothing subtle about the way she was looking him over.

'Why, Sergeant,' she purred, 'what a nice surprise. Have you come for that game I suggested?'

'Err, no, not exactly,' Slater said, awkwardly. 'I'm afraid we need to talk to you.'

She looked past him, 'We?' she asked.

'My colleague.' Slater indicated Norman puffing towards them from the car. 'DS Norman.'

Her smile faded at the sight of the untidy bundle that was Norman. 'Oh, him,' she said, sounding dismayed. 'I suppose you'd better come in then.'

She was suitably distraught, almost verging on hysteria, when he broke the news to her, but when he looked across at Norman, it was obvious his colleague was unimpressed with her performance.

When she eventually calmed down enough to talk, and Slater told her about the cause of death, she was adamant her sister avoided Brazil nuts like the plague. She told them she would never eat any food if she thought there was even the slightest risk of contamination with nuts of any sort, especially Brazil nuts.

They kept the news of Ruth's pregnancy until last. But when Slater told her, to his great surprise, she said she had guessed as much.

'A woman can tell, you know,' she said in a condescending tone. When pressed about whom the father might be, she claimed Ruth had never discussed the matter with her and that she had no idea. Her best guess would be the boyfriend, Tony Warwick, she suggested. 'But frankly I didn't think he had it in him.'

Slater figured she was probably experienced enough to be a good judge, and then felt guilty for thinking that way about someone who had just been told their sister was dead. But only slightly guilty.

Having done his mournful duty, Slater just wanted to get away and be somewhere else, but before he made his escape, he asked if he could call anyone for her. She told him that wasn't necessary as a good friend would be arriving shortly. She assured him that would be sufficient comfort for her.

'Life has to go on, Sergeant,' she told him. 'One can't dwell on these tragic events.'

* * *

'Did you buy any of that crap?' asked Norman as he drove slowly back down from the house. He hadn't bought Beverley Green's theatrics. 'You must have done this shitty part of the job before. Have you ever seen anyone react like that? Or perhaps I should say have you ever seen anyone over-react like that?'

'It was a bit hysterical wasn't it?' agreed Slater.

'Yeah! For a couple of minutes,' said Norman. 'Then she just turned it off like it was a tap. I'm telling you, that was bollocks. And do you think a woman like that would keep her nose out of her younger sister's pregnancy? No. I don't buy it.'

They passed through the gated entrance to the estate and out onto the road.

'Just pull up here for a few minutes,' said Slater.

Norman pulled the car over and looked quizzically at Slater.

'Just give it a couple of minutes,' said Slater, in response to the look. 'I want to see if I'm right about her good friend. Going back to what you were saying, yes I agree. It was a bit like a prepared statement, wasn't it?'

He was looking back over his shoulder along the road.

'What are we waiting for?' asked Norman.

'I think this is it, coming now,' said Slater, smiling broadly.

Norman looked in his mirror to see what Slater was talking about. In the distance, heading their way, a young man pedalled furiously on his bicycle.

'Who's this?' asked Norman.

'This is Sebastian. He's Beverley's tennis coach. She likes to play mixed doubles with him, and he's happy to play with her.'

'Yeah. I bet he is.' Norman sighed. 'That was the one nice thing about her, her body. She'd like to play mixed doubles with you too.'

'Oh, cobblers!' said Slater.

'Please don't treat me like an idiot,' said Norman. 'You know I'm right. You saw the way she was looking you up and down. If I hadn't been with you, she'd a had you for breakfast.'

'Not while I'm on duty, mate,' Slater assured him. 'And anyway she's not my type.'

'I'm beginning to wonder if you really know what type you're looking for,' said Norman.

'What's that supposed to mean?' said Slater, indignantly.

'Don't start getting uppity. I don't care what your preferences are. I have friends who are gay. It's not a problem for me.'

Norman put the car in gear and started to pull away.

'I'm not gay,' said Slater, shaking his head. 'What is it with people trying to put a bloody label on me? First I'm negative, now I'm gay. Not so long ago I was told I was a bloody stalker.'

'Now just hold on a minute,' said Norman soothingly. 'I didn't say you were gay. I just said I wouldn't have a problem if you were, that's all.'

'Well, I'm bloody not, alright?' snapped Slater. 'So you don't need to worry about whether you would have a problem. Got it?'

'Okay, okay.' Norman held up a pacifying hand. 'I got it.'

He smiled quietly to himself. The thing was, he just couldn't stop himself sometimes, and Slater was so very easy to wind up.

* * *

Back at the ranch, Biddeford had clearly been digging furiously while they were gone. As soon as they got back, he told them: far from being only recently acquainted by the disappearance of Ruth, Jenny and Beverley were in fact old friends. They belonged to the same tennis club, and played doubles together. They even shared the same tennis coach.

'That would be Sebastian, right?' asked Slater.

'That's him,' said Biddeford, nodding. 'Sebastian Coombes. He's not the club coach though. He seems to be some sort of private coach.'

'Yeah,' added Norman. 'We saw him. Apparently he's into mixed doubles. I'm sure he's up there comforting Beverley Green with a game, right now.' Then as an afterthought he added, 'Do you think he plays mixed doubles with Jenny Radstock too?'

'I wouldn't be at all surprised,' said Slater, grimly. 'See if you can find anything out about him too, will you, Steve?'

'Are you two off out again?' asked Biddeford.

'Norm and me are going up to see an old lady and show her some photos. Maybe we'll get lucky and she'll recognise one of our suspects.'

'Before you go,' said Biddeford hesitantly, 'I've got this idea nagging away in my head.'

'A problem shared is a problem halved,' said Norman. 'Come on, let's hear it.'

'It's not really a problem,' explained Biddeford. 'And it's probably nothing anyway.'

'Steve,' pleaded Slater, 'just tell us, please?'

'It's probably just a coincidence, but I seem to recall watching a TV show recently where a woman was murdered by anaphylaxis. I can't remember what exactly happened, but I know it was to do with Brazil nuts.'

Slater and Norman looked at each other, and then back at Biddeford.

'And this helps us how?' asked Norman.

'I just thought maybe if I could find the programme it might tell us how it happened. Maybe our murderer saw the programme too.'

Slater felt a bit embarrassed for Biddeford. 'Murder by copying a TV show? It's a little unlikely, don't you think?' said Slater.

'Not to mention the fact that our murder was committed six months ago,' added Norman. 'And you say this TV show was in the last few weeks? Are we looking for Doctor Who, d'you think? Or is there someone else who travels through time we should be questioning?'

Biddeford blushed scarlet.

'I'm sorry, Steve,' said Norman. 'I don't mean to make you look stupid, but let's be honest, as theories go that's pretty wild, isn't it?'

'I suppose,' sighed Biddeford, sadly.

'Put it on the back burner,' suggested Slater, not wishing to extinguish the fire of Biddeford's enthusiasm. 'We can always take a closer look at it if we find we run into another roadblock, okay?'

Biddeford nodded, but still looked unhappy.

'Right,' Slater said to Norman. 'Let's get going.'

As they left he turned back to Biddeford. 'Don't stop coming up with ideas, Steve,' he said. 'We all come up with some wild theories at times, but sometimes it's the wild theories that provide a breakthrough. Okay?'

'Yeah. Okay, boss. Thank you.' Biddeford smiled. 'And don't worry about Norman taking the piss out of me. I can handle it. And I'll get my own back in time, don't you worry.'

'I'm sure you will,' Slater said, smiling back.

* * *

Much to Slater's dismay, Norman had insisted on driving all the way up to Clapham. He was quite sure they would probably spend half the day stuck in traffic, but he'd forgotten that Norman used to work up in town. And there was obviously nothing wrong with his memory. His extensive knowledge of back roads and side streets enabled them to dodge all the usual black spots. Slater was impressed. Norman had promised it would be quicker than the train, and he was right.

The last time Slater had knocked on Mrs Webster's door, she had been hostility personified. This time he had chosen to phone ahead and warn her he was on the way. As soon as they stepped from Norman's car, her front door opened. She waved them across the road and ushered them inside. Slater assumed she didn't get many visitors, and regarded their visit as a rare treat.

She fussed around them, making tea and producing what she called 'me posh crockery' to serve it to them.

'Oh, and I got some nice biscuits from the corner shop, special like.' She beamed at them.

'This is really nice of you, Mrs Webster,' said Slater. 'But you didn't have to go to all this trouble.'

'It's no trouble for proper policemen,' she said. 'You're not like the useless idiots we get round here. Wankers, the lot of 'em. They're more interested in lining their pockets than solving crimes.'

Mrs Webster was evidently a firm believer in saying it how she saw it and not mincing her words. Having given her opinion of the local police, she now turned her attention to Norman.

'And who's this nice young man?' She squinted at Norman. 'Has 'e got a name?'

'I'm DS Norman,' said Norman. 'I'm very pleased to meet you, Mrs Webster.'

'You're a big 'un, ain't you?'

'I'm afraid I'm not as slim as I used to be,' admitted Norman with good grace. 'But my excuse is I'm getting older.'

'So am I, son,' she said, wagging a finger at him. 'But I haven't doubled in size, have I?'

Slater tried to disguise a smile as he watched Norman take the insult firmly on the chin. He was sure his colleague had heard much worse in the past.

'So what can I do for you, Mr Slater?' said the old lady, turning her attention back to him. 'You said something about some photos. Is it still to do with that girl from across the road?'

'Yes, it is,' said Slater. 'I've got some photos for you to look at. I'm hoping you might be able to tell us if any of them ever visited her.'

He pulled the photos from his pocket and passed the first one over. It was Tony Warwick. She looked long and hard at it.

'He's not a very happy soul, is 'e?' she observed. 'But I don't recognise him. I'm sure he's never been there. I'd remember an ugly mug like that, wouldn't I?'

She passed the photo back and Slater gave her the next one. This was Jimmy Jones. Again, she studied it long and hard.

'Looks like a crook,' she said. 'But his face doesn't ring any bells. I'm sorry.'

'No need to apologise,' said Norman. 'It might be you don't recognise any of them. We understand that.'

Slater handed her another photo. This one was a tester. If she didn't know Mr Chan, they would know they were wasting their time.

'Ha! Charlie Chan,' she said straightaway. 'He lives over there, don't 'e? He might have been one of her visitors, but I never seen 'em together. Everyone around 'ere knows 'im. Nasty piece of work if you get on the wrong side of 'im.'

The next photo was Mark Clinton. Mrs Webster didn't take long to recognise him.

'Now this one was a regular,' she told them. 'Tuesday afternoons. And sometimes on a Friday morning.'

Norman looked at her and raised an eyebrow.

'What?' she asked. 'I suppose you think I'm a nosey old git, don'tcha? Well, you wait until you're my age and you're sat 'ere day after day, on your own, with nothin' to do, and no one to talk to. There's bugger all worth watching on the telly most days, so I look out the window. Is that so wrong?'

'I'm sorry,' said Norman. 'That wasn't what I meant to imply. I was actually impressed your memory is so good.'

'Ha! It's good for some things,' she said. 'But bleedin' useless for others. One day you'll see what I mean. You'll find you can remember all the things you'd like to forget, and you forget all the memories you'd like to hang on to.'

'Really?' said Norman, gloomily. 'Jeez, I hope it's not like that. I've only got memories to cling to as it is.'

They allowed Mrs Webster to reminisce for another ten minutes or so, and then Slater thought it was probably time they made a move.

'Thank you, Mrs Webster,' he said, as they got ready to leave. 'You've been very helpful.'

'Have I?' she said doubtfully. 'I only recognised two of 'em.'

'Yes, but that means we don't have to waste time on the ones who haven't been here, and that is very helpful, believe me.'

She looked at the empty plate on the table.

'That's why you're so big, son,' she said to Norman. 'It's got nothin' to do with your age. It's all to do with bein' a pig. You've eaten a whole packet of biscuits!'

'Did I eat all of them?' Norman looked deeply embarrassed. 'I didn't realise. There's a shop on the corner back there. Let me go and get you some more.'

'Don't be silly.' She laughed. 'Who's going to eat them if you do that? No, it's alright. I bought them for you two. I just hope Mr Slater's not disappointed he didn't get to eat any.'

'That's alright,' said Slater, with a sly grin. 'I'm used to it.'

They headed towards the front door.

'Oooh! Just a minute,' cried Mrs Webster. 'I nearly forgot.' She rushed over to an ancient sideboard in the corner of the room and pulled open a drawer. She rummaged around briefly and then turned to them holding aloft what looked like a newspaper cutting.

'See what I mean about my memory? I nearly forgot about this.'

She bustled across to Slater, holding the cutting out to him. 'I saw this and I thought of you, so I cut it from the paper,' she said, handing it to him.

'It's a good job you said you was coming or I might have forgotten all about it. I suppose you calling must have made me more aware or something like that.'

It had been cut from the local newspaper. It was a story about a donation being made to the local community. Slater didn't get the point at first, then he looked at the photograph accompanying the story. It showed a man in a suit presenting a cheque. He was smiling to the camera.

'That bloke in the photo,' she said. 'The paper says he's some banker or something. I wouldn't know about that, of course, but I knew his face as soon as I saw it. 'E used to visit. Every Wednesday, like clockwork. He'd arrive mid-afternoon and stay all night, sometimes on a Thursday as well.'

Slater was staring at the photograph. He'd seen that face before. This was a surprise. He handed it across to Norman.

'Does it help?' she asked.

'Oh, I think it might be quite useful, Mrs Webster. Thank you very much.'

When they finally got back into Norman's car, he handed the cutting back to Slater.

'I saw his photo earlier, right?' he asked.

'You certainly did,' Slater confirmed.

'You think he's the mystery boyfriend?'

'That thought had crossed my mind,' said Slater.

'He'd have an awful lot to lose if there was a big scandal, wouldn't he?'

'Indeed, he would.'

'That's one hell of a motive, don't you think?'

'The best one yet,' agreed Slater.

* * *

Not long after Slater and Norman had left, Biddeford became aware of the muffled sound of a mobile phone ringing. He knew by the awful ringtone that it was Slater's phone. It stopped before he found it, but then as soon as he sat down it started again. He figured this meant it was probably important so he hunted in earnest this time and soon found the phone behind a seat cushion.

'DS Slater's phone,' he said.

'Is he there?' asked a voice.

'He's out,' said Biddeford. 'But I can take a message.'

'I'm not sure about that. Who am I talking to?' said the voice.

'It's DC Steve Biddeford.'

'Oh, that's okay then. I can tell you. It's Sid Murgatroyd here. I've got a blood result for you.'

'Hi, Sid. That's quick work. Let me just grab a pen.'

'It's an easy test these days,' explained Murgatroyd. 'Especially when you've got a nice big lab of your own to get things done.'

'Right. Fire away,' said Biddeford, pen at the ready.

'The blood group is AB Rhesus negative.'

'That's quite rare, isn't it?' asked Biddeford as he scribbled away.

'Just nought point five percent of the population,' confirmed Murgatroyd. 'Which sounds great on paper, but with the population of London being about eight million that means you've still got forty thousand people to choose from.'

'Christ!' said Biddeford. 'Not exactly pinpoint accuracy, then?'

'Best I can do, I'm afraid,' agreed Murgatroyd. 'If you had the budget I could do DNA. That's the only really accurate thing these days. The blood group helps but it's not DNA.'

'I think Dave will be pushing for DNA, but the boss won't okay it unless we've got good grounds for doing it.'

'Pity,' said Murgatroyd. 'If there's anything else I can do, just let me know.'

'Since you're offering,' said Biddeford, 'can I run something by you?'

'Sure. Go ahead.'

'Ruth Thornhill died of anaphylaxis, caused by Brazil nuts, right?' he began. 'Now there was a TV show on a few weeks ago where a girl died of the same thing. It wasn't a murder, but she'd had sex shortly before she died. The boyfriend had eaten Brazil nuts beforehand. They reckoned she died because his semen carried something from the Brazil nuts and that's what caused her anaphylaxis. But that was just a TV show, wasn't it?'

'You mean is it for real, or not?' asked Murgatroyd. 'It sounds really unlikely doesn't it? But it is genuine. It's called seminal plasma protein allergy, or SPPA for short. If a guy eats Brazil nuts, waits a few hours and then has sex with a girl who's allergic, then yes, she can easily die as a result. It's a genuine allergic reaction to a protein derived from Brazil nuts.'

'Is there any way of checking this out?' asked Biddeford. 'Only Dave and Norm think I'm being stupid.'

'I can test the semen. If the protein's there it'll show up alright. I'll do it right now, and get back to you.'

'You can do that?' asked Biddeford, surprised by what he was hearing.

'Sure I can. It's not a difficult test to do. I know exactly what I'm looking for and I know exactly what to do to identify it. It's either there or it's not. Simples, as they say. I'll call you back later.'

'Great,' said Biddeford, smiling happily as he ended the call. Maybe it wasn't such a wild theory after all, he thought.

* * *

The moment Slater and Norman got back, Biddeford knew they'd had a successful trip. There was a spring in Slater's step that hadn't been there earlier, and Norman was grinning like a Cheshire Cat.

'What do we know about Paul Green?' Slater asked him.

'He's Beverley Green's husband?' said Biddeford, hopefully.

'Is that it?' asked Slater.

'Up until now he's not been mentioned,' Biddeford pointed out. 'So there's been no reason to check him out.'

'Well, there is now,' said Norman.

'He's in the running now, is he?' asked Biddeford.

'He's just come from nowhere and taken the lead down the home straight,' said Norman, beaming. 'It looks like our boy Paul is the mystery boyfriend. He's been bonking his wife's little sister for quite some time, and if she got pregnant without him realising, that gives him one seriously strong motive. I wouldn't want to be in his shoes if Beverley ever found out. I reckon she's the sort who would make sure he was totally ruined, and then she'd want revenge on top.'

'You don't happen to know his blood group, do you?' asked Biddeford.

'Oh no,' said Norman to Slater, his voice dripping with sarcasm, 'I knew there was something we forgot to ask Mrs Webster.'

'You've heard from the lab?' asked Slater. 'Do we have a blood group?'

'AB Rhesus negative,' said Biddeford, grandly. 'It's pretty rare.'

'Now we're starting to get somewhere, at last.' Slater sighed happily. 'If Paul Green's a match he's in serious trouble.'

'Do you think we should ask Beverley?' asked Norman.

'No!' said Slater, shaking his head vehemently. 'I want him picked up and brought down here tonight. I don't want him warned and given a chance to run. We can check his blood group when we've got him here.'

While he was talking, the annoying ringtone of Slater's mobile phone began to sound. Biddeford watched Slater check his pocket, and then, with a start, looked down at the phone in front of him. He checked the incoming number and snatched it before Slater could have the chance to ask him what was going on. 'Hello, Sid. Steve here.'

Biddeford saw Slater look at Norman quizzically. No doubt he was confused as to why he had Slater's phone — and was answering it.

'Really? It's there? You're quite sure? Fantastic! They won't believe this when I tell them. Yeah.' He laughed. 'I'll do that if they don't believe me. Yes, thanks. This is fantastic. Cheers.'

He cut the call and turned to Slater. 'Sorry about that.' He nodded at the phone. 'You left it here and it kept ringing earlier so I had to answer it in case it was urgent.'

'So who was calling earlier?' asked Slater.

'It was Sid from the lab with the blood test results.'

'Fine,' said Slater. 'And who was it this time?'

'It was Sid again. I asked him to check something out for me.'

'Well? Are you going to tell us what it was? Or is it a secret?'

'Remember that wild theory I had before you went out? About Brazil nuts being killers on a TV show?'

They both looked doubtful, and Norman heaved a heavy, impatient sigh. But Biddeford didn't back down. This time he had scientific backing. It wasn't just a wild theory anymore.

'Well,' he continued, 'Sid confirms it is possible for someone to be affected by the protein that causes the Brazil nut allergy without actually eating Brazil nuts themselves.'

'Right. So how does that work?' asked Norman. 'It sounds unlikely to me.'

'That's exactly what Sid told me,' said Biddeford. 'His exact words were, "it sounds really unlikely, but it is genuine". It's called seminal plasma protein allergy, or SPPA for short.'

'Did you say seminal plasma?' asked Norman. 'Isn't that something to do with having sex?'

'Exactly,' said Biddeford, smugly. 'It's transferred in the seminal fluid. If a guy eats Brazil nuts, waits a few hours and then has sex with a girl who's allergic, then yes, she can easily die as a result.'

'Jesus!' said Norman. 'So he literally screws her to death? I swear this is the weirdest case I've ever worked on.'

Slater hadn't said a thing so far, but now he spoke. 'So let me get this straight. If Paul Green's blood group is AB Rhesus negative we can more or less prove he was the person who had sex with Ruby before she died, and if we can prove he'd eaten Brazil nuts at some stage before that, we can prove he killed her.'

'That's what Sid reckons. Of course, DNA would be better, but the blood group is pretty conclusive,' said Biddeford.

'Can you do me a favour, Steve?' asked Norman. 'Next time I suggest you're barking up the wrong tree, please tell me to shut up and listen.'

'Right,' said Slater, 'we'd better locate Paul Green and send a set of uniformed chauffeurs to pick him up. We'll start questioning him in the morning.'

CHAPTER TWENTY-NINE

Slater had never really considered the effect a night spent in a cell might have on someone. Of course, for the hardened criminal it was nothing more than an inconvenience that came with the territory. However, for someone like Paul Green, used to being able to afford only the very best in life, it must have come as an enormous shock.

Looking across the table at him now, Slater thought he appeared to be even more untidy and crumpled than Norman, sitting alongside him. His face bore the haunted look of a man caught in a trap, desperately seeking a means of escape.

'I want it put on record that my client is extremely unhappy with the way he's been treated. He was brought here under the impression he was under arrest and then locked up in a cell all night. Now you tell him he's not under arrest. If you want to play games, Sergeant, you've chosen the wrong opponent. We're leaving right now, and I can assure you, you have not heard the last of this.'

The speech was delivered by Melvyn Spencer, Paul Green's oily-looking lawyer. He'd done nothing but complain and make loud tutting noises ever since he had arrived. Slater waited until Spencer began to push his seat back to stand up before he responded.

'Your client is not under arrest, yet,' he said quietly. 'But the choice is entirely yours. He can volunteer to help us with our enquiries, or we can arrest him right now.'

'And what trumped-up charge do you propose to arrest him for? It had better be good,' sneered Spencer.

Slater made a big deal of thumbing through his paperwork, as if to make sure he got it right. 'Let me see, now,' he said slowly and deliberately. 'Oh yes. Here's one we thought we'd try. How about murder? Is that good enough for you?'

'Murder?' repeated Spencer scornfully. He was so full of his own importance he didn't notice Paul Green bury his head in his hands. His client began to cry quietly and then a low moan began to escape from him.

'No, no,' he groaned quietly. 'I didn't murder her. It wasn't like that!'

'Keep quiet, Paul. Say nothing,' hissed Spencer to his client. Then he turned his attention back to Slater, raising his voice to add extra emphasis to his words.

'This is preposterous. My client happens to be a man of excellent character. He's a very well-respected banker in the City of London. A man of impeccable integrity—'

'Who just happens to have been having an affair, with a high-class hooker, who just happens to be his sister-in-law, and who also happens to be dead,' Slater interrupted.

There was a stunned silence from Spencer while he tried to take in what Slater had said.

'Your blood group is AB Rhesus negative. Isn't that right, Mr Green?' asked Slater. 'You were the last person to see Ruby alive, weren't you? You had sex with her shortly before she died.'

'I didn't kill her,' burbled Green. 'I would never have hurt her. She had some sort of fit or something. I just panicked. I didn't know what to do.'

'My client has nothing to say,' said Spencer. 'We're leaving. Now!' Once again, Spencer began to push back his chair. 'Come on, Paul, we're leaving,' he said, pulling at Green's arm.

'Very well,' sighed Slater. 'If you want to do it the hard way.' He nodded to Norman, who climbed to his feet.

'Paul Green,' began Norman, 'I'm arresting you on suspicion of the murder of Ruth Thornhill, aka Ruby Rider, on or around—'

'Wait!' yelled Green. 'There's no need for that. I'll talk to you. I want to talk to you.'

'No, you don't,' snapped Spencer. 'As your lawyer I'm advising you—'

'And as your client,' Green said, glaring at him. 'I'm telling you I want to talk to them.'

'But you can't—' began Spencer.

'Yes, I can, and I'm going to. I'll discharge you if I have to.'

'But I can't let you—'

'Then you'd better go home, Melvyn,' said Green decisively. 'Don't you understand? I don't want your advice. I promise you I didn't murder her, but I want to get this all out in the open. I can't live with it anymore.'

Green slumped in his seat, seemingly exhausted by his little speech. Spencer looked around the room, obviously realised he wasn't going to change Green's mind, and then, muttering things like 'wasting my time' and 'ignoring sound advice', he finally settled back in his seat. But he wouldn't look Slater or Norman in the eye.

'Right, Paul,' said Slater, once they'd all settled again, 'why don't you tell us all about Ruth, or was it Ruby?'

And so Paul Green told them all about Ruth. About how she'd been his wife's little sister, and how she had always been treated pretty badly by her family, especially by Beverley. Apparently it was Beverley who insisted Ruth wore those awful clothes and looked like a fifties throwback.

'Why do you think that was?' Norman asked.

'Because Beverley could see Ruth was much prettier than she would ever be,' he replied. 'Beverley has to work bloody hard to look as good as she does, but under those dreadful clothes, Ruth was beautiful, and it was effortless.

Beverley couldn't have that, could she? So she bullied Ruth, tried to wear her down, and break her spirit. But Ruth knew what she was doing. I used to try to stop Beverley. I never realised Ruth knew what she was trying to do all along. She just played Beverley for years and years.'

Then he went on to explain how one day, when he was at home on his own and Beverley was away, Ruth had come to his bedroom dressed as Ruby.

'She was sensational,' he marvelled. 'Absolutely stunning. And all the time I'd thought she was the hen-pecked little sister.'

'And that's when the affair started?' asked Slater.

'I just couldn't resist her,' said Green. 'She was amazing. After that we'd get together any time we could when Beverley was out of the way, but it was risky, and when we nearly got caught we decided we'd have to do something about the situation. That's when I got her the job in London, and the flat. I used to stay there with her one or two nights a week.'

'So it was your flat,' said Slater, as another piece of the puzzle dropped into place. 'Did you know she was working as a hooker out of there?'

Green looked disappointed.

'I didn't know at first, and I certainly didn't want her to do it,' he said sadly. 'But she said if I wasn't going to leave Beverley, she needed to make sure she could make a decent living on her own.

'It was a tough decision, because it meant leaving the children. But I was in love with her, and I wanted to be with her, so I agreed to leave as soon as she stopped working. We even planned to get married and have children of our own.'

Slater was beginning to feel this story was just a little too convenient, but then again, it was also plausible. They couldn't deny Ruth/Ruby could play both characters and did so very successfully. And there was no denying she put Beverley into the shadows when she was Ruby.

'This is all very nice and cosy, Paul,' said Norman, 'but what about the night she died? You were there, right?'

'I swear I didn't kill her,' he said, becoming upset again. 'I shouldn't have left her, but I didn't kill her. Honestly. On my children's lives.'

'Whoa,' said Norman. 'Just try and calm down. Can you just try to talk us through what happened that night?'

'It was a Wednesday. I always used to stay over on Wednesday nights. We'd had dinner, gone to bed, made love and we were lying together talking about our future plans when she suddenly started struggling for breath. It all happened so quickly I didn't have time to do anything. Before I knew it she was dead.'

He nearly choked over that final word. He was distraught even now, several months after the event. Slater thought it was a very good act. Quite convincing.

'So what happened after that, Paul?' he asked.

'I didn't know what to do.' Green sighed. 'I thought I'd lose my job, my children, and everything. So, instead of doing the right thing and calling for help, I acted like a coward and sneaked away into the night.'

He seemed to be reliving the events of that night, and the consequences of his actions. The tears were flowing in earnest now.

'I'm so sorry I left her,' he said again. 'She deserved better than that.'

Slater and Norman exchanged looks. They knew he hadn't just left her, and he must be aware they knew that, so why was he lying like this?

'I kept looking in the newspapers,' said Green, interrupting Slater's thoughts. 'I was expecting to see her picture and a story. I thought maybe the police would come calling, but weeks went by and nothing. Why is it you've only just got to me?'

'Come on, Paul,' said Norman, wearily. 'You know we've only just found the body.'

'You mean she's been lying there all this time? But it's been months. Poor Ruby, she must have decomposed by the time you found her.'

'Alright,' said Slater, sternly, 'let's stop playing around, shall we, Paul? We all know Ruby's body wasn't left in the room. It's been in a deep freeze for months. Now why don't you tell us the truth and stop wasting our time.'

Green looked confused. He looked to his lawyer for support, but Spencer just shrugged his shoulders.

'I don't understand,' said Green. 'She was lying in the bed when I left.'

'Yeah. Right,' said Norman. 'Maybe I should tell you what we think happened. It might help you to remember a little better.'

Green flapped his lips, but no sounds emerged. He looked genuinely baffled, and Slater began to wonder if there was something more to this story.

'See, we think the story goes something like this,' Norman began. 'We think Ruby wanted you all to herself, but you were quite happy having her as your bit on the side. Hell, what guy wouldn't want a beautiful girl waiting every time he came up to town?

'Anyway Ruby doesn't want to wait, so she sets a little trap for you. She gets pregnant, thinking then you'll have to leave your wife and kids.'

'Pregnant?' said Green. 'She wasn't pregnant, was she?'

'The thing is,' continued Norman, ignoring Green's questions, 'you didn't like her holding a gun to your head like that, so we think you decided she had to go. You knew she was allergic to Brazil nuts, didn't you? And you saw that TV show about how someone could be killed by a protein in Brazil nuts that transfers via semen. You had sex with her one last time and then watched her suffocate. Isn't that how it really was, Paul?'

Green looked as if he'd just been assaulted by a team of mastermind questioners. To say he looked confused would be an understatement.

'Pregnant?' he said, looking desperately from one to the other. 'Allergic? Brazil nuts? TV show? I've told you what happened. Why won't you believe me?'

'I really think this has gone far enough,' stormed Spencer, as if he'd suddenly been awakened from a deep sleep. 'My client has been happy to tell you what happened that night, but that's not good enough for you, is it? So now you're trying to put words into his mouth with some cock and bull story about Brazil nuts! That's an awfully elaborate way of murdering someone, don't you think? Paul could easily pay a hit man and not risk being involved at all if he really wanted to murder someone. This whole thing is going beyond a joke. I demand you let him go or charge him.'

Slater and Norman exchanged a long look.

'Ok, Norm,' said Slater. 'You know the drill.'

Norman climbed to his feet.

'Paul Green I'm arresting you on susp . . .'

But Paul Green had stopped listening, and looked utterly broken.

CHAPTER THIRTY

Once Paul Green had been taken back to his cell, the three detectives gathered to discuss the interview. While Slater and Norman had been in with Paul Green, Biddeford had been sat in the observation suite watching the whole thing.

'Ok, Mr Observer,' Norman said, smiling, 'what do you think?'

'Honestly?' said Biddeford. 'I think he's telling the truth.'

'Really?' said Norman. 'You're buying all this "I panicked and ran" crap?'

'His story sounds perfectly plausible to me,' said Biddeford, sticking to his guns. 'And there's something I think we've all missed anyway.'

'What's that?' asked Slater.

'Even the smoothie lawyer had a good point about it being an elaborate way to murder someone when he could easily afford to pay someone to do it for him. And even if he did kill her the way we're saying, how are we going to prove he did it on purpose? Even if he knew she was allergic, and he seemed pretty adamant that he didn't know, how are we going to prove beyond reasonable doubt that he knew it would kill her?'

'Hmm,' said Slater gloomily. 'That's a fair point, but I think it's the least of our problems at the moment.'

'Don't tell me, you believe this guy's innocent?' said Norman.

'I do and I don't,' said Slater. 'He's not denying he was there, or that he was having an affair with her, or even that he'd made love to her, so it's possible.'

He was struggling to make his mind up one way or the other, so right now they had Norman saying 'guilty', Biddeford saying 'not guilty' and Slater undecided.

'This is not going to help us close this case,' said Norman, stating the obvious.

'So how about,' suggested Biddeford, 'we come at it from the other direction? What if we take what we know, and try to prove it wasn't Paul Green.'

'You're kidding, right?' said Norman. 'We've got a case here.'

'Steve's right, Norm,' said Slater. 'There are enough ifs, buts, and maybes, to create plenty of doubt. We need to be a bit more convincing. Let's take a closer look at the things Green said that didn't fit with what we wanted him to say. Let's check some of this stuff out, see if he is telling the truth.'

There was a knock on the door and a head appeared.

'Sergeant Slater? Your prisoner wants a word. Says he'll only talk to you.'

'Okay. I'll be right down,' he said, heading for the door. 'I wonder what this is all about.'

* * *

'I honestly didn't kill her, Sergeant,' insisted Paul Green. 'I know I was wrong to run away, and I'll regret that for the rest of my life, but I swear she was still in the bed when I left her. If she was murdered, it wasn't by me. If her body was moved, it wasn't by me. I loved that girl. I would never have hurt her. We were planning a future together. Why would I want to kill her?'

Slater looked at Green's face. He certainly seemed genuine enough.

'Ok, Paul. If you want me to believe your story you're going to have to give me some help. There are some things we believe we know to be true that you don't even seem to know about.'

'What things?' said Green.

And so they talked . . .

* * *

It was an hour later when Slater returned. He scribbled an address on a piece of paper and handed it to Norman.

'Norm, can you take Steve with you and go and find our friend Sebastian, the tennis coach? I want you to lean on him and make him feel uncomfortable. See if you can find out what he does for Beverley Green apart from mixed doubles. Paul Green seems to think he likes to play chauffeur. Let's find out if that's true, shall we?'

'You look like you suddenly have the bit between your teeth,' said Norman. 'Would you care to share?'

'I have two phone calls to make,' said Slater. 'By the time you come back, I think we might just have collected the missing pieces of our puzzle.'

'Alright,' said Norman. 'We're on it.' Then, turning to Biddeford as he gathered his car keys, he said, 'Come on, Brains, let's go.'

Slater watched as they left and then turned back to his desk. Paul Green had given him two phone numbers. Both could provide vital evidence, but which one first, he thought. Eeny, meeny . . .

Half an hour later, he sat back and looked at his notes. It occurred to him that they could have checked this out much earlier in this case, but then they had been following where the evidence took them, and it had all been pretty compelling. There had never been the slightest hint of this.

A knock on the door interrupted his thoughts. It opened a little way and a pretty face popped into sight.

'Ah!' smiled Slater. 'PC Flighty. Thank goodness there's one good-looking face in this place. Do come in.'

'As you well know,' she said firmly, 'it's PC Flight, and flattery won't get you anywhere. And nor will asking for a date.'

'You know you'll give in to my charms one day,' he said, jokingly.

'Not in your wildest dreams,' she said, firmly. 'By the time that day comes, I'll be old and wrinkly and you'll be past it. Dream on, buddy.'

Slater played his part in the repartee by pouting his mock disappointment. 'Is that all you came up here for?' he asked. 'Just to shatter my dreams?'

'Actually, I've been sent with an urgent message, the keyword here being *urgent*,' she said. 'The duty sergeant downstairs says you've to get down there right now. Apparently some woman's creating merry hell because you've locked up her husband. So the sergeant says, as it's your problem, you can come down and deal with it.'

'Is she slim and expensive looking? Possibly dressed for tennis, filled with her own importance, and likes the sound of her own voice?'

'I haven't actually seen her,' said PC Flight. 'But she certainly sounds as if she likes the sound of her own voice.'

'Hmm. Yes. I think I know who that is,' said Slater.

'Well, don't just sit there,' she said. 'He's under siege.'

'Alright, alright,' Slater said, climbing reluctantly to his feet. 'I'm on my way.'

As Slater descended the stairs, he could hear the commotion he was walking into. It sounded as though Beverley Green's strident tones were rapidly erasing the duty sergeant's patience, and he was already resorting to threats to try to control the situation.

As Slater entered the room, he clearly heard the sergeant's booming voice. 'Any more language like that, madam, and I shall be forced to arrest you for abusive behaviour!'

The threat was enough to silence her for just a moment. She was standing barely inches away from the sergeant's desk with her back to Slater as he made his entrance from the far side of the room.

'Why, Detective Sergeant Slater,' boomed the sergeant, his weary voice heavily laden with sarcasm. 'Thank you so much for sparing the time to join us. This "lady" seems to think you have made a mistake by arresting her husband. Perhaps you would care to take her into one of the interview rooms and explain the situation to her, and perhaps you could also explain to her that using the "f" word ten times in every sentence still doesn't make her right.'

He glared at Beverley Green. 'Here you are, *madam*. The nice detective sergeant will be happy to listen to your abuse,' he finished.

With that, he backed away from his desk and walked out of sight behind the partition wall to the rear of the desk. As Beverley Green turned to face Slater, her face full of venom, there was a loud crash from the background as the duty sergeant took his feelings out on a wastepaper bin.

'Sergeant!' snapped Beverley. 'What the f—'

'Let's go in here to discuss this, shall we?' interrupted Slater, directing her to one of the interview rooms. 'I'll explain everything in there.'

'I demand to see my husband,' she yelled as soon as they were inside the room.

'I'm afraid that's not possible, right now,' said Slater.

'What do you mean it's not possible? I asked you to find out what happened to my sister, not arrest my fucking husband! And now you tell me I can't see him? Who the hell do you think you are?'

'Your husband has said he doesn't want to see anyone right now,' explained Slater patiently.

'But I want to see him!' she screamed. 'You can't stop me.'

'I can,' he interrupted. 'Especially if he chooses not to see you.'

'But I demand—'

'Do you always get what you want, Mrs Green?'

'I beg your pardon?' She gasped at his audacity.

'I've already told you, your husband has made it quite clear he doesn't want to see you, yet you don't seem to be listening to me. I wonder is that because you always get what you want?'

She looked as though she couldn't believe her ears.

'And while we're at it,' he went on. 'The desk sergeant is right. We don't give in to your demands just because you know how to use the "f" word. You went to a good school. I'm sure they taught you good manners there, or perhaps you were away that day? Just in case you were, let me make it clear for you. One more "f" and I'll arrest you myself. Are we clear?'

She had been red-faced and breathing heavily from her anger. Now she simply gulped a few times like a stranded fish, but no words came out. The look on her face told Slater she wasn't used to being spoken to like this, but he didn't care. As far as he was concerned, far too many people seemed to think it was just fine to swear and curse at the police anytime they felt like it, but this was one occasion when he was going to make sure he didn't take a load of abuse for doing his job. Especially from this particular woman.

'Right,' he said firmly, pulling out a chair and sitting down at the table in the centre of the room. 'If you sit down and behave yourself I'll tell you what's going on.'

She looked daggers at him.

'Your choice, Mrs Green,' he said.

Eventually, reluctantly, she pulled a chair out and sat down opposite him. For the first time she looked around the room.

'Is this an interview room?' she asked.

'Yes.' He nodded.

'Am I being interviewed?'

'No, you're not,' he said. 'I'm just going to tell you why Paul's sitting in a cell right now.'

'This had better be very, very good,' she said, clearly trying to assert some sort of authority and regain control of the situation.

'Oh, I think you'll find it quite interesting,' said Slater. He steepled his fingers and thought about what he was going to say.

'There's no easy way to put this,' he said. 'You remember we told you Ruth lived as another person up in London?'

'You mean that stupid rubbish about her being a high-class hooker?' she said derisively.

'That's right. If you choose not to believe it, that's your affair,' he said. 'We know it's the truth, and so did your husband, Paul.'

'What's that supposed to mean?' she shot back, looking horrified. 'What could Paul possibly have to do with any of that?'

'He paid the rent on the flat she lived in,' said Slater.

'This is ridiculous,' she stormed. 'My husband had hardly anything to do with Ruth. He wouldn't have paid for her flat. I know my husband. He would have told me.'

'Maybe you don't know him quite as well as you think,' said Slater.

'But, but . . . No. This can't be true. You've got it all wrong.' She was starting to run out of steam and all that was left now was bluster. Finally, even that fizzled out. Now she looked stunned and shocked.

'I'm afraid Paul was having an affair with your sister,' said Slater, gently. 'He paid for the flat and he often stayed up there with her one or two nights a week. We believe she got pregnant to try and trap him into leaving you, and when he found out, he killed her.'

'Paul's not capable of any of this,' she said, adamantly. 'You've got it all wrong. How is he supposed to have killed her?'

'That's the clever part,' said Slater. 'He used her allergy to Brazil nuts to kill her.'

'But she would never have eaten nuts,' she said.

'She didn't have to. Somehow Paul found out it's possible to pass the protein that killed her through his semen. He had sex with her and she died shortly afterwards. Then he hid the body until he thought it was safe.'

She looked stunned and said nothing at first, then a look of horror filled her face.

'Oh my God,' she said. 'We watched a TV show where they showed that. I thought he was strangely interested in it, but I never thought for one moment . . .'

She sighed heavily and slumped back in her chair. 'You do your best for people,' she said, sadly. 'You think you know them. And then something like this happens. Did he really say he didn't want to see me?'

'Maybe he's just too ashamed to face you right now,' Slater suggested, quietly.

A few tears escaped from her eyes and slid down her cheeks. Slater pulled a couple of tissues from a box and passed them to her.

'I'm really sorry,' he said. 'It's not the ending we envisaged when we started this case.'

He let her sob quietly for a minute or two. When he thought she'd had sufficient time, he decided it was time for her to go. He had things to do and comforting someone like Beverley Green was not one of them.

'Can I get someone to drive you home?' he asked.

'No. It's ok, thank you. My car's outside and I need to collect the children later.'

As he escorted her out to her car, he agreed he would go up to the house in a day or two, when they had more information. Then he could fill in the blanks for her. Maybe Paul would agree to see her by then, he suggested.

* * *

'How did you get on with our local neighbourhood tennis coach?' Slater asked Norman when he came back a little later.

'He was full of all that "I know my rights" bullshit when we started asking about Beverley, but as soon as we mentioned being her driver, he went a funny colour and started crapping himself. We didn't need to do any more than that. Trust me, he's looking seriously shaky right now. I wouldn't be surprised if he does a runner, so Steve's up there now keeping a look out. He's going to follow him if he does anything suspicious.'

'Yeah. That figures,' said Slater happily. 'Care to guess why he's crapping himself?'

'Well, you obviously know,' said Norman. 'So, instead of sitting looking like the cat that got the cream, why don't you tell me?'

'I'm sure we've got the wrong man,' said Slater.

'But doesn't all the DNA evidence prove Paul Green was there?' said Norman. 'I thought he got the idea from a TV show, had sex with her, planted the killer protein in the process, and then waited for her to die. Case closed.'

'That's all correct up until the point where he waited for her to die,' agreed Slater. 'I don't believe he knew she was going to die.'

'So what are we saying?' said an irritated Norman. 'That this is some sort of accident?'

'Not exactly,' said Slater. 'While you were out, Beverley Green came in. When I told her why we'd arrested Paul, she remembered he'd watched the infamous TV show with her, and she says he was very interested in it.'

'Okay,' said Norman. 'But doesn't that just add even more weight to our case.'

Slater grinned at him.

'Well, that's one way of looking at it, but there is an alternative view.'

'Well, don't keep it all to yourself,' said Norman.

'When Steve saw that TV show the other week, it was a repeat,' explained Slater, 'so he thought he'd check out when it was first screened. That's what he was doing when you two rushed off to find Sebastian, so it was there on his computer. It was first shown on September twelfth, last year. So that's what? Nine months ago?'

'I'd say that fits into our Paul Green theory pretty well,' said Norman. 'So what's the problem?'

'September twelfth was a Wednesday,' said Slater.

The significance eluded Norman for a couple of seconds, but then he realised what Slater was saying.

'A Wednesday night?' said Norman, finally. 'So Green would have been up in Clapham with Ruby.'

'Looks that way, doesn't it?' agreed Slater. 'I think maybe we need to have another little chat with Paul, don't you?'

Suddenly the door burst open and an excited Steve Biddeford rushed in.

'What the hell are you doing back here?' asked Norman. 'You're supposed to be keeping tabs on Shaky Sebastian.'

'He's downstairs,' said Biddeford, looking very pleased with himself. 'Waiting to talk to us.'

'What?'

'I was sat watching his house,' explained Biddeford. 'I hadn't been there twenty minutes and he came out to the car and asked me if we could talk. Then he asked me if he could do a deal. Would we keep him out of trouble if he came clean? I told him I didn't have the authority to make such a promise but if he came in voluntarily and helped with our enquiries, we might be able to help him. He jumped in the car, and here we are.'

'Did he say anything on the way down?' asked Norman.

'Not a peep. But he has been crying. He's in a right old state. He's guilty as hell about something, that's for sure.'

'Come on, lads,' said Slater. 'Let's go and see what he's got to say for himself.'

CHAPTER THIRTY-ONE

Slater and his two colleagues had decided to wait until mid-morning to make sure the children were at school and out of the way before they made their way up to Old Shrubs Cottage. Their usual banter was missing, but then, bringing Beverley Green up to speed regarding her sister's killer was no joking matter.

They lined up at the front door and Slater rang the bell. Beverley Green must have been at the back of the house because it took a good few seconds before the door opened. She was dressed in her tennis outfit once again, and was looking back into the house as she opened the door.

'Where the bloody hell have you been?' she asked angrily, turning to face them.

The look of shock on her face made it clear they weren't the visitor she was expecting.

'Expecting someone else?' asked Slater. 'Sebastian, perhaps?'

'Very clever deduction, Sergeant,' she said, drily. 'Why else would I be dressed like this?'

'Some might say over-dressed for mixed doubles,' said Norman, unable to stop himself.

Her eyes flashed angrily. 'I beg your pardon?' she said. 'Are you trying to imply—'

'I'm not trying to imply anything, Mrs Green,' Norman assured her, putting great emphasis on the word 'trying' but she either missed it, or chose to ignore it.

'What do you want?' she said, glaring at Slater.

'I did say I'd come up and see you when we'd finished our enquiries,' he explained.

'Does it really need three of you?'

'These are the two colleagues who've helped me complete this inquiry, Mrs Green,' he said. 'It seems only right they should be here to help me explain everything to you.'

She looked as though she was going to tell them to go away.

'Isn't it bad enough I have to deal with my sister being found dead, learning my husband had made her pregnant, and then that he was a murderer?' she cried. 'And now I have to put up with three of you turning up unannounced. What more can you possibly expect from me at a time like this?'

'If you don't mind me saying,' interrupted Norman, 'you look as if you're coping extremely well with your grief.' He indicated her tennis outfit. 'I mean, if I didn't know all the things that have just happened, I would never have guessed how grief-stricken you must be feeling right now.'

It looked, briefly, as if she was going to explode, but somehow she managed to keep her temper.

'We all have our own way of coping with situations,' she said, snootily. 'I do it by trying to carry on as though nothing has happened.'

'Wow!' said Norman. 'That's very heroic of you.'

'Are you trying to be funny?' she snapped.

'Who me?' asked Norman. 'No, ma'am. Humour and me just don't go together. I just think it's great you can carry on like nothing happened. I mean most people would be in bits, but you? Well, you're something else, you really are.'

Beverley Green glared at Norman, and Slater knew she was trying to figure out if he was being sarcastic or not.

'Is this going to take long? Only I'm very busy and my tennis coach will be here any minute.'

'If you mean Sebastian, he said to tell you he wasn't coming today,' said Slater.

A faint look of alarm flashed across her face, but it was gone as soon as it appeared.

'Typical man,' she tutted. 'So bloody unreliable.'

'I guess that means you're not quite so busy, right now,' said Slater, making sure she knew it wasn't a question. 'So why don't you let us in and we'll be as quick as we can.'

'Oh, come on in then.' She sighed impatiently. 'But make it quick.'

'Oh, I don't think we'll be long.' He smiled.

She turned her back and led the way through to the huge kitchen. Slater couldn't help but admire her tanned, toned legs as she walked ahead of him. He thought it was a pity her personality didn't match.

'Right.' She turned on them, once they were all in the kitchen. 'Get on with it.'

'Any chance of a cup of tea?' asked Slater.

'Absolutely none,' she said firmly, crossing her arms.

Slater made a mental note of her changed body language, from attacking to defensive. Then he made a big deal out of finding his notebook, ignoring her heavy sigh of impatience.

'There are just a couple of questions I need to ask you. Little details, you know?' He smiled.

'What questions? What details?' she snapped. 'I've told you all I know.'

'Mmmm,' he said, mulling over her last few words. 'The thing is, I'm not sure you have told us all you know.'

'It's a fact,' added Norman. 'We often think we've told everything we know about something, and then when someone asks the right questions they can get a whole lot more out of us.' He smiled encouragingly at her. 'DS Slater here is very good at asking the right questions.'

She looked down her nose at Norman. Slater got the distinct impression she regarded him as nothing more than a nuisance.

'Is there any chance this person could be removed from here?' she asked Slater.

'Who? Norm? Absolutely not.' Slater smiled, shaking his head. 'He's a key part of my team.'

'I find that very difficult to believe,' she sneered.

'Yes, you probably do,' agreed Slater. 'But I don't give a damn what you find hard to believe. He stays.'

He smiled sweetly at her. She scowled back at him.

'Now then, Mrs Green,' he began, looking at his notepad. 'Just a few short questions.'

'Yes, alright. If it means you'll go away and leave me alone, ask your damned questions!'

'Question one. Where were you on the night of September twelfth last year?'

'Good God. That's months ago. How am I supposed to remember that?'

'It was a Wednesday, does that help?' he said.

'Then I would have been out with my girlfriends, playing bridge,' she said.

'How about the twenty-sixth of September?'

'Is that a Wednesday too? Then I would have been playing bridge that night too?'

'October the tenth?'

'That's another Wednesday. I already told you I would have been playing bridge. I always play bridge on a Wednesday night. What's this got to do with my sister's murder anyway?' she cried, her patience clearly in shreds.

'You're sure about this?' asked Slater, carefully.

'Of course. Wednesday night is bridge night. Every week, without fail.' She was getting really angry now.

'Tell her, Steve.' Slater nodded to Biddeford who thumbed to a page in his own notebook.

'According to your bridge partners you didn't show up on the twelfth or the twenty-sixth of September, or on the tenth of October.'

'They must be mistaken,' she said, red-faced.

They said nothing.

'Oh wait. The kids were ill around that time. They all had colds, one after the other. I was probably at home looking after them. You can't go out and leave them when they're ill, now, can you?'

'Apparently you can,' said Norman cheerfully. 'According to your babysitting service, you had babysitters for all those nights.'

She began to pace nervously. They could see she was thinking hard.

'We're not here to judge whether you were right to leave your kids with a babysitter when they had colds, Beverley,' Slater soothed her. 'We're not here to question anyone's morals either. We're just curious to know where you were and who you were with.'

'Perhaps you were with Sebastian,' suggested Norman. 'Playing the other sort of mixed doubles. If that was the case, then everything would be okay.'

'Yes. Alright,' she said, seizing the lifeline Norman had thrown her. 'I was with Sebastian, but there's no need for anyone to know about this, is there? Especially not my husband, although I suppose it doesn't really matter what he thinks anymore, does it? Not where he's going for the rest of his life.'

'Where were you with Sebastian?' asked Slater.

'In bed, of course,' she snapped.

'In bed, where?' he persisted.

'What bloody difference does it make?' she shrieked. 'What's my private life got to do with this, anyway? You're just prying for the sake of it, aren't you? Well, you won't embarrass me. I'm not ashamed, I can tell you that for sure.'

'Oh, we're quite sure you have no shame, Mrs Green,' Norman said, smiling. 'But we'd still like an answer to the question.'

'Well hard luck. I'm not going to answer any more of your nosy, privacy-invading questions until you tell me why.' She stamped her foot to emphasise her determination.

Slater shook his head and tutted.

'Now that's a pity,' he said, 'because we were rather hoping you could confirm what Sebastian said, and then we could all go home.'

'What? What did he say?' She was sounding desperate now.

'You tell me,' said Slater. 'If you've got nothing to hide, and you're not ashamed, you've got nothing to worry about, have you?'

'Perhaps you were in his bed that night,' suggested Norman.

'Oh, alright.' She sighed. 'I give in. I was at his house, in his bed.'

'You sure you weren't in his car?' asked Slater.

'Oh Sergeant, please! I stopped having sex in cars when I was a teenager. Doing contortions in the back seat is definitely for the young or desperate. A girl like me needs a bit of space so she can really enjoy the experience.'

Slater pursed his lips and shook his head.

'Oh dear, what a pity,' he said, sadly. 'You were doing so well up to that point.'

She looked shocked, but said nothing.

'Now you have a problem,' added Norman. 'You see Sebastian has told us a different story. According to him, you weren't in his bed at all. You didn't even go to his house. But you were in his car, right?'

She said nothing.

'Do you know a place called Mistral Court, Beverley?' asked Slater.

She stared at him open-mouthed.

'It's in Clapham,' he continued, 'but then you know that, don't you? You know exactly where Mistral Court is because Sebastian drove you up there on September the twelfth, and the twenty-sixth, and again on the tenth of October. The first two times you just sat outside and watched one of the houses, but on the third occasion you brought something back with you, didn't you?'

'He's lying,' she said. 'I don't know what you're talking about. He's making this all up.'

'Call 'em in, Steve,' Slater advised Biddeford.

Biddeford pulled his mobile phone from his pocket as he left the room.

'What's he doing? Call who in?' she stammered. 'I don't understand. What's going on?'

'I'll tell you, shall I, Beverely?' said Slater. 'You found out what your husband was up to with your sister. You got Sebastian to drive you up there to make sure, and then you planned her murder.'

'This is rubbish,' she said. 'I was the one who wanted you to find her. I wouldn't have done that if I had killed her, would I?'

'Yes,' said Slater, 'I must admit I had to think about that one, but then I realised, it wasn't you who wanted the case re-investigated, was it? It was Jenny Radstock. She was the one who pushed for us to get involved, and then once the ball was rolling you couldn't stop it, could you?'

'You thought making out you were keen to find out what really happened would be way too clever for the stupid policemen, right?' said Norman. 'But I'm afraid you're not as clever as you think you are, and we're not quite as stupid as you think we are. All the clues led to your husband just as you had intended, but you made a couple of mistakes that didn't quite fit, and that made us re-examine our evidence.'

'You see no one's ever excluded until we're sure we've got the right person,' said Slater.

'I want my lawyer,' she demanded, heading for the phone in the hallway.

'Don't worry,' Slater assured her. 'You can make that call from the station. Okay Norm, take her away.'

Norman read Beverley Green her rights, and then led her towards their car. As they got to the front door, a van pulled up and the forensic technicians began to gather their equipment, ready to go through the freezers with a fine-toothed comb. They weren't sure they would find anything, but according to Sebastian, they needed to take a good close look at the one in the garage.

CHAPTER THIRTY-TWO

It was nine p.m. on Friday evening. Dave Slater climbed from the shower and towelled himself dry. It had been a late finish, and he was tired and hungry, but he felt pretty good. And so he should, he thought. It wasn't every week you got to solve so many major crimes at once.

He'd thought about getting dressed up and going down the pub but, quite frankly, he just couldn't be bothered. Instead of dressing up, he dressed down in his pyjamas. He figured by the time he'd thrown together some sort of meal and watched an hour's TV he'd be ready to hit the sack anyway. He knew he was being pretty boring, but that's just how he felt tonight.

He made his way into the kitchen and pulled open the fridge door. He wasn't really surprised to find there was very little inside. A few limp vegetables and a pack of sausages that were a full week past their sell-by date didn't exactly inspire his inner chef. He gathered the contents from the fridge, stepped on the pedal and dropped the lot into the bin. Oh well, he could always phone for a takeaway.

He was trying to decide if he fancied Chinese or Indian, when his doorbell rang. He looked at his watch. Who the hell was ringing his bell at gone nine? He thought about ignoring it, but whoever it was wasn't going to give up. The bell rang again.

'Bollocks!' he said quietly to himself. Then, much louder, 'Alright, alright. I'm coming.'

He swung the door open. A woman stood before him, her face hidden behind the carrier she was holding aloft in her left hand, obviously filled with food. It was Indian, he could smell the spices. The carrier slowly lowered and Jenny Radstock peeped over the top.

She smiled cautiously, and then brought her right arm from behind her back. In her right hand, she held a bottle of champagne by the neck. Her red hair had been released from the bun she often wore when working, and it flowed over her shoulders, framing her face.

'I come in peace,' she said. 'I heard you'd got a result so I thought congratulations were in order. I thought you might be hungry. And I was hoping you might like some company.'

He looked at her in surprise. They hadn't parted on very good terms last time they had spoken and he really hadn't expected to see her again, so this really was a surprise.

She looked disappointed.

'I can go away if you'd prefer,' she said. 'I do understand. I was a bit selfish, wasn't I?'

She'd lowered the bag and the bottle to her sides now, and he could see she was dressed in jeans, designer, of course, and a thin T-shirt. He could see quite clearly there was nothing under the T-shirt. And she had open-toed shoes with four-inch heels and ankle straps. Oh my. How had she known he had a thing about ankle straps and high heels?

He suddenly realised he was in his pyjamas.

'Err, I'm not exactly dressed for guests,' he began.

'I'll go then, shall I?' She pouted.

'No! No. That's not what I mean at all,' he said. 'I just wasn't expecting anyone. I certainly didn't expect you to turn up on my doorstep clutching a takeaway and a bottle.'

'So, is that a yes?' she asked. 'Only this food's going to get cold.'

'I'm sorry,' he said, stepping back. 'Please come in.'

She came through the door, carrying her gifts, lingering in front of him long enough for him to inhale her perfume as she passed. Ah yes, he remembered, Chanel Number Five. He thought she smelled every bit as good as she looked, and right now, she looked pretty fabulous.

She marched straight through to his tiny kitchen and began opening cupboards looking for plates and dishes.

'Here,' she instructed, offering him the bottle. 'You find some glasses and open this, while I sort out this food.'

Obediently, he did as he was told. Suddenly he didn't feel so tired. Maybe tonight wouldn't be quite so boring after all.

By the time he'd found two glasses, opened the champagne, poured the drinks and handed one to her, she had the food laid out on the table. It was very cramped, and one or two dishes steamed away on the side, but there was more than enough to be going on with. He sat opposite her.

'I think we should toast Detective Sergeant David Slater and his dogged persistence.' She smiled, her green eyes sparkling.

They clinked glasses and sipped their drinks.

'It was a team effort,' he said, slightly embarrassed at her praise.

'I think we should also toast the fact that I can see I was behaving very badly and being very selfish,' she said.

She raised her glass and clinked it against his again.

'No hard feelings?' she asked.

'No hard feelings,' he agreed.

They took another drink.

'Can I also ask you to toast the resumption of friendly relations between us?' she asked.

They clinked glasses and drank again. She reached for the bottle and topped up their glasses.

'Whoa,' said Slater. 'You're in a hurry! Are you trying to get me drunk?'

'Good heavens no.' She gave him a coy smile. 'I'm trying to get both of us drunk.'

'Do you think that's necessary?' he asked.

'Oh, it's not necessary,' she agreed. 'But it does help to remove any inhibitions, don't you think?'

'We'll just have to wait and see, won't we?' he said.

There was an awkward silence while they sat and watched each other. It was one of those 'what's going to happen next' situations, but the moment was lost when Slater's stomach began growling loudly.

'I think we should probably eat,' he said, red-faced. 'I haven't eaten all day, and we don't want it to get cold.'

* * *

As they began to eat, the tension between them eased and Slater began to relax. He had to admit she was very good company, very easy to be with, and very easy on the eye, too. She had that great talent of being a good listener as well as a good talker. She soon got him talking about the Ruth Thornhill case and how they'd come to the conclusion Beverley Green was the murderer.

'So how does it all fit together?' she asked him.

'You're not asking about this because you're going to be defending her, are you?' asked Slater, wary of letting his guard down too far.

'Good God, no! I'm far too close to get involved. Conflict of interest and all that,' she explained. 'I'm just curious to know how you did it, that's all.'

And so he told her about Ruth and her double life as Ruby. He told her about Beverley carrying on for years behind Paul's back thinking he didn't know, but he had known all along. About how Beverley had tried to make Ruth's life a misery and how Ruth had gained her revenge by becoming Ruby and seducing Paul.

He told her about how Paul had found Ruth a job up in London, and then found a flat where he could be with her up in town. But, somehow, Beverley had found out and wanted revenge.

So she'd persuaded Sebastian to drive her up to Clapham so she could spy on Paul and Ruby. Then she'd heard about the Brazil nut protein and how it could be transmitted through sex. All she had to do was arrange for Paul to eat some Brazil nuts before he had sex with Ruby.

'But how did she get him to eat Brazil nuts at the right time?' Jenny asked.

'She used to pack him a bag full of healthy snacks to take with him every week. You know the sort of thing — dried fruits and seeds, energy bars, that sort of thing. Then on the week that mattered, she added Brazil nuts. She knew what would happen because she knew about Ruth's allergy, but Paul had no idea. He was like a walking time bomb for Ruby that week.'

'But how did she know about that, what's it called? SPPA?' she asked.

'There was a TV show that featured it,' he told her. 'She says Paul watched it with her and he was really interested, but it was on a Wednesday. Paul was in London with Ruby.'

'And I suppose Beverley knew that Paul's rare blood group would lead you to him quite easily?' she suggested.

'Exactly,' confirmed Slater. 'She was pretty cute about the whole thing. But we think we've found evidence to prove Ruby's body was kept in the freezer in Beverley's garage, and they've found Ruby's mobile phone. I'm betting Beverley's fingerprints will be all over it.'

'But don't you think your case is a bit flaky?' she asked. 'There's plenty of circumstantial evidence against her, but there's just as much against him. It's his word against hers about the Brazil nuts. And can you really believe he didn't know about her allergy? I'd fight tooth and nail on that if I was defending her. And what about the TV show? He could have seen it when he was with Ruby. And how could she have seen it if she was with Sebastian, sat outside Ruby's flat? Then there's the freezer. He's got access to it as well, you know. And she could argue he hid the mobile phone.'

'Ah!' said Slater, triumphantly. 'That's why it's a good job we've got our secret weapon. Sebastian can prove where she was on the night of the murder. He was her accomplice in removing the body and bringing it back down here and storing it in her freezer. He also helped by taking the frozen body back up there and dumping it in the river. Sadly, for Beverley, her accomplice isn't made from the same stuff she is. No amount of sex with her could ease his conscience in the end.'

'Now that does make a difference,' she agreed.

'You know him too, don't you?' he asked.

'If you mean do I know Sebastian, yes I do,' she said. 'If you mean is he my tennis coach, then yes, sort of. Beverley and I play doubles together, and at one time she insisted he coach us, but frankly he's got no idea.

'However, if you mean am I having sex with him, no I am not. He's not my type. I like a man who wants to be a man. Sebastian doesn't screw Beverley, she screws him. It's a subtle difference, but it's real enough.'

'Yeah. He's not exactly the hero type,' he agreed.

'Well, I'm glad you've got him to complete your case,' she said. 'Otherwise you'd have to prove Beverley had found out about SPPA some other way.'

'Like how?' he asked.

'Maybe she had a friend who saw the programme and told her about it,' she suggested, mysteriously.

Slater sat there for a moment as her words slowly sunk in. What had she just said? His mind was buzzing, but she was talking again.

'Now I don't know about you,' she murmured, 'but I'm going upstairs to find your bed.'

She got up from her chair and moved around the table. As she passed him, she ran her hands across his shoulders and through his hair.

'Don't be long,' she whispered, as she walked towards the stairs.

'But you're a friend of hers,' he said. 'Aren't you?'

'Of course I am,' she said. 'One of dozens.'

He thought about this.

'Are you telling me you told her?'

But there was no reply. She'd already gone upstairs. All he heard was the slight creak of the floorboards above him as she climbed into his bed.

THE END

THE JOFFE BOOKS STORY

We began in 2014 when Jasper agreed to publish his mum's much-rejected romance novel and it became a bestseller.

Since then we've grown into the largest independent publisher in the UK. We're extremely proud to publish some of the very best writers in the world, including Joy Ellis, Faith Martin, Caro Ramsay, Helen Forrester, Simon Brett and Robert Goddard. Everyone at Joffe Books loves reading and we never forget that it all begins with the magic of an author telling a story.

We are proud to publish talented first-time authors, as well as established writers whose books we love introducing to a new generation of readers.

We won Trade Publisher of the Year at the Independent Publishing Awards in 2023. We have been shortlisted for Independent Publisher of the Year at the British Book Awards for the last four years, and were shortlisted for the Diversity and Inclusivity Award at the 2022 Independent Publishing Awards. In 2023 we were shortlisted for Publisher of the Year at the RNA Industry Awards.

We built this company with your help, and we love to hear from you, so please email us about absolutely anything bookish at feedback@joffebooks.com

If you want to receive free books every Friday and hear about all our new releases, join our mailing list: www.joffebooks.com/contact

And when you tell your friends about us, just remember: it's pronounced Joffe as in coffee or toffee!

ALSO BY P.F. FORD

SLATER AND NORMAN MYSTERIES
Book 1: DEATH BY CARPET

THE WEST WALES MURDER MYSTERIES
Prequel: A DATE WITH DEATH
Book 1: A BODY ON THE BEACH
Book 2: A BODY OUT AT SEA
Book 3: A BODY DOWN THE LANE
Book 4: A BODY AT THE FARMHOUSE
Book 5: A BODY IN THE COTTAGE

Printed in Great Britain
by Amazon

48228406R00169